MURDER
IN THE
SCOTTISH
HILLS

BOOKS BY LYDIA TRAVERS

THE SCOTTISH LADIES' DETECTIVE AGENCY SERIES

The Scottish Ladies' Detective Agency

MURDER
IN THE
SCOTTISH
HILLS

LYDIA TRAVERS

Bookouture

Published by Bookouture in 2023

An imprint of Storyfire Ltd.
Carmelite House
50 Victoria Embankment
London EC4Y 0DZ

www.bookouture.com

ISBN: 978-1-83790-184-5
eBook ISBN: 978-1-83790-183-8

To my husband, Jon

ONE

It was six o'clock on a warm weekday afternoon and Maud was attempting a graceful arabesque when it occurred to her that she was having some difficulty with the position.

With a sigh, she lowered her leg and released her hold on the back of the dining chair. Hadn't she seen an advertisement in a recent newspaper for a novel way to exercise? She searched through the little pile by the side of the hearth.

Success! *Indian Clubs: Swing Your Way to Health.* Bare-chested men in loose trousers were doing interesting exercises with their clubs: manly-looking lunges and so forth. And there was a young lady featured in a sailor dress with a club resting on each shoulder. The woman wasn't actually swinging her clubs, but Maud felt sure that she herself could.

She was filling in the coupon when her friend walked into

the room. Daisy came to stand next to her and raised her eyebrows as she pulled the pin from her purple velvet hat.

'Clubs? Would that be to knock our quarries senseless?'

'Not at all. They're to improve my strength, agility, balance and physical ability.'

'Perhaps they could improve my strength, agility... all those other things you mentioned.' Daisy sounded doubtful.

What her friend lacked in height, Maud thought, as she watched her friend remove her hat, she more than made up for in a pink blouse with that red hair.

'You'd have to actually *use* the clubs,' Maud said, smiling, knowing Daisy's dislike of what she termed too-strenuous physical exercise.

'Aye. Perhaps not, then.' Daisy sat on the sofa and tossed her hat onto the seat beside her.

'Anything to report?' Maud asked, sitting in the armchair opposite.

It had been a week since Maud had returned to Edinburgh from a short stay at her father's house in the country, and, during that time, the M. McIntyre Agency had been quiet. She'd opened the business last month, with Daisy, who had been her lady's maid when Maud lived at home, and was now her assistant. The two of them had been very busy, solving the cases of Lady Argyll's missing Pekingese, Lord Urquhart's stolen love letters, Mr Laing's runaway bride-to-be and the jewellery theft and murder at Duddingston House. And Laing had even attempted to murder Maud and Daisy. His trial would take place in due course, and she and Daisy would be called as witnesses, which was a slightly unnerving prospect Maud was trying not to think about.

But at present... nothing.

'Definitely no letters at the office?'

Daisy shook her head.

'Or messages by telephone?'

'Nae.'

'Or—?'

Daisy folded her arms across her chest. 'Nae *nothing*.'

Maud ignored the double negative. 'We are in credit at the bank, thanks to the success of our first cases, but you'd think that our reputation might encourage others to come forward.'

'They will, just as soon as they have cause to. Until then, we'll just have to be a wee bit more patient.'

Maud sighed. 'Give me work to do, problems to analyse, and I am content.'

'Aye, me too,' said Daisy. 'Though I wouldna have put it into such flowery words.'

'They were not my words, Daisy; I was paraphrasing Sherlock Holmes speaking in *The Sign of Four*.' Maud smiled. 'The case at Duddingston House was our finest, don't you think?'

Daisy uncrossed her arms and nodded. 'It was fortunate for us that the thief turned up that night and swiped the diamond necklace. It put our wee agency on the map and no mistaking.'

'I only wish we could have averted the murder of the poor Viscountess...'

'She wasna so poor.'

'I meant poor in the sense of unfortunate.'

'Aye, she was that all right.'

Maud let out an exasperated sigh. 'Oh, dash it all, Daisy. Are we just to sit here twiddling our thumbs for weeks or, worse, months?'

'There'll be another case soon, I'm sure.'

Maud hoped so. The agency had been doing so well.

'Thank you for waiting a little longer at the office anyway.' Maud rose. 'I'm going to take a bath now and then get ready for Eleanor's dinner party. Martha has put a pie in the oven for you,' she said over her shoulder as she left the room, 'so you won't starve.'

'What is it?' Daisy called. 'I hope it's nae fish again.'

'Haddock.' Maud's voice floated back into the sitting room. 'Fish is good for the brain.'

'Maud, dear!' Eleanor came into the hall to welcome her, as Maud was removing her emerald green hat with matching feathers. 'I'm so glad you could make it to my little dinner party.'

Maud slipped off her green wrap edged with sable and handed it to the butler. She hugged her friend before stepping back and looking at her.

'You look as delightful as ever.'

For a brief moment, Maud envied her old school friend's dark curls, blue eyes and *petite* build. It would make a nice change to be able to look up, rather than down, at a person when talking to them. Maud's hair was fair, her eyes grey and her height a willowy five feet seven inches. But no point in worrying about what can't be changed, she thought.

'As do you, my dear,' Eleanor said, casting an admiring look at Maud's beaded sea-green chiffon gown. 'Now, come into the drawing room.'

Smoothing her long cream gloves, Maud followed her friend. In front of the open french windows, looking out into the garden, stood a distinguished-looking man. He turned to face them.

'Maud, let me introduce Mr Edward Ogilvie.' Eleanor gestured to the tall, late middle-aged man who stepped forward. 'Edward, this is Miss Maud McIntyre, a friend from my school days in Lausanne.'

'Miss McIntyre,' he said in a pleasant voice. 'How do you do.'

'I'm pleased to meet you, sir.' Maud held out a hand and he took it. 'Your name is familiar,' she said, 'although I cannot think why.'

'Mr Ogilvie is the editor of the *Edinburgh Times*,' said Eleanor, with a smile up at him.

Maud was pleased to note that he was a little taller than her. His evening clothes were well-cut, his smile dazzling and his manners impeccable.

Eleanor glanced uneasily at the clock on the mantlepiece. 'I wonder where the Paines are. They are usually the first to arrive.'

Somewhere in the distance the doorbell rang.

'That might be them now,' Eleanor said, sweeping her deep red gown behind her and turning to face the double doors, ready to receive the awaited guests.

'Mr and Mrs Paine,' announced the butler from the doorway.

Mr Paine was an elderly, delicate-looking man with a stoop to his shoulders. Exactly what a parish minister should look like, thought Maud, before transferring her attention to his wife. Close observation was an important skill for a detective. The draped bodice of Mrs Paine's lilac dress gave the sense of a woman who had shrunk in older age.

'We lack only one more to make the dinner party complete,' Eleanor said.

Maud frowned. 'Is George not yet home from the bank?'

'Did I not tell you, my dear? My husband is visiting his mama who has developed lumbago. It's another gentleman guest I'm expecting.'

Before Maud could ask the name of the third man, a heavy knock resounded through the hall as the clock on the mantle struck eight. Low murmuring, followed by long footsteps striding towards the drawing room, and a smiling Lord Hamish Urquhart stepped unannounced into the room.

'Good heavens, that man again,' Maud murmured, as her heart picked up speed.

He was very tall and dark, with broad shoulders and what

some might call noble features: high cheekbones, straight nose, strong chin. She chastised herself. The modern businesswoman had higher thoughts on her mind. Their paths had crossed on two occasions during the course of her work, the first time as a suspect, and here Lord Urquhart was, inserting himself into her life once again. She watched as he walked over to where she stood with Eleanor.

'Hello, Eleanor, light of my eyes.' He took Eleanor's outstretched hand and his lips lightly brushed the back of her hand.

'Hamish,' Eleanor said, with mock severity. 'You are almost late.'

'Almost, but not quite.' He smiled at his hostess, turned to Maud and looked down at her. Not in the figurative sense, but literally.

'Good evening, Miss McIntyre.'

'This is a... pleasant coincidence,' Maud said.

'Oh, do you two know each other?' Eleanor looked from one to the other. 'I had no idea.'

'We've met a couple of times,' he said.

Eleanor laughed. 'Do I sense an intrigue?'

With a start Maud realised that, not having seen her friend for some months, Eleanor did not yet know about the detective agency. She would have to draw her aside when she got the chance, for it wouldn't do to let it be known Lord Urquhart was a past client of her business. Discretion was Maud's byword.

No sooner had the other guests been introduced to Lord Urquhart than the butler appeared in the doorway. 'Dinner is served, madam.'

The dining room lay at the end of the hall. It was as large as the drawing-room and as comfortable, but it lacked the other room's long windows and its furniture was darker and heavier.

'I've put Edward opposite me at the end of the table,' said Eleanor. 'Mrs Paine, if you will take the seat on his right and Mr

Paine on my right. That leaves Maud to your left, Edward, and Hamish here on my left.'

The gentlemen quickly moved to hold the chairs for the ladies and all took their places at the table.

'It's just a simple meal,' Eleanor told them. 'Soup, *poulet rôti au cresson* and, to finish, mixed sorbet.'

'It sounds perfect,' said Lord Urquhart. 'When I was in Paris, the food was delicious, as you would expect, but judging by the number of advertisements for indigestion pills, it seems their culinary excesses take their toll on the digestive system.'

'You have been to Paris?' Maud asked.

'I have, Miss McIntyre.' He smiled. 'The French have a saying about dining. Conversation at table should always be light so as not to distract from the main interest, which is the food. The arrival of soup is followed by a silence. Until the third course, there should be no talk about anything except what one was eating, what one has eaten and what one will eat. But after one has eaten well, one has a duty to make witty conversation. *La crise de foie.*'

Maud blinked.

'Liver attack,' he helpfully explained.

'I understand the French language, Lord Urquhart,' Maud replied.

'Oh? I thought you looked bemused just now.'

'We will not be following that rule here,' said Eleanor, her blue eyes sparkling in the candlelight. 'Witty conversation is an absolute *must*. I will brook no silence at my dining table, if you please.'

'In that case,' said Lord Urquhart, and he began a series of reminiscences which Eleanor and the Paines found diverting. He certainly was an excellent speaker and fond of a lively story. Maud found herself half-vexed, half-fascinated, and wasn't sure which feeling predominated.

'You don't seem particularly amused by our friend's tales,' Mr Ogilvie murmured to her after a while.

'He's rather fond of the sound of his own voice,' Maud replied, keeping her voice low.

Mr Ogilvie smiled. 'That is often the case with young men these days, but I'm sure there's no harm in him.'

'That seems to be the best one can say about him.' Maud sighed. 'Shall we change the subject?'

Maud and Mr Ogilvie moved on to a variety of topics, including the launching of the luxury ocean liner RMS *Titanic* in Belfast in May, yet to make its maiden voyage, and the discovery by the American explorer of Machu Picchu, the Lost City of the Incas, in July. When the newspaper man introduced the theft of the *Mona Lisa* painting from the Louvre in Paris in August, Maud felt her pulse begin to race. Here was a subject she found most interesting.

'Imagine,' she said, 'da Vinci's masterpiece disappeared, leaving only the broken frame and four nails for hanging. I wonder how the thief managed to get into the building, and out again carrying that rectangle of wood. There was no sign of a break-in...'

'The police are of the opinion that the thief had entered with the public at some time the previous day and hidden until nightfall.'

Maud swallowed a mouthful of chicken too hastily and almost choked. 'Oh, the police! I read in *The Scotsman* that they thought the painting must have been taken by someone who really appreciated art and tried to arrest Picasso. How utterly bizarre.'

Mr Ogilvie laughed. 'It does indeed seem a rather large leap.' He took a sip of wine. 'And now many people come to the Louvre to stare at the space.'

It was Maud's turn to laugh. 'What would da Vinci think of that?'

He smiled. 'Now tell me, Miss McIntyre, what do you like to do with your time?'

I'm a detective and I like to solve crimes... is what Maud didn't say. Mr Ogilvie appeared to be genuinely interested, but what should she reveal? It would be good publicity for the agency to feature in his newspaper, but there was also the danger that it could attract not just new clients, but the simply impertinent.

'You hesitate, Miss McIntyre, and yet I feel you are a young lady of strong feelings. Tell me, perhaps, your opinion of the suffragette movement.'

Now here was something Maud could talk about without hesitation. 'I consider it a great shame that women in this day and age should need to campaign for such a basic right as that to vote.'

He nodded. 'The Prime Minister's delay is truly shocking.'

'Only last month the Commons reduced the power of the Lords and awarded its MPs annual salaries, but they could find no time to allow women's suffrage. It's a disgrace.'

'I agree.'

'What, sir, does your wife think of the issue?'

'I regret to say that I never found the right woman and, therefore, I am a bachelor. But I try to keep up with all matters, including those of interest to ladies, and have a page devoted to fashion in my newspaper.'

Maud had seen it. 'Fashion, Mr Ogilvie,' she said in a severe voice, 'is simply one of the subjects that ladies enjoy.'

He smiled. 'I thought you might say that. Indeed, I hoped you would. Tell me, would you be interested in writing an article for the page, seeing that you are a young woman with strong views and a good knowledge of what is happening in the country?'

'On what subject, pray?'

'On anything you wish that would be of interest to the modern-day woman.'

'Really? I'd love to,' Maud said, smiling.

'We could publish it under your own name, a pseudonym or without a name at all, whichever you prefer.'

She became aware that the conversation around the table had fallen silent. Mr Ogilvie and Maud turned towards the other guests.

'Is something the matter?' she enquired.

'I thought I heard Mr Ogilvie offer you a column in his newspaper.' Lord Urquhart looked at Maud.

'You heard correctly, Lord Urquhart,' said Mr Ogilvie.

'How delightful for Miss McIntyre.'

'I believe so.' She smiled at Lord Urquhart. 'Mr Ogilvie wishes me to write an article on women's suffrage, rather than frivolous topics such as the well-dressed woman about town.' A hurt look crossed Lord Urquhart's face and she immediately felt chastened, without knowing why he had reacted in this way. 'Although fashion, of course, has a role to play in modern society...'

'Heavens!' exclaimed Eleanor, coming to the rescue. 'It is time for the ladies to leave the gentlemen to port and cigars.'

One day, Maud thought crossly as she dutifully rose from the table, women will stay and drink and smoke at table and talk politics with the men.

But today was not that day.

The Indian clubs arrived a few days later. Maud opened the box on the kitchen table and lifted out the slim book lying inside the packaging.

'*The Indian Club Exercise Book*. With twenty different diagrammed movements,' she read aloud to Daisy from the cover. She opened it. 'This one looks like fun. The Windmill.'

The drawing depicted a boy in what she took to be a Boy Scouts' uniform, whirling his clubs in a series of concentric circles.

'I dinna ken about fun,' said Daisy. 'More like dislocate your shoulders.'

Maud put the book down and reached into the box to remove the first club. She grasped the handle, lifted it and swung the object in a circle. She immediately felt the weight in its head and toppled backwards onto the rug to land on her backside.

'Maud!' Daisy dashed forward.

'That was... deceptive.' Maud sat up. Tentatively, she rotated her shoulder. 'It's still in its socket.'

'Thank goodness for that,' said Daisy, crouching down beside her. 'Perhaps you should do the exercises on the floor?'

'I'm fine.'

Daisy helped her friend to her feet. More carefully this time, Maud took up the club. 'I can see how the exercises build grip strength and shoulder endurance. Which will be very useful,' she added firmly, 'should I be attacked again.' She'd been assaulted twice in their earlier cases. The next time – there was certain to be a next, given the nature of the work – she would be ready.

Maud removed the second club from the box. She positioned her feet firmly on the rug and, with a club in each hand, began a rhythmic swinging back and forth. Gripping the handles tighter as the clubs rose higher with each swing, she smiled encouragingly at the dubious-looking Daisy. 'Would you like a turn after me?'

The club in Maud's left hand slipped out of her grip and flew across the room, sending the brass candlestick on the mantelpiece crashing to the floor.

'I suppose it'll get easier,' Daisy said, crossing the room to pick up the candlestick. 'But I'll nae be standing anywhere near when you're using them.'

Maud retrieved the club and placed both carefully back in the box. Her hands trembling from the unaccustomed exercise, she opened the instruction book again and read aloud: 'Avoid standing near windows or valuable objects, in order not to break anything with an accidental flying club.'

She averted her gaze from Daisy.

TWO

The next morning, looking businesslike in a white cotton crêpe blouse with a lace panel down the front and a dark brown high-waisted skirt, Maud sat at her desk at the agency.

Newly filled fountain pen in hand, she considered what to write. Mr Ogilvie wouldn't want a history of women's patience and constant disappointment on the subject of female suffrage. Maud looked up as Daisy, in a cream blouse less alarming than the pink one, set a cup of tea in front of her. She thanked her and returned to frowning at the blank sheet of paper.

'How's the article going for the newspaper mannie?' Daisy asked.

Maud sighed. 'If I could just get started, I'm sure then the words would flow.'

Daisy put her own cup and saucer on the desk and dropped into the chair opposite. 'Tell me the first thing that comes into your heid on the topic.'

'The failure of the Conciliation Bill, which was hardly perfect anyway as it excluded several classes of women who could have voted if they were men.'

'On you go, then,' Daisy said. 'Put that down. You can polish it later.'

Maud's pen scratched out a few basic sentences as Daisy sipped her tea.

'I want the Prime Minister to explain why he refused to grant it further Parliamentary time.' Maud put down her fountain pen. 'But is this going to be too political a piece?'

'How can the issue of women's rights be dealt with without politics?' said Daisy, setting down her cup and crossing her arms. 'You have to write it, Maud. You owe it to Mrs Pankhurst and all the women who were assaulted and arrested on Black Friday.'

'And still nothing has changed,' Maud said hotly. She bent her head and scribbled furiously.

'Say something about the awfa force-feeding of suffragettes on hunger strike in English prisons,' added Daisy. 'That news was applauded by some of those muckle gowps in Parliament.'

Maud wrote, then leaned back in her chair. 'Now I need a title. *No Laughing Matter?*'

'Nae, that would put people off reading it in the first place. What about *Passions Run High?*'

'That sounds like a romantic story.' Maud pursed her lips. 'I have it. *Change in the Air.*'

'I'm delighted to say your article was a huge success,' said Mr Ogilvie, when a week later Maud attended the meeting they'd arranged to discuss her piece. 'We've received a large number of letters from our readers, both male and female.'

'Oh?' She arranged the skirts of her fawn silk dress. 'What do they say?'

'You can see for yourself.' He pushed towards her the stack of correspondence on his desk.

'These are all in response to my article?'

'They are. And more than that, a number of them have a variety of questions for you.'

Intrigued, she took the top envelope from the pile and slid out the letter. '*Can you please give me some advice?*' she read aloud. '*My husband has been away at sea for some months and during that time I became very good friends with another man.*' Maud raised her eyes from the sheet of paper. 'She has underlined the word very.'

Mr Ogilvie nodded. 'Go on.'

Slightly hesitant, Maud continued. '*Is this wrong of me? I was so lonely. My friendship with the other man is now over, but should I tell my husband when he returns home? I feel sure you, as a woman of the world, will know what course I should take.*'

Maud put the letter on the desk. 'How can I reply? I have no experience of such things.'

'No matter,' he said. 'You are a sensible woman and there are many people out there, men and women, who need advice but have no one to turn to. You would be helping them.'

Who didn't want to think their advice was useful? 'I'm happy to dispense advice, depending upon its nature, but I don't feel qualified to comment on clandestine relationships.'

'Have you heard of the *Athenian Gazette?*' Mr Ogilvie asked.

'I'm afraid not.'

'In the 1690s, a London bookseller by the name of John Dunton published a new periodical, the *Athenian Gazette*, and in it he began an advice column. He wrote it with a group of male friends. How much experience of life do you think they had?'

'Probably a lot more than me,' Maud said dryly.

Mr Ogilvie smiled at her. 'What I meant was, what these men didn't know – and they could have no experience of matters that you have, as a woman, Miss McIntyre – they made up. Why don't you try replying to these letters? Only those you are comfortable with.'

Maud took a deep breath. Could she do what Mr Ogilvie asked? Yes, she could – and she could speak out in favour of women's rights!

'I would need to present myself as a married lady with two small children, to establish credibility.'

'Accepted. Choose your name.'

Maud thought for a moment. 'Mrs Fraser. That has a respectable ring to it, don't you think?'

Other people's problems were endlessly fascinating. Maud supposed that was one reason why she wanted to be a detective. The following day, gazing at the pile of correspondence Mr Ogilvie had arranged to be delivered to her apartment, she estimated there were enough problems to keep her occupied for some time.

'Just as well you didna tell the editor that you run a detective agency.' Daisy was also staring at the letters. 'Or he might have thought you were touting for custom.'

Maud looked horrified, and Daisy laughed. 'I ken you'd never do such a thing, Maud. I was only saying just as well.'

'Will you give me a hand replying to them?' she asked, spreading the letters across her desk. 'Mr Ogilvie is paying for the column, and we can put it into the business.' She had done the same with the money she'd received for the article.

Daisy pushed up her sleeves. 'Let me at 'em.'

'Be respectful, Daisy,' Maud cautioned.

'Aye.' Daisy flexed her fingers and spat on her palms.

Maud pretended she hadn't seen. 'Shall I read each letter in turn and then we can decide which of us should answer?'

'Go ahead.'

Maud opened the first letter, put the envelope in the

wastepaper bin under the desk and began to read. '*Can you please tell me where I can get a husband?*'

'Glory be!' Daisy said. 'I thought that sort of question went out with the ark.'

Seeing the mischief in Daisy's eyes, Maud said firmly, 'I will reply to this lady and tell her to put aside her own troubles to help women less fortunate than herself.'

She opened the next letter. 'This one is from a woman concerned that her daughter's health is being affected by the tight corsets the girl is forced to wear at boarding school.'

'We can't approve of tight lacings, right enough.'

'Can you reply to the effect that the boarding school is a little old-fashioned and that the s-shaped silhouette will surely soon be a thing of the past.' Maud paused. 'In fact, I remember reading that a rubberised material is being developed and this will replace the corset.'

'I could try the patriotic approach.' Daisy grinned. 'If there's to be a war – and God kens no one wants one – say that if women didn't buy corsets, there would be enough metal to build a battleship.'

Despite the thought of a possible war, Maud laughed at the image of a ship sailing along, its corsets flapping in the breeze.

She turned to the next letter.

'What do you think about this one, Daisy? The writer is a housemaid in the Highlands. She says she's very happy in her work, likes her employer and is well treated, but she is worried as she feels that something not-quite-right is going on in the house.'

'What sort of not-quite-right?'

Maud frowned and looked again at the letter. 'She doesn't say. She adds she's a good Christian and is unsure if she should leave her employment or stay and ignore her suspicions. She signs herself Rose.' Maud glanced up at Daisy.

'I dinna see how Mrs Fraser can answer that without knowing a wee bitty more.'

'I agree. I'll reply through the women's page saying that I can't comment as I don't know the facts of the situation. It's not a very satisfactory answer, but it can't be helped.'

Over breakfast a couple of days later, Daisy opened the morning's post. 'This is from the editor. He's enclosed a letter addressed to Mrs Fraser care of the *Edinburgh Times*.'

'That sounds intriguing,' Maud said, pouring more tea for them both. 'Open it, do.'

Daisy did so and pulled out a single sheet of writing paper.

From where she sat at the other side of the desk, Maud could see it was good-quality paper in pale blue.

Daisy read the letter quickly. 'It's from that housemaid Rose, with the not-quite-right household.'

'She's in Edinburgh,' Maud said.

Daisy looked up. 'How did you ken that?'

Maud nodded at the envelope. 'From the postmark. What does she say?'

'She doesna want to put her concerns in writing, but she will meet you – Mrs Fraser, that is.'

Maud hesitated. On the one hand, the agency had no work at present, but on the other hand, they couldn't really afford to take on a case pro bono. Could they?

Daisy must have guessed Maud's thoughts, for she said, 'A maid canna afford to pay us, but what about the money we've made from the two columns? In a way it seems fair, as that's how Rose came to us.'

'Very well, Daisy. Does she say where and when she would like to meet?'

Daisy checked the letter. 'Rose is here for an event her employer's organised for Monday evening. She's got that afternoon off and asks Mrs Fraser to meet her in the tea shop at the Old Waverley Hotel on Princes Street at four o'clock, if that is convenient.'

Maud didn't need the consult the diary; she knew it was empty.

Maud and Daisy were sitting in the busy tearoom in good time the next day, chatting while keeping an eye on the door. Exactly on time a solitary woman came in, wearing a neat hat trimmed with a sprig of lavender. Maud judged her to be a couple of years younger than her, perhaps twenty-three. The young woman looked shyly around the room and, not seeing a lady seated alone of an age to have two small children, she flushed and turned to leave. Maud rose hurriedly and, weaving between the tables, caught up with the young woman who already had her hand on the door.

'Rose?' asked Maud in a soft voice.

'Yes?' The girl's voice was barely above a whisper. 'How do you know my name?'

'I'm the woman you are here to meet.'

Rose let herself be led to where Daisy sat. 'We're pleased to meet you, Rose.' Daisy gave her a big smile and gestured to the empty chair at their table.

Still looking fearful, Rose perched on the edge of the seat, gripping the bag on her lap.

'I'm Maud McIntyre and I run a detective agency,' Maud began.

Rose gave a little gasp and made to rise.

'Please dinna go,' said Daisy, putting out a hand.

Rose reluctantly resumed her seat.

'I'm Daisy Cameron,' added Daisy. 'Together, Maud and I make up Mrs Fraser.'

'It's really quite simple,' said Maud. 'The editor of the *Edin-*

burgh Times asked me to write a column for his newspaper, which I agreed to do under another name. Rather a lot of letters arrived, so I asked my friend and assistant to help me reply to them all.'

'When your letter came in,' went on Daisy, taking up the story, 'we realised it was an out-of-the-ordinary problem and decided to help you.' She beamed.

'But I can't afford to pay a private detective,' Rose whispered.

'Dinna worry,' said Daisy, 'we're not going to charge you. Because of the money we got from writing the column, we've decided to work on your case pro...' She turned to Maud.

'Pro bono?'

'Nae, not that. The other one.'

'Quid pro quo?'

'Aye, that's it.'

Maud didn't think that was quite the right phrase here, but she let it go.

'So,' she said to Rose, 'we'd very much like to help you.'

Maud noticed Rose's clutch relax a little on her bag, and went on in a low, confiding tone. 'What is it you are worried about, Rose?'

Rose glanced around, saw the waitress making her way over and gripped her bag again.

'Tea for three, please,' Maud said. The waitress nodded and left.

'You were saying, Rose?' Maud smiled at her. The young woman hadn't been saying anything at all and she needed to be drawn out.

Taking a deep breath, Rose fixed her gaze on Maud. 'My name is Rose Gilmour and my employer is an art dealer. He owns a big gallery in Edinburgh and a small one in Braemar. The family house is in Braemar and that's where I work as a live-in maid, but he also has a large house in Royal Circus where he stays most of the time.' She paused for breath.

Royal Circus in the Stockbridge area of Edinburgh. It was part of the New Town, most of which favoured straight lines, but Royal Circus was a beautiful curved street of Georgian houses and apartments. They housed the great and the good of Edinburgh's society, Maud knew, from doctors and solicitors to businessmen and church ministers. And art dealers, as it turned out. She nodded encouragingly.

'My employer' – Rose dropped her voice to whisper his name – 'Mr Anderson, buys paintings from large houses around Scotland and sells them in his gallery in Dundas Street. His son, Mr David, runs the Braemar gallery. My fear is...' she glanced down at her white-knuckled hands on her bag.

'He's got the *Mona Lisa!*' Daisy exclaimed.

'What?' Rose looked up, startled.

'Hush, Daisy,' Maud hissed, 'keep your voice down.' She glanced quickly round the tea shop, her heart thumping. Thank goodness the general hubbub from the chatting customers had drowned out Daisy's excited voice.

'No, not a stolen painting, but something worse,' whispered Rose. 'I think my employer and his son are working with a forger.'

There was a pause as they digested what Rose had said.

'And what makes you think that?' Maud asked.

'A man comes to the Braemar house with paintings and then they sell for a lot of money in the village gallery.'

The waitress approached with a tray. They waited until their order was placed on the table and the waitress had again departed.

'But isna that what art dealers do?' said Daisy. 'Buy pictures and sell them for a profit?'

'Yes, but these paintings are brought to the house late at night. I've never seen the seller's face as he wears a hat pulled low, but his boots are brown and very scuffed.' Seeing the blank expressions on Maud and Daisy's faces, she went on, 'The paintings are by Zurbarán.'

Maud had no idea who Zurbarán was.

'I take it this artist's work goes for a lot of money?' said Daisy.

Rose nodded. 'One of his paintings would sell for more than I could earn in fifteen years.'

And yet the fellow who sold them couldn't afford new boots, Maud thought. 'When did this man first come to the house?' she asked.

'I can't be certain as I've been employed in Mr David's house for only five months, but I believe it was four months ago.'

'And how many paintings have there been during that time?'

'Two. And just before I wrote to you, another painting by the same artist was brought to the house by the same man.'

'Perhaps the artist fellow you mentioned just paints an awfa lot,' Daisy said.

'Zurbarán died in the seventeenth century!' Tears shone in Rose's eyes.

'So you think that the mannie who comes to the house is painting them himself?' Daisy glanced at Maud.

'And this third picture has also sold for a large sum of money?' Maud asked.

'I don't know,' Rose said. 'It hadn't been put into the gallery when I left the village.'

'Hmm.' Maud poured tea for the three of them. 'Tell me about the Andersons.'

'There are only the two. Mrs Anderson died many years ago, I've been told. Mr Anderson comes to Braemar every month to see how the small gallery is doing. His son, Mr David, is unmarried, lives in the Braemar house and goes down to

Edinburgh from time to time. He started work in his father's business about two years ago.'

'And this evening's event?' asked Maud.

Rose turned pale. 'It's a private viewing for Mr Anderson's best customers. He asked me to help the other maids, those employed at his Edinburgh house, to serve the refreshments. I'm so afraid that this new painting is going to be being exhibited and that one of the experts tonight will see it is not a genuine Zurbarán, and my employer will be sent to prison.'

Maud glanced at Daisy. It was clear that her assistant wanted to take the case.

'We'd like to investigate further, if you agree,' Maud said. 'Miss Cameron and I will be very discreet, so you need have no concern on that score about losing your employment.'

Rose nodded slowly, her eyes a little red as she clutched her handkerchief. Daisy made a note of the Andersons' two addresses and a few other details, while Rose drank her tea.

'I'd better go.' Rose got to her feet. 'I'm returning tomorrow in the motor car with Mr Anderson. There's a nice hotel in the village where you could stay. The Braemar Arms.'

'Miss Cameron and I will travel up by train tomorrow. Oh, one further thing, Rose. Can you describe the supposed old masters?'

'No, I'm sorry I can't. I only caught a glimpse of the first two paintings, and they were small – less than a foot square – and what are known as still lifes.' Her voice wavered. 'I hope it's nothing, but I can't stop thinking... I might be working for a criminal.'

The following morning Maud left a note for Martha, their daily maid, before finishing her packing. She reluctantly decided there was no room in the Gladstone bag for a single disguise. Besides, until they reached Braemar, she had no idea what, if any, disguise might be needed. She and Daisy set off for Waverley station.

'What on earth have you got in there, Maud?' Daisy said, when Maud stopped in the street for the second time to shift her bag to the other hand. 'Anyone would think—' She caught sight of Maud's sheepish look. 'You havena? Dinna tell me you've packed those clubs?'

'There was no point my buying them if I don't use them,' Maud said sharply.

'Keep your bonnet on,' Daisy told her. 'Never mind, we're almost there.'

Inside the great cavern of Waverley station, whistles sounded, doors slammed and everywhere steam billowed. A paper boy at his stand, waving a copy of the daily newspaper above his head, bawled out the headlines: '*Scott and Amundsen race to the South Pole latest!*'

The guard was already raising his flag as the pair dashed onto the platform. Maud swung open a third-class door, and they scrambled in. To her relief, the compartment was empty. She had barely closed the door when the whistle went. With a hiss of steam the train pulled out.

The towers and spires of the capital's grand buildings slid by the window. Through the other side of the tunnel and they were met with the ever-splendid sight of Edinburgh Castle, perched high on its volcanic rock. It had been home to Scottish royalty for nine hundred years, including Mary, Queen of Scots and her son James, the monarch who joined the crowns of England and Ireland after the death of the childless Queen Elizabeth.

The train steamed across the magnificent Forth Rail Bridge as the estuary glittered below them. They were to follow the North Sea up the coast and would see mountains looming in the misty distance beyond the water. Maud and Daisy settled down in contentment.

Two hours later, they were approaching a long, curved bridge.

'The Tay Bridge,' Daisy whispered.

'It's been rebuilt, Daisy, and this one is perfectly safe.' Some thirty years ago, during a violent storm one December night, the central span of the bridge collapsed into the river, taking with it the train travelling from Edinburgh and killing all seventy-five souls aboard. Maud knew it was foolish, yet as they passed over the bridge, she couldn't help but cross her fingers to be absolutely sure.

Green fields dotted with sheep and cows, fields of golden stubble with sheaves of hay formed into stooks, the glittering grey of the North Sea, misty mountains – all was delightful.

As the train pulled into Aberdeen, the end of the line, Daisy leaned towards Maud. 'Just think, we've travelled over one hundred and fifty miles!'

Maud smiled. 'And it's not over yet. We've still got more than fifty miles to go.'

They hurried to buy tickets for the Great North of Scotland Railway. Barely had they finished a hasty luncheon in the station buffet than there came the call for Ballater.

In the compartment, Maud just had time to note there were three other passengers before they were off again, travelling inland now, on their way into the wild and rugged Highlands.

'Famous for its mountains and stags, loch and men in kilts,' Daisy murmured to Maud. 'I wonder if we'll see any of those – braw laddies in kilts, that is.'

Before she could reply, the older gentleman seated in the opposite corner spoke. 'We are fortunate to be travelling in autumn and not winter.' He lowered his copy of the *Aberdeen Journal*, revealing a face notably pale against his dark suit, and folded the newspaper neatly in his lap. Schoolteacher or bank manager, Maud thought, as she politely inclined her head.

He took her gesture as an invitation to continue. 'The High-

lands have an average of thirty-six to one hundred and five days
of snow each year.'

A teacher, she decided. Thanking him for the information,
she pulled a book from her commodious bag, and a pair of plain-
glass pince-nez, which she settled on the bridge of her nose.
This journey was an opportunity to hone her observation skills.
Opening *Lady Molly of Scotland Yard*, she held it a few inches
from her face to imitate short-sightedness. She turned her attention to the young man slumped in the far corner. His pulled-
down cap, drawn-up jacket collar and whiff of whisky suggested
an unsavoury character.

Maud's pulse quickened. Could the fellow be in disguise?
Sherlock Holmes could disguise himself so effectively that even
Dr Watson failed to recognise him. In *The Adventure of the
Final Problem*, Holmes tells his friend he will meet him on the
Continental express at Victoria Station. When Watson boards
the boat train, the only other passenger in their reserved
compartment is an elderly priest dressed in black cassock and
hat. Once the doors had been shut and the whistle blown,
Watson hears Holmes speak to him. Astonished, he turns to see
the aged cleric straighten in his seat and become Holmes.

She smiled inwardly as the train pulled into Banchory
station. No one in the carriage moved or spoke, and none
entered their compartment. The train chugged forward again.

Maud peered over her book to study the woman seated
opposite the young man. She wore red lipstick, a smart suit and
a large hat set at a jaunty angle, yet couldn't be more than
twenty. The girl rummaged in her leather handbag, took a
cigarette from a silver case and lit it. Inhaling deeply, she leaned
back against the upholstery and let out a smoke-filled sigh.

'This is a non-smoking compartment,' said the teacher.

'Then move if you don't like it,' the girl suggested without
looking at him.

'He's right, you ken.' Daisy pointed to the window. 'It doesna say Smoking.'

Casting a stony glare at Daisy, the girl took two more pulls on her cigarette before dropping it to the floor and grinding it under her buckled shoe.

The teacher continued. 'I remember when—'

'If I have to listen to you drivelling on, I'll need a stiff drink.' The slumped man struggled to sit up.

The teacher straightened his shoulders. 'I think you've had quite enough to drink already.'

The young man rose, swaying with the movement of the train. 'Get on your feet, man.'

The teacher's face flushed.

'Stop that.'

To Maud's surprise, it was the girl who had spoken, her voice sharp. 'Sit down.'

He shrugged and dropped back into his seat.

Maud turned to the teacher. 'Are you all right?'

'Yes, thank you.' His heightened colour deepened. He raised his newspaper and stayed behind it until the train slowed to a halt at the next station.

'Ballater station,' called the guard, passing down the platform outside. 'All change.'

Maud and Daisy rose. The young man pulled his knapsack from the netting rack overhead, then pushed his way past everyone to get to the door. He released the leather strap, the window thudding down, and leaned out to turn the handle. The door swung open and he stumbled down onto the platform, his foot glancing off the running board. The girl alighted next, her haste almost as swift.

The teacher touched his hat to Maud and Daisy, then followed the girl across to the other platform, where a single-carriage train idled. The girl stood casting her gaze around until he boarded the first compartment, then seeing Maud and Daisy, she stepped into the next one and closed the door.

'That must be for Braemar,' said Daisy, and they, too, crossed to the opposite platform.

They walked along the side of the train, glancing in the windows as they went.

'There's that crabbit fellow,' said Daisy, seeing the young man slumped in the third compartment. 'We dinna want to travel with him again.'

'We're in luck.' Maud glanced into the fourth one. 'An empty compartment at the back of the train.'

She put out a hand and turned the brass handle.

The door flew open and out rolled the body of a man.

THREE

Maud gasped at the dead weight of the corpse. Her Gladstone went flying as she staggered backwards in an attempt to catch the man before he hit the platform.

Daisy shrieked, dropped her own bag and jumped forward to help Maud, who was already kneeling on the ground, the man's bloodied head in her lap.

Maud stared into the compartment. A small revolver lay on the floor. Blood had splattered the back of the seat and a glistening red pool had formed on the wooden floor. She looked down at the dead man, crumpled on the concrete platform. There was an ugly wound in the right temple of his fleshy face.

A guard came running. 'What—?' He took one look at the man, turned pale and called, 'Mr Harrison!'

The portly stationmaster had already come out of his office at Daisy's scream and now he jostled the younger man out of the way.

'Good grief!' Mr Harrison said. 'In all my years working at this station, I've never had anything like this happen before. Nabbs, telephone Sergeant Peebles,' he ordered.

'Yes, sir.' The guard ran off towards the stationmaster's office.

'Don't touch anything until the sergeant gets here,' Mr Harrison warned Maud and Daisy. 'That applies to everyone,' he added, seeing the other compartment doors on the train open and the occupants climb back down onto the platform.

'Surely not Maud, though,' Daisy pointed out. 'She canna be expected to sit there with his heid in her lap until the policeman arrives.'

'No, of course not; you're right. Here, miss, let me help you.'

Mr Harrison knelt on the platform beside Maud, and together they lifted the man's head and shoulders from her lap with as much reverence as the situation allowed. Once Maud was free, Daisy helped her to her feet.

'Your skirt,' she said, taking in the dark smear on the front of Maud's blue tweed. She picked up her friend's bag, brushed it down and placed it next to hers on the platform.

'What is the hold-up?' called the young woman. 'I must get to Braemar before dinner or my father will be cross.' Suddenly, she sounded young and fretful.

'Please stay back there,' cried the stationmaster, positioning himself so that the body was not clearly visible.

Nabbs emerged from the office and joined the trio gathered round the body on the platform.

'Should I get a tarpaulin to cover the gentleman, Mr Harrison?' asked Nabbs. 'It seems disrespectful to be staring at him.'

The stationmaster considered. 'You're right, Nabbs. It can't do any harm. Go and fetch one.'

The guard ran off again and returned within minutes carrying a heavy cloth, grey with ingrained coal dust. He and Mr Harrison carefully laid the tarpaulin over the dead man. One huge, raw-looking hand with thick fingers stuck out from under the cloth.

A farmer, Maud thought, or the owner of some small business; someone who had lately come into, or decided to spend, money. She had noticed, too, before he was covered, that the short, stocky man was of late middle age, nearer to sixty than fifty, and his clothes were startling. A tweed suit of the loudest check imaginable – a light-coloured background with lines of orange, blue and brown. He was like a caricature of a Scottish country gentleman. Perhaps, she wondered, he dressed like that because he thought that was how one ought to dress in a village in the Highlands.

The hiss of steam jerked Maud from her thoughts. There were a couple of clunks as the engine was uncoupled, taken round on the adjacent track and coupled to what was now the front of the train.

'How long will we have to wait?' The young woman, her tone petulant, had come to stand beside Maud.

'It'll take as long as it takes, miss,' said Mr Harrison.

She pouted and Maud waited to see what she would say next, but to everyone's evident relief, the police sergeant and a gentleman with a doctor's bag arrived.

'*Feasgar math*, Bert,' said Sergeant Peebles.

'It was a good afternoon, until this happened.' Bert Harrison grimaced at the tarpaulin-covered mound.

'Aye.' The sergeant's gaze went to the gun lying on the floor of the blood-splattered compartment. 'I can see at a glance that this is no accident. But suicide or murder, it's a bad business.' He shook his head.

The doctor was already crouching down and peeling back the cloth from the top half of the dead man.

'Were you first on the scene, Nabbs?' asked Sergeant Peebles.

'No, sir,' said Nabbs, looking fearful. 'It was these two young ladies. More particularly this young lady.' He indicated Maud. 'The body fell on top of her.'

'*Fell* on the young lady, you say?' Sergeant Peebles raised his eyebrows. 'I hope you weren't hurt, miss.'

'Not at all,' said Maud, privately giving thanks for her Indian club arm- and shoulder-strengthening exercises. 'Miss Cameron and I managed to lower the poor gentleman to the ground.'

'And what might your name be, miss?' he asked Maud.

'I am Miss Maud McIntyre.'

'Did you know the deceased, Miss McIntyre?'

'I have never seen him before.'

Out of the corner of her eye, Maud saw the young woman take a step closer to the body half-uncovered on the platform and heard the instant sharp breath. Maud wasn't the only one to turn to look at the girl, who was staring, white-faced, at the dead man.

'Father!' The girl let out a piercing scream.

The assembled group on the platform all turned to stare at the girl. To Maud's surprise, the obnoxious young man stepped forward and put an arm around the young woman's shoulders to comfort her.

'Sorry, miss, but is this man your father?' said the sergeant, finding his voice.

The girl nodded, tearful.

Maud removed a clean white handkerchief from her bag and handed it to the girl, who took it and dabbed at her eyes.

'What is your name, miss?' Sergeant Peebles asked.

'Bisset. Lilias Bisset.' Her voice was barely above a whisper.

'Do you have any idea why he was on this train?'

'No.'

'Or why he would want to kill himself?'

Or, thought Maud, who might want to murder him?

Miss Bisset shook her head, blew her nose into the handkerchief and passed it back to Maud.

'Do please keep it,' Maud murmured.

The sergeant crouched down to the body and carefully slid his hand into the inside pocket of the dead man's lurid jacket. He withdrew a wallet and opened it. Maud positioned herself so that she could see its contents. A wedge of bank notes. If he had been murdered, then the motive wasn't robbery.

'Not robbery then.' The sergeant replaced the wallet, stood again and glanced down at the body. 'Seems likely it was suicide.'

The girl let out a wail.

'Apologies, miss,' the policeman said quickly.

'Come and sit over here,' Daisy said to the distraught young woman.

'I'll take her.' The young man, his arm still around her shoulders, led Miss Bisset to the seat on the platform and made sure she was comfortable.

The shock appeared to have sobered him up, Maud thought, watching them. And if he was an acquaintance of Miss Bisset, it was possible that he had also known her father.

'I have seen the man in Braemar,' the schoolteacher stepped forward and spoke, looking down at the dead man. 'On one or two occasions, but I don't know him. I believe the family moved to the village just a few months ago, and they haven't fitted in.'

'Would you say he has been dead for only a short time?' Maud asked the doctor, before turning her frowning gaze on the body.

The doctor covered the man with the tarpaulin again and got to his feet. 'I would, by the look of it. Less than an hour, it would have to be.'

'Indeed,' Maud said. 'It takes no more than thirty minutes for the train to reach here from Braemar.'

The doctor turned to face Sergeant Peebles. 'I'll get him moved.'

'That would be for the best. Will you be wanting a cart? I'm sure there's a spare one around the station.'

'Already in hand. The station guard was away to... ah,' said the doctor, gesturing to the uniformed man arriving with a canvas stretcher over his shoulder. 'There it is now, if I'm not mistaken.'

The sergeant addressed Mr Harrison. 'Do you know if the stationmaster at either Braemar or Bridge of Gairn noticed anything unusual, Bert?'

'I'll go and telephone them now.'

Maud watched as the uniformed man placed the stretcher on the ground beside the body. The dead man was then lifted by him and Nabbs onto the stretcher and carried to the horse-drawn ambulance waiting at the station entrance.

Bert Harrison returned. 'Nothing out of the ordinary was spotted at Braemar, Douggie,' he reported to the sergeant.

'Ah,' said Maud, her eyes lighting up, 'then something was noticed between Braemar and here?'

'I can't say for sure, miss, but Fred at Bridge of Gairn said an agitated man with unkempt whiskers, and wearing trousers splashed with brown paint, had hurried from train, pushed his ticket into Fred's hand and disappeared down the road.'

'That doesn't exactly sound like a man running from the scene of the crime,' said Sergeant Peebles. 'More like a man late home and in trouble with his woman.'

He and Bert Harrison laughed.

Maud felt herself bristle, offended that they were joking over the body of so recently deceased a person. And at the expense of a woman, no less. She pushed the feeling aside. There were important questions to be asked.

'What colour were the man's whiskers?'

Mr Harrison turned to look at her. 'Let me think.' He

frowned. 'Aye, Fred said they were fair or white, he couldn't be rightly sure as the man dashed past him, but they were a light colour.'

'What else was he wearing?'

'Jacket and flat cap, Fred said.' Mr Harrison stared at her. 'Why do you ask?'

'I thought perhaps I might have seen him from the train window, but alas I don't believe I did.' Maud didn't intend to reveal her real purpose in asking the questions. From what she had noted so far, it was evident the police officer would have found the notion of a female detective an amusing one.

The sergeant clearly felt he needed to take charge of the questioning. 'Was the train running on time?' he asked Mr Harrison.

'Aye. It left Braemar at one-twenty and Bridge of Gairn at one-fifty, arriving here at two o'clock.'

'I'll need to speak to the two stationmasters, but it looks like Mr Bisset boarded the train at Braemar and shot himself somewhere on the journey between there and here.'

'That's about it,' said Bert Harrison. 'Although Fred saw no occupants in the train when it left Bridge of Gairn, so likely the poor man was already dead and slumped over, out of Fred's sight.'

The sergeant gave a sad shake of his head. 'It looks very much like an ordinary suicide.' He pursed his lips.

'It certainly does look like that.' Maud's gaze rested for a moment on the revolver and the spent cartridge lying on the compartment floor.

Sergeant Peebles sent her a sharp look. 'It fits together. The man was newly in the village, knowing no one here by the sound of it and, probably homesick for wherever he'd come from, put a bullet through his head. It fits.'

'It fits perfectly,' Maud said.

The sergeant sent her another suspicious glance.

'The thing is, the question that came to mind as I was cradling his head in my lap was why would someone shoot themselves on a train?' In fact, there was more than one question, but she wanted to keep it simple.

'I don't suppose a suicidal man would weigh up the different methods or location.'

And yet he had the foresight to carry a gun with him. 'Will there need to be an investigation by the Procurator Fiscal?' she asked.

'It's not an accidental or a sudden or unexplained death, but it is a suspicious one, right enough,' said the sergeant. 'I'll need to report it to the PF. He'll order a post-mortem, and I'll be gathering witness statements, but it's my betting that the Fiscal will agree it's a suicide. That word won't be put on the death certificate, mind, but gun wound or such like.'

'What about the Railway Police?' put in Daisy.

'You ladies are well-informed,' said Sergeant Peebles, his tone decidedly unfriendly as he directed his glare at both Maud and Daisy.

'We like to keep up-to-date,' she said, adjusting her hat with its green ribbon.

'Well, that's as may be.' He turned at the sound of the horse-drawn ambulance moving off with the dead man. 'There's no Railway Police hereabouts,' he continued to Maud and Daisy, 'so I'll see what the Procurator Fiscal says.'

He climbed into the compartment, edged carefully round the pool of blood on the floor and picked up the revolver and then the empty cartridge case. The blood on the back of the seat near the open door indicated where the dead man must have been sitting when the gun was fired, Maud thought. The movement of the train, and in particular the momentum when it juddered to a halt must have caused his body to fall against the door.

The sergeant slid the gun and cartridge into the trouser pocket of his uniform and stepped back onto the platform.

'Now, if everyone could let me have their names and addresses, starting with you, Miss McIntyre.' He pulled his notebook and pencil from his jacket pocket and licked the end of his pencil.

'Bert,' the police sergeant threw over his shoulder to the stationmaster, 'can you get this compartment locked? Then the train can be on its way. Once it's back at Braemar, I'll examine the compartment in more detail, and after that, you can get your cleaners in.'

Maud and Daisy gave their names and address in Edinburgh, adding that they would be staying at the Braemar Arms for the time being.

'If you could board, please, ladies.' Sergeant Peebles nodded towards the waiting train.

Maud held Daisy back, pretending to search for something in her bag, while she listened to the details given by their fellow passengers. The older man was, as Maud had surmised, a teacher, for he gave his name as Mr Shepherd of the School House, Braemar. He then got onto the train.

The sergeant glared at Maud, so she and Daisy could delay no longer. They walked past the now-locked door to the next compartment, climbed inside and swung the door shut. Maud let down the window to listen to the information the remaining two travellers supplied to the policeman.

Sergeant Peebles walked over to where the young woman still sat on the platform bench, the young man standing a little awkwardly beside her. No matter how much she tried, Maud could not hear the replies Miss Bisset or the young man gave. Yet watching them, Maud felt sure they were a couple.

Their details given, the man assisted Miss Bisset up the step and onto the train, though he didn't board himself. He leaned in and murmured something to her. She gave an agitated reply.

Maud strained to hear their conversation, but it was impossible for at that moment the guard's whistle blew. The young man hurriedly made up his mind, jumped into the compartment and slammed the door shut.

Maud wondered about the young couple as the train began to move away. They appeared to know each other, yet had pretended to be strangers. Why? Mr Shepherd and the Bissets lived in the same small village, but they didn't know each other. Or perhaps they didn't want to know each other. What was it the schoolteacher had said? *They haven't fitted in.* Why was that?

FOUR

'So,' said Maud to Daisy, as she made herself as comfortable as possible. The shuttle train had thinly padded seats. At least it was clean, she thought, unlike the bloodied front of her skirt. 'What do you make of the dead Mr Bisset?'

'I canna believe it's suicide. It would be a strange way to kill yourself – getting on a train to shoot yourself in the heid. Wouldna most people just step in front of the train?'

Maud nodded her agreement. 'I'm not a pistol-shot,' she went on, 'but I know a little about guns from my father.'

'Aye?' Daisy leaned forward eagerly in her seat.

'The cartridge case was in the wrong place.'

Daisy frowned. 'I dinna ken what you mean.'

'Let us say that the man was seated on the right-hand side of the compartment and near the door where he got on, which we must assume was the case, given the blood on the back of the seat and on the floor. You'll have noticed there were only a few splashes on the mirror in the centre of the wall behind the seats. If the man put the revolver to his right temple—'

'And assuming he was right-handed...'

Maud nodded. 'And he then pulled the trigger, the empty

cartridge case ought to be somewhere close to that spot and not where it was – by the far door.'

'You mean,' said Daisy, thinking it through, 'that the gun *wasna* held against his heid?'

'That's exactly what I mean. Whoever killed him was standing by the far door when he – or she – fired. They remembered to place the gun on the floor near the body, but did not think to do the same with the cartridge case.'

Maud glanced out of the window and saw that the large, prosperous-looking houses in grey stone had been replaced by hills and trees. To her left, the Dee wound and sparkled its way along the riverbed. The landscape was magnificent, with just the occasional farmhouse and sheep grazing in fields. In the distance, there were dark mountains with their tops covered in snow.

'Snaw in September,' said Daisy, following her friend's gaze. 'Who'd have ken it?' She gave a theatrical shiver and leaned back in her seat.

Within a short time, the train began to slow down.

'Bridge of Gairn,' said Maud, reading the station sign. 'Where it would seem our murderer alighted from the train.'

'Should we get off here and have a wee chat with the stationmaster?'

'We're not working on this case, Daisy,' Maud reminded her. 'Although I do confess to a certain curiosity. Let's first see what happens with our new investigation.'

The stationmaster came out of his office and stood on the platform ready to take tickets, but no one got on or off the train, and, within minutes, they were jolting on their way again.

'Did anything strike you about the description the stationmaster gave of the man hurrying away from the station?' Maud asked.

'Aye. First, his breeks. They were splattered with brown

paint, the station mannie said. That colour could easily hide any splashes of blood.'

'I agree. And I thought it interesting that he made no mention of paint on the jacket.'

'I suppose a painter could take it off to work?' Daisy suggested doubtfully.

'But over time, and given the weather generally in this country, a painter and decorator would have accrued some marks on his jacket. Did anything else strike you about the man's appearance?'

Daisy thought for a moment. 'You'd expect his whiskers to be unkempt, whether he'd just murdered a man or finished work for the day, so nae that... They were fair or white, which means he could be young or old.'

'My thoughts too.'

They passed a white suspension bridge over the river, then the Dee wound away and disappeared from sight. Maud could see tall birches and pines, rocky ground and drystone dykes, then lush rolling fields with sheep grazing, a path winding up to some distant cottage. A pretty castle perched precariously on the riverbank came into view. Tree branches swayed in the breeze, making patterns of light like a kaleidoscope. It was all idyllic. Far too beautiful for murder.

They travelled ever westwards. A delightful little stone church appeared and slowly disappeared as the train trundled past. The road was visible now and a government van appeared, travelling in the same direction. With a merry toot of its horn, the motor van overtook the train. Maud suspected even a bicyclist could overtake them, so slowly were they rumbling and jolting along. Cycling might be good fun, but first she'd have to learn how to ride such a machine...

The motor van turned into a long wide avenue, which curved away to the right.

'That must have been Crathie Kirk just now, where the

royal family worship,' said Daisy, 'and that the driveway to
Balmoral Castle. Perhaps the van is delivering supplies from
Ballater for the royals.'

The spires on the corners of the tower were just visible
above the trees. Rising from the tower was the red, gold and
blue of the Royal Standard of the United Kingdom.

'Look!' cried Daisy, pointing to the flag. 'The King is in
residence!'

Maud smiled. 'Then we might see him in Braemar, if we're
lucky.'

'I hope so. We'd get a much better look at him here than in
Edinburgh. When he and the Queen came on their coronation
tour in July, the city was hoatching.'

The landscape became wild and rocky again. At some stage,
the river had reappeared and shimmered its way under a second
suspension bridge strung high across the Dee. Within minutes,
it seemed, the scenery was again green and lush. A mansion
house came into sight – presumably the laird's residence. Then
Braemar Castle loomed, an old toll house, a graveyard, and the
train reached its destination.

'Braemar station!' called the guard. 'End of the line.'

'And the beginning of our investigation.' Maud smiled at
her friend.

She picked up her bag and climbed down onto the platform,
glancing along the length of the short train as she did so. She
saw Mr Shepherd alight, and then Miss Bisset, and they each
walked out of the tiny station. Maud looked around for the
remaining passenger. The young man was nowhere to be seen.

Maud and Daisy passed under the station canopy painted
in a pretty green and white, crossed the road and walked along
the main street. Maud's first impressions of this little Highland
village were distinctly favourable: a row of charming cottages
set back from the road – the cottages had no gardens, but all had
contrived to grow colourful dahlias and gladioli in pots at their

front doors – a green with Highland cattle grazing, the ruins of a castle, church spires and mountains in every direction.

'It's awfa bonnie,' Daisy observed.

'It is,' said Maud, 'and compact too. If I'm not mistaken, that's the hotel.'

They crossed the stone bridge over the river and came to a two-storey inn displaying the name of the Braemar Arms. It was a long, handsome building with bay windows. The tiled canopy over the wide front door was supported in a manner by gnarled tree trunks painted in green.

A gentleman of middle years standing outside the hotel raised his bowler hat and stepped forward to welcome them.

'*Fáilte*, ladies. I am Mr Wallace, the hotel proprietor.'

'Thank you, Mr Wallace. We are Miss McIntyre and Miss Cameron. I believe you are expecting us.'

He held the door open for them. 'My good lady will see to your requirements.'

The late afternoon had turned a little chilly, and when Maud caught sight of the banked-up fire in the hearth and the floral overstuffed armchairs beside it, she thought it a most welcoming place.

They moved forward to make themselves known to Mrs Wallace, a plump woman who looked to be about forty years of age, the same as her husband. Her mass of salt-and-pepper hair was pulled not very expertly into a bun. She wore a royal blue silk day dress with cream lace on the bodice. Maud immediately liked Mrs Wallace's warm smile as the woman came out from behind the desk.

'*Feasgar math.*'

When neither Maud nor Daisy replied immediately, Mrs Wallace said, 'You will not have the Gaelic?'

'No, I'm afraid not,' Maud said.

'I was after bidding you good afternoon,' Mrs Wallace said in her soft accent.

'Oh yes, of course.' Maud attempted to repeat her greeting.

She laughed. 'It's pronounced *fesgur mah*. But don't be worrying yourself. You will pick it up in no time. You'll be here on holiday?'

'Aye, from Edinburgh,' put in Daisy.

'Edinburgh? My goodness. Such a busy place, I hear. You'll be tired after such a long journey. Mind, it would have been even longer if Queen Victoria, God bless Her late Majesty, had had her way. You'll have noticed the turrets and spires of Balmoral Castle above the trees on your way here?'

Daisy nodded eagerly.

'The Queen was against the line running too close to Balmoral and she wanted the train service to end at Ballater. That would have meant a long omnibus ride for the last part of the journey here.' Mrs Wallace smiled. 'Well, now, I'll have some tea sent up to you both. If you'd just like to sign your names.' She turned the open book on the desk round to face Maud and Daisy.

As Maud picked up the fountain pen and signed, Mrs Wallace continued, 'There's a horse charabanc that goes from here every Wednesday on a scenic tour of the area, if you are interested?'

'Thank you,' said Maud, sliding the book and pen across to Daisy, 'but our preference is to enjoy the peace and quiet of the village.'

'Peace and quiet, aye,' muttered Daisy. She wrote her name neatly, recapped the pen and put it down on the desk.

'You'll be getting plenty of that,' went on Mrs Wallace, smiling. 'Nothing ever happens in the village.'

Although it hadn't taken place *in* the village, she will hear of something soon, thought Maud.

Mrs Wallace nodded at their Gladstones. 'Leave your bags there, and the boy will have them in your rooms in no time. Will you be wanting dinner with us? You'll find we eat earlier here than in the big cities. Dinner is from half past six.'

'That's braw news, Mrs Wallace.' Daisy smiled. 'I'm starving.'

Maud found a fire waiting to warm her in her prettily furnished bedroom on the first floor. The red wallpaper with a white floral pattern, and the small vase of pink roses on the dressing table, was as cheerful as the hotelier's wife. Maud's window looked onto the hotel's well-maintained garden. She began to feel more like a lady on holiday than a detective come to investigate a possible crime. The death on the train seemed almost like a bad dream.

Unsure what to do with her stained skirt, Maud stepped out of it and laid it on the back of a chair. She washed and unpacked before unpinning her hair. Although the advisability of brushing hair was a debated point, many specialists highly recommended this and Maud was of the same opinion. Five to ten minutes at least once a day was beneficial both in terms of giving one's hair a healthy sheen, stated *Every Woman's Encyclopaedia*, and in order to raise one's spirits. Maud's spirits were high – she and Daisy were embarked on their latest case, after all, a distinctly possible art fraud – but it felt delightful to brush her long fair tresses and shed the dust from the long journey.

She let her hair rest from its pins as she drank the tea brought up by a chambermaid. Then Maud examined the slim contents of her wardrobe and dressed in the raspberry linen blouse with matching bolero jacket and a pale grey skirt. She caught up her hair, twisted it into a French bun at the back of her head and pinned the coiffure in position. Satisfied with her low pompadour, Maud rose from the dressing table stool and sailed downstairs to meet Daisy in the parlour. This proved to be another welcoming room with a large round table in the centre holding a vase of hydrangea, panelled walls and a portrait of a past local worthy over the mantle. She and Daisy made themselves comfortable before the fire, aware of the murmur of voices through the slightly open door into the small entrance hall.

'What have you done with your tweed skirt?' Daisy asked.

'I'm afraid I'm not sure how to remove the stain,' Maud admitted. 'It's in my room.'

'Give it to me when we go back upstairs. I'll get a bit of soda from the kitchen and sort that out for you.'

'Thank you, Daisy.' Maud was grateful that her previous lady's maid knew all the techniques for the care of garments.

Mr Wallace appeared wearing a serviceable brown apron over his white shirt and dark waistcoat. Now he was without his bowler, Maud could see him more clearly. Unlike his wife whose hair was plentiful, his hair was receding, but he had the same pleasant countenance.

'Dinner is ready, ladies, if I can tempt you?' he asked.

'Aye, we're tempted, right enough,' Daisy said, getting to her feet.

They followed him into the dining room, where there wafted the rich smells of roasted meat and warm baked pastry. He led them to a table at a window overlooking the river. The sun wouldn't set for another hour, so they were able to enjoy the view of the water tumbling over the stony bed on its way to the sea.

'We have home-made broth, roast beef and apple pie with cream,' Mr Wallace said.

'Sounds delightful,' Maud said.

'And to drink?'

Maud looked at Daisy. 'Shall we splash out on a half-bottle of claret?'

Daisy gave a pleased nod.

As soon as Mr Wallace was out of earshot, Maud said to Daisy, 'We need to look like two ladies on holiday, after all.'

'Dinna worry, it's not as if we're going to get blootered,' Daisy said with a grin.

'Indeed. Tomorrow we start work and then we will need to keep a clear head.'

Soon they were eating heartily, while discussing their plans for the following day.

'We'll keep our story as close as possible to the truth when we visit the Anderson house,' Maud said between spoonfuls of delicious broth. 'We are a private detective agency and are engaged on an investigation. Our client has reported concerns regarding the provenance of a painting their gallery has sold.'

'Dinna you think it might be better if we go in some sort of a disguise?' Daisy looked hopeful, as she always did when this subject arose.

'I'm afraid there was no room in my bag for disguises, Daisy.'

Daisy opened her mouth, saw the warning look in Maud's eye and closed it again.

'However,' Maud went on, 'we can approach Mr Anderson, whichever one is at home, and pretend that, having heard of his wonderful reputation in the art world, we wish to purchase one of his paintings.'

Daisy nodded. 'It would help if the gallery were closed, then we can say we're here only for a wee visit and couldna wait about.'

'An excellent idea, my friend.'

'What happens when we see Rose, as we're sure to?'

Maud had no intention of doing anything to jeopardise Rose's position in the household. 'We must act as if we have never met. And we can rely on her to do the same.'

When the waiter removed their empty soup plates, Maud

said to him, 'I believe there is a particularly fine art gallery in the village.'

'I've not been in myself,' the young lad said, 'but I've heard they've sold some grand paintings in the last few months.'

'Perhaps we will find something bonnie then,' put in Daisy.

'It's just a short walk from here. At the west end of the village. The owner's house, An Taigh Mòr, is the next place after that.'

FIVE

Outside the Braemar Arms the following morning stood a smart little two-horse charabanc.

'Scenic tour, ladies?' called the driver, raising his top hat to them.

'No thank you,' Maud replied firmly. She and Daisy had a case to solve.

Following the waiter's directions from last night, they set off along the high street, past the general store and the post office. Daisy had cleverly managed to remove the blood stain yesterday evening from Maud's skirt, but it was still damp, and so today Maud wore the blue tweed coat with a slim pale grey skirt.

'I wonder when something will be said in the village about Mr Bisset's death,' Maud mused aloud.

'Perhaps it has,' Daisy replied. 'But we've nae heard.'

'But if the Bissets aren't part of the community and the schoolteacher isn't a gossip...' For all his little speeches yesterday, Maud didn't believe Mr Shepherd was fond of scandal.

'And that gowp on the train has disappeared.'

'If he has.' She would need to see if Mrs Wallace had any news.

'Here's the gallery,' said Daisy, coming to a halt outside the shop.

They peered in through the window and saw paintings of various sizes and in different styles displayed on walls and on easels around the shop. There was no sign of the owner or any customers inside.

'It looks like they're closed.' Daisy moved round to the door and tried the handle. 'Nae note of opening hours either.'

'Which is perfect for our purpose. Let us continue to the Anderson house.'

They walked on and came to a large house, its stone mellow as it bathed in the morning sun. An Taigh Mòr, announced the wrought-iron sign on a pillar at the entrance.

'If this is the wee house for the son, heaven knows what the muckle one in Edinburgh is like,' Daisy said.

'It certainly looks like the home of a prosperous family,' Maud agreed, as they approached and mounted the stone steps.

She lifted the heavy knocker and rapped on the dark red front door. After a short wait, it was opened by Rose. Her face under her frilly white cap went pale when she saw them.

'We would like to see Mr Anderson,' Maud said. She could not give her card, as it stated the name of the detective agency.

'Yes, miss,' Rose all but whispered. 'Please wait in the hall, and I will let the master know.'

She went off quickly along the passage, the bow on the back of her white frilled apron bobbing up and down in her haste, and returned within a few minutes. 'Come this way, please.'

She showed them into the drawing room, not meeting their eyes, and closed the door. A tall, plump man stood in the centre of the room. He wore one of those extraordinary Lord Dundreary facial trims. It suited him because of his height and it certainly gave him a distinguished look. But the white moustache grown down almost to the chest, with the ends of the whiskers trimmed to a point and the chin shaved, was not a good look in Maud's opinion.

'Good day, ladies.' The gentleman smiled through the hairy growth. 'I am Mr Anderson. How can I help you?'

Ah, Maud thought, Mr Anderson *senior*. He had not yet returned to Edinburgh. Was the son also here?

'Good day to you, Mr Anderson,' she said, moving towards him. 'I am Miss McIntyre and this is my friend, Miss Cameron.'

'How do you do.' He nodded and waited, looking enquiringly at them.

'We've heard of your reputation for buying and selling some rather splendid paintings, Mr Anderson, and we wondered if we might be permitted to look at your latest acquisitions with a view to making a purchase.'

'I'm very pleased to hear that, Miss McIntyre, but I'm afraid I do not keep such pictures in the house. You will need to visit my gallery in the village or the larger one on Dundas Street in the capital. I have a number of exceptional works of art which may be viewed there.'

Maud noticed that he made no mention of his son running the village gallery. Did that rankle with Anderson junior?

'Sadly, sir, we are on a touring holiday—' Maud began.

'Visiting Braemar for just the day,' put in Daisy.

'And we took it upon ourselves to come to your house—' Maud continued.

'Because the gallery is closed,' Daisy finished triumphantly, with a smile.

Goodness, thought Maud, we sound like a music hall double act.

'Closed?' Mr Anderson looked puzzled. 'It shouldn't be.' Recovering his poise, he went on, 'If you could tell me what particularly interests you, I might be able to help.'

He gestured for them to take a seat on the sofa and lowered

himself into a chair opposite. Maud noticed that he did so with
surprising grace for a man of his build.

'I have a fancy for a still life, in oil. Something small as we
are travelling.'

'I regret, Miss McIntyre, that you are too late. The village
gallery sold two paintings of that description only recently.'

'And you have nothing similar?' asked Daisy, in a fair imitation of Maud's accent.

'Unfortunately not.'

Really? Maud wondered. There were no indications in his
manner or expression that he wasn't telling the truth. Then
where was the third picture Rose had seen?

He smiled. 'Can I interest you ladies in any other
paintings?'

There was nothing for it. She would have to tell Mr
Anderson the truth. Or part of it anyway.

Glancing at Daisy, Maud began, 'We have not been entirely
honest with you, sir. We are staying in the village, but I am Miss
McIntyre of the M. McIntyre Agency' – it still gave her a little
thrill to say that – 'and Miss Cameron is my assistant.' She
reached into her bag and handed him one of her business cards.

'The M. McIntyre Agency?' He glanced at the card and
frowned. 'Do you purchase paintings for clients?

'We are a private detective agency and are engaged on an
investigation. Our client has reported concerns regarding the
provenance of one of the paintings sold from the Braemar
gallery.'

'I don't understand. Someone who bought a painting has
made a complaint to you that it isn't by the artist the gallery
represented it to be?'

That wasn't quite what Maud had said, but it was a good
enough cover. Daisy withdrew her notebook from her bag and
waited, pencil poised.

'Our client does not wish to make an official complaint,'

Maud went on, neatly avoiding a direct answer to his question, 'merely to ascertain that you are not knowingly selling forgeries.'

He passed a hand over his brow. 'Can you tell me which picture it was?'

'A still life by Zurbarán.'

He thought for a moment. 'It will be *An apple and a rose,* or *A broken cup and a pomegranate.*'

Daisy snorted softly at the second title. Maud sent her a warning look. Mr Anderson did not appear to have noticed, as he continued, 'Oil on canvas. I remember my son telling me of them.'

'You did not see them yourself?' Maud asked.

'No. My son has responsibility for purchasing and selling from this gallery. Early examples of the artist's work, he thought, but nonetheless fine pieces from the 1600s. Did you know that pomegranates have diverse cultural–religious significance? They are a symbol of life and fertility owing to the fruit's many seeds, but also a symbol of power, blood and death. My son's description of the juxtaposition of the broken cup to the fruit I found particularly interesting.' He paused. 'But you are saying they are forgeries?'

'It's possible. I understand they came with no paperwork.'

'With a painting of such age, it's not possible to give a written guarantee of genuineness. If it is a forgery, it could take years – ten, twenty, perhaps even fifty – to determine the truth. I can say only that David would have bought them in good faith.'

'I'm sure that is the case, Mr Anderson.' Maud paused. 'Can you tell me who sold the paintings to the gallery?'

He stiffened. 'No, I cannot. A dealer would never reveal such information.'

'Then how do you and your son find your contacts?'

'We do not approach potential clients, Miss McIntyre,' he

said, his tone still chilly. 'Our good name ensures they contact us. Some of those requiring my services are impoverished lairds and the recently widowed. You will understand that, reluctant to enter the gallery and risk speculation as to their finances, such people usually request that I visit their country establishments and examine whatever works of art they possess.'

'Was that how your son was able to buy those paintings?' asked Daisy, glancing up from writing in her notebook.

'He told me so.'

'Is he here at present?' Maud asked.

'He should be working in the village gallery.'

Perhaps he had been there, she thought. Presumably there was an office of sorts at the rear. They would try the gallery again after this interview.

'David has been involved in the business for a couple of years,' said Mr Anderson, 'but I was becoming concerned that he didn't seem to have the flair for spotting good works of art. Until, that is, the Zurbaráns. I confess that I was delighted when he came across the paintings. It was just the opportunity he was looking for to improve his standing in the business.'

'Nae doubt,' Daisy murmured.

Mr Anderson glanced at her. 'I'm sure my son did not represent the painting to be by Zurbarán. If a buyer wants a picture to be by a particular artist, then that's what the buyer sees.'

Rather like the disguises of a private detective, Maud thought. She nodded for him to continue.

'As you no doubt know, both the paintings sold for a high price. I cannot say I was surprised, as such newly discovered works by the artist are rare.'

'Hen's teeth,' muttered Daisy.

He looked at her sharply. 'I'm sorry, did you say something, Miss Cameron? I didn't quite catch it.'

'Good grief. I said good grief, Mr Anderson.' She sent him an innocent smile.

'Did anyone authenticate the pictures?' Maud asked. 'An auction house, for example?'

'An auctioneer is not in the business of identification.'

'Can you tell me what terms are used when a painting is sold?'

'There are six basic terms used by dealers. "Work by the master" signifies an original whose artist is undisputed. Then there is "attributed to," which means that it's more likely than not to have been created by the master. A third category is "in the circle of the master," that is, work done by an artist associated with him, but not one of his pupils.'

Maud interrupted his recitation. 'Would this painting have come under one of these terms?'

'It's not possible to be completely certain, so David asked for them to be sold under the "attributed to" banner.'

'Out of interest,' said Daisy, 'what are the other three?'

'You understand that we are now moving down the desirability list. These are "in the style of", "in the manner of" and, finally, "after" the master.'

'So paintings in these three are nae actual forgeries?' Daisy asked.

'No, there are three general categories of forgery.'

'We *are* learning a lot,' murmured Daisy.

'One is the straight copy,' he went on. 'This is where the artist copies exactly an existing work. The second is the pastiche. Here the forger pastes together a mixture of details copied from several works. The third is what we can call the original fake. Here, the forger creates a work of art in order to pass it off as the work of another.'

'Which may be what we have in this case,' Maud said.

'This news you bring me, ladies, is not good. A dealer's reputation is invaluable in the art world and goes before him.'

Maud felt sorry for Mr Anderson. He was committed to his work and, after all, it was his business at risk. And perhaps it was his son who was creating that risk. 'As I said, Mr Anderson, our client has not made a formal complaint to the police, does not intend to do so and is not requesting a return of any or part of the purchase money. I'm satisfied that you did not sell the works knowing they were forgeries—'

'If indeed they are.'

'Indeed.' It's a pity they couldn't speak to the son's good name, Maud thought, and then nodded to Daisy, who closed her notebook. They got to their feet.

'Thank you for your time,' she said.

Mr Anderson rose and pressed the servants' bell. 'My maid will show you out. I hope there will be no need to see you again.'

'We hope so too,' Maud told him.

Rose appeared and led them through the hall and to the front door. Clearly too afraid to ask the question she longed to, she instead raised her eyebrows at them.

Daisy mouthed *Don't worry,* and Maud gave what she hoped was a reassuring smile. There was nothing more they could say to the young woman for the time being.

Maud felt certain that Rose wasn't mistaken about the third painting. Were the Andersons involved together in forgery or only one of them? If the latter, was the father an accomplished liar or did his son have the picture hidden away?

SIX

Maud and Daisy retraced their steps to the village, glancing in the window of the closed gallery.

'Shall I try the handle again?' asked Daisy.

'Tea first,' Maud said. 'Let's visit the village's establishment.'

They walked on, past the shops and the hotel, and soon were seated at a table in the busy little tea shop. Their seats by the window looked onto the main street, where people hurried past on errands or stopped to chat with neighbours. The position was perfect for keeping an eye on those going hither and yon, Maud thought, as Daisy placed their order.

'What do you think of Mr Anderson senior?' Daisy said.

'I think he's telling the truth,' Maud replied. 'It looks like his son might be the culprit. He's not the forger, but he's the one who bought and sold the paintings.'

'He might have got away with saying the first one he bought was a genuine mistake, especially as he doesn't seem to know much about pictures according to his own faither. But you heard Mr Anderson say his son had bought the paintings from private houses. That doesna tally with Rose's account. A mistake, my... oxter.'

Maud couldn't see what Daisy's armpit had to do with anything.

Daisy continued, 'Rose said the fellow came to their house late in the evening too.'

'It does smack of dishonesty, rather than a mistaken attribution.'

'What we've learned should settle Rose's mind as to the honesty of her employer, Mr Anderson the elder,' Daisy said, 'but then there's the younger. He's part of the family and will take over the business at some stage. Rose will still be worried, won't she?'

Maud shrugged. 'What can we do? Let's hope the father mentions our visit to the son, and that he doesn't buy from this seller in the future. It's also unlikely that the forger – I think we can call him that – now alerted, will try to pass off any more pictures in this way.'

Despite what she had just said, Maud still felt uneasy. If the forgeries were at an end, Rose would be relieved and her conscience might allow her to stay with her employer. But Maud disliked an inconclusive investigation – and the thought that someone was deceiving her.

A man entered the tea shop. He caught her attention at once, which wasn't surprising. Artist was stamped upon him. His black hair was long, there was a carelessly tied piece of silk around his neck, and on his head sat a broad-brimmed, floppy hat.

'Michty me,' murmured Daisy. 'I didna think artists really dressed in that way.'

He walked unsteadily up to the counter and leaning across it, said, 'Whisky.'

The young waitress stared fearfully at him, but did not move.

He banged his open hand down on the counter and she jumped with fright.

'I am not drunk, so give me what I ask for.'

'Leave the poor lass alone!' Daisy called. 'She canna give you a dram. This is a tea shop, nae a public house.'

He turned, his gaze wandering around the room to find the speaker, and alighted on Daisy. A smile very much like a leer curled his mouth. He pushed himself away from the counter and made his way between the tables to where they sat. He stood and looked down, first at Daisy and then Maud.

The fellow placed a hand with paint-encrusted fingernails on their table to steady himself. 'Two bonnie lassies out on their own.' He raised an imaginary glass. 'A toast! To beauty!'

Maud watched him from under her frowning eyebrows.

He laughed and his hazy stare fixed on her face. 'You're awfa quiet.' He pulled out the empty chair from the table and collapsed into it. 'Don't you speak?'

'What would you care to talk about?' she said.

'*What would you care to talk about?*' He mimicked her Edinburgh accent. 'Great art, of course. What else is there to talk about? One day my work will be famous.' He crossed his arms and started to chuckle.

An older woman in a black silk dress now appeared. She bustled over and addressed Maud and Daisy. 'Good morning, ladies. I am the manageress and I must apologise for this gentleman's behaviour.'

She turned to the artist. 'I will have to ask you to leave, sir. You are making a nuisance of yourself.'

The artist turned on her with a snarl. 'Philistine! You can't tell me what to do. I am Adam McGonagall, and there is not another in the country who can paint as I paint.'

'I'm sure your pictures are wonderful, Mr McGonagall,' the woman said in a soothing voice.

He swayed and looked at her through half-shut eyes. 'You won't be so patronising when I move to Paris. There, they understand great work.'

'These ladies don't want to be disturbed, so come along now.'

To Maud's surprise, he allowed himself to be helped out of his chair and assisted across the room to the door. As soon as he had disappeared, Maud gestured to the manageress.

'Who was that?' she asked, when the woman returned to their table.

'He's the local artist, miss.'

Maud's pulse jumped. 'Where does he live?' She tried to keep the eagerness out of her question.

'The last house in the village; the white cottage that looks like it's falling down. Làrach Cottage it's called, which is about right as it's a scar on the landscape. Are you interested in buying one of his pictures?'

'Possibly.'

In fact, not at all, Maud thought.

'If you want to see him at work, he spends the afternoons at the Linn of Dee.'

'The Linn of Dee? Where is that?'

'It's about five miles or so west of here. It was a favourite picnic spot of Queen Victoria, so it's bonny enough. Linn means gorge, and it's quite something to watch the Dee squeeze through the narrow gap in the rocks.' She smiled. 'Not that you'd know what you were looking at from one of Mr McGonagall's pictures.'

'Isna there something called artist's impression?' Daisy said.

'Artist's nightmare, more like.'

'Perhaps it's something to do with the drink he takes.'

'He isn't often like you saw him today. But when the drink is in him, he insists on coming in and asking for a whisky, even though he knows fine this is a tea shop.' The manageress sighed. 'His pictures must be doing well, mind, as he's been going on lately about moving to Paris.'

'Yes, I heard him say that. Is he well known in the village?'

'I can't say, but I've got used to him and I've never heard he did anyone any harm. Now if you'll excuse me, ladies.' She moved away.

'That was interesting,' Daisy said thoughtfully.

'Are you thinking what I'm thinking?' Maud asked.

'That our order should have arrived by now?'

'Well, yes, there is that.'

'And that we've just met a crabbit artist whose work is suddenly selling?'

Maud nodded. 'It is well known,' she said, pausing as the young waitress arrived and set their tea things in front of them, 'that you can't set much store by what a drunken man may say...'

'But on the other hand,' continued Daisy, 'dinna they say that alcohol makes you tell the truth?'

'Something like that,' Maud agreed. 'Mr McGonagall may be worth a little closer investigation.'

'You think he's our forger?'

'I don't know. In truth, we don't even know for certain there is a forger at work.' Although she was beginning to think there might well be.

'I wonder why Rose doesna know of the fellow.'

'Perhaps she does and doesn't want to point the finger. It doesn't have to be a local artist, after all, who's involved. Or perhaps she doesn't know, not having worked here long.'

Daisy nodded. 'Five months, she said.'

'That's just a few months.' A sudden thought came to Maud. Hadn't the schoolteacher said the Bissets moved into the village only a few months ago? What possible connection could there be? Surely none?

She pushed the thought aside before continuing. 'And Rose might well keep herself to herself.'

'She seems the quiet type, right enough.'

They drank their tea in silence for a while.

'One of us should walk to the Linn of Dee.' Maud replaced

her cup on its saucer. 'The manageress told us he likes to paint *en plein air,* so he should be easy to spot. Then we can express an interest in seeing his work.'

'Five or so miles from here,' Daisy said slowly, 'and nae bus. Presumably the other one of us should try the gallery again?'

'Yes.' Maud smiled.

'Then I'll do that.'

They finished their tea, paid and left. They walked past the hotel, general store and post office, and came to the gallery. A younger, slightly slimmer version of Mr Anderson senior, his hair fair rather than white and his whiskers cut in a less flamboyant style, was seated at a desk, engaged in making an entry in a ledger.

'That must be the son,' Maud said. 'See what you can find out, Daisy. My skirt must be dry by now. I'll change, walk to the Linn of Dee and meet you back at the hotel later this afternoon.'

A warm sun slanted out of the autumn sky, and the golds and yellows, oranges and reds of the leaves glowed. A brisk walk of some hour and a half on the country road brought Maud to a gentle downhill footpath. She could hear the thundering river before she saw it, then suddenly it came into view.

One of Scotland's mightiest rivers abruptly reduced to just a few feet wide as it squeezed through a long rocky chasm under an old stone bridge before it dropped into rocky pools below and on to the sea. The view was so delightful that Maud began to feel more hopeful about Mr McGonagall's work. She left the grassy bank and carefully made her way to the rocky edge above the water.

And then she spotted him. He was a little way ahead of her, dressed in a shabby tweed jacket and seated on a low campstool in front of an easel. She would see what the artist had made of such a wild and beautiful scene.

Mr McGonagall no longer appeared to be under the influence of alcohol, but was a man entirely absorbed in his work. It wasn't until Maud stopped at his elbow that he looked round. He glared up at her out of bloodshot eyes. Had he recognised her from their earlier encounter in the tea shop? He frowned a little, as if he wasn't sure, but then lost interest and returned to his picture.

She stole a glance at his boots. They were brown, badly scuffed and in need of a clean, but did that make the man a forger? Any fellow with little money might have brown, scuffed boots.

She addressed him in a pleasant voice. 'Good afternoon. If I may so say, you are drawing a most remarkable picture.'

It was the truth. The gorge, stone bridge and river had been reduced to a green smudge on the side of the picture, a brown line smeared along the top and a smattering of blue-grey blobs in the centre. Yet although his drawing could hardly be said to represent the scene in front of them, Maud could see that it was executed with a certain skill.

'With this picture, I will make my name, my own name,' he muttered.

'Very few people have the eye to see the river like that,' Maud continued.

He joined the blue-grey blobs by a couple of wavy lines. 'That is true.' He was using some sort of a soft pastel stick and he drew in a few more lines. 'These sketches inform my final work, you understand. They are a starting point. I am concerned with capturing contours, light and shade.'

'The Highlands are indeed fortunate to have one who is so obviously a genius to capture them in such a way.'

He threw down his blue-coloured stick, where fortunately it landed on a small patch of grass. 'Do you think I stay here because I choose?' His anger was clear. 'One day soon I will live in Paris, where someone with my talent belongs.'

'You expect, then, to sell your picture for a very large sum?'

At this, Mr McGonagall shot her a quick look, picked up the pastel stick and bent his gaze on his sketch again. 'It's good. You said so yourself.' He hunched his shoulders like a peevish child.

There seemed to be little hope of getting anything more out of him, at least for the time being, so Maud prepared to leave. 'I hope to see your picture again once it is finished.'

He glanced up at her. 'Would you like to see more of my work?' He looked hopeful, and she immediately felt guilt wash over her. 'I have a number of completed drawings in my cottage, perhaps not as fine as this will be, but all full of my genius. Perhaps you will see something you would like to buy.'

'I might, yes,' Maud said slowly, hoping a purchase would not be necessary.

'Come soon and I will show you my best work. Are you free tomorrow?'

Maud wanted very much to see inside his cottage, and it looked like she was about to have her wish. 'Thank you. I'd like to, if I may. Shall we say about this time?' She glanced at her wristwatch. 'Three o'clock?'

'I will be available.'

'My name is Miss McIntyre. And you are...?' She was already aware of his name, of course, but he didn't seem to remember the encounter in the tea shop.

'McGonagall. Adam McGonagall.'

'Goodbye, Mr McGonagall,' she said. 'I will see you tomorrow afternoon.'

Leaving the idyllic scene behind, Maud strolled back to the village, going over what he had said to her as she walked. One thing seemed clear enough: he was hoping to make his name in the art world using this unusual style of drawing. She'd heard of a movement in France in which the subjects are broken up into pieces and rearranged in an abstract form, but she didn't think what Mr McGonagall was doing could be considered Cubism.

There was also a Spanish artist, a man living in France who had produced an extraordinary depiction of an interior scene of a Barcelona brothel. Whilst she had never been inside a brothel, in Barcelona or elsewhere, at least the women in Picasso's *Les Demoiselles d'Avignon* looked like women. She wasn't sure that Mr McGonagall's bridge looked like a bridge. Or indeed that his river could be considered a river.

And there was the matter of his material. The soft pastels were pleasing, but she doubted they would ever be considered to produce real works of art, like those painted in oil.

One of Mr McGonagall's sentences came back into her mind. '*With this picture, I will make my name, my own name.*' It was the use of the words, 'my own name'. Did this mean that he was copying another person's work, and passing off the pictures as having been painted by that other artist?

Her best hope now was that on the following day she might, by buying one of his pictures, induce him to disclose more. It was possible he wasn't their forger and that it was another individual entirely, but Maud felt that purchasing his smallest drawing was something that had to be faced. Even if it meant she would end up with a picture she might otherwise not buy. And where would she hang it? Her apartment in Edinburgh, where she would see it every day? She shuddered at the thought of having to face squiggles or cubes on a regular basis. Hang it on the agency wall then? That would be no better. Give it away as a gift at Christmas, perhaps?

No, she thought. That would be unkind to the recipient.

SEVEN

Maud and Daisy were seated by the hearth in the snug little parlour at the hotel, cups of tea to hand on the low table.

'How did you get on at the gallery?' Maud asked Daisy.

'I canna say I warmed to the younger Anderson. Once it was obvious I wasna going to buy anything, he lost interest.'

'No Lord Dundreary trim, I noticed.' Maud smiled.

Daisy laughed. 'His moustache was the military type. Curling up at the ends. Though I personally would say his face is too round to carry it off.'

'And what about the paintings on display? What would you personally say about them?'

Daisy grimaced. 'Those he has for sale are awfa expensive. Who can afford that sort of money in this small village?'

'I suppose well-heeled tourists. Since Queen Victoria bought Balmoral, the Highlands are popular with wealthy merchants and the gentry.'

'Aye, well, no one else came into the shop while I was there. It's probably out of season now for city folk. I dinna know how Mr Anderson the younger sells anything anyway, opening whenever it suits him by the look of it. I put on a posh accent like yours,' Daisy said with a grin, 'so I could get him thinking I was interested in buying a picture and he was soon boasting about his recent sales.'

'What did he say about how he'd obtained the paintings?'

'When I said how clever he was, finding such rare works as he was talking about, he clammed up and said – just as his faither had – that an art dealer never reveals his sources.'

'Two paintings from the same seventeenth-century artist. Isn't that too much of a coincidence?'

'One collector could have two – what did Mr Anderson senior call them? – Zubaroos.'

'Zurbaráns,' Maud said. 'Did you see the other painting Rose referred to when we met in Edinburgh?'

Daisy wrinkled her nose. 'There was something on an easel with a title like *A squashed plum and a fancy jug.*'

'Daisy!' Maud looked at her friend and saw the laughter in her eyes. 'You know very well it wouldn't have been called that.'

'Och, well, near enough.' She became serious again. 'Aye, Maud. It was there all right, in the gallery. When I went to get a proper look at it, he dashed across and turned the painting to face the easel, telling me it was sold. I dinna believe him, else why was it on display like that?'

'Hmm,' said Maud. 'I thought he'd keep it under wraps for a while.'

'And his faither hasna told him about our visit?'

'Why would Mr Anderson senior do that, if he thinks there's no truth in our story?'

'Aye... Well, I hope the younger Anderson wasna getting suspicious, telling me that picture was sold.'

'How much—'

Daisy shook her head. 'There was nae price on it. I think it was a case of if you have to ask the price, you canna afford it.'

Maud sighed. 'We don't seem to be making much progress on Rose Gilmour's case.'

'There's the dead man on the train.' Daisy's eyes lit up. 'We could investigate that.'

'Daisy,' Maud said with a frown, 'we can't afford to look into every possible crime without payment.'

It was Daisy's turn to sigh. 'I ken. How did you get on with our artist?'

'I watched him draw a very odd picture.'

Daisy pulled a face. 'Not one of those semi-naked women jobs?'

'I don't think so, but who knows?'

'When I look at a painting, I like to be able to see what it's meant to be. Call me old-fashioned.'

Maud laughed. 'That description hardly suits you.' Daisy was all in favour of social reform, especially with women's lot in life.

'So what did the mannie say?' she demanded.

'Not as much as I would have liked. But he did use what might be a telling phrase about how his pictures in this new, abstract style would be the ones to make his name – "my own name", he said.'

'That *is* a telling phrase.'

'I'm going to view his work for sale tomorrow afternoon. Come with me this time, Daisy. As I am to enter his cottage, it will look better if there are two ladies. And I can say I need a friend's advice as to which picture to buy. You can also tell me your opinion of the man himself.'

They looked up as the door to the parlour opened and Mrs Wallace came in carrying a small tapestry bag. She smiled as her gaze lighted on Maud and Daisy.

'You won't mind if I sit with you two ladies for a wee while?' she asked. 'I like to chat to our visitors when I get the chance.'

'Of course.' Maud gestured to the empty chair by them.

Mrs Wallace set down her bag on the floor beside her and pulled out a half-formed shape of knitting. 'You've come all the way from the metropolis to this sleepy wee spot?'

'Not so sleepy, Mrs Wallace,' Maud said.

The older woman's face clouded. 'You'll be referring to the death of Mr Bisset, I take it?'

'You've heard about that?'

'Everyone in the village has. And on the same train you travelled on too.' She consulted her pattern for a moment. 'Knit ten, purl ten,' she murmured to herself and began to work across the row of stitches on the small garment in pink wool. 'Well now, if you had asked me a couple of months ago, I would have said no one new ever came to live in the village. But the Bissets recently took Woodend, a large house that had been empty for some time, since an elderly relation of the laird died.'

'Was it the Dowager House?'

'Och, no, nothing as grand as that, but grand enough all the same.' She came to the end of the row and turned the garment. 'The Bisset girl is quite nice-looking, but she puts colour on her lips and she's thrawn.' Mrs Wallace tutted loudly and silence fell as she concentrated on her knitting.

Miss Bisset certainly seemed to be a difficult young woman, Maud thought. 'I suppose she's typical for a young girl and wants the bright lights of the city.'

'Where have the family moved from?' Daisy asked.

'Inverness.'

Daisy sniffed. 'That's nae a city.'

Mrs Wallace smiled at her and returned to her knitting. 'This wee pink bonnet is for our lassie's third. Her other two are boys, but Flora is her first wee quine.' She sighed with pleasure.

'You must be very happy, Mrs Wallace,' Maud said.

'That I am.' She nodded.

Another row as if by magic developed under Mrs Wallace's quick fingers before she continued. 'From what I gather, Miss Bisset wanted to move down to Edinburgh, but for some reason her father moved the family here. We're only about a hundred miles south from Inverness.' The needles switched places again. 'Perhaps Mr Bisset was looking to be a big person in a small village. That's the way he's behaved since they've been here anyway. Inverness wasn't lively enough for the daughter, so she's definitely not at all happy to be in Braemar.'

She looked up from her knitting and fixed Maud with her gaze. 'The mother says she wants to fit in with life in the village. Which is very good, as there are always meetings of the Rural to attend, village concerts in the winter and fetes in the summer to be organised in aid of the school or the church. But she's not yet done anything to help.'

Mrs Wallace glanced towards the door where a waitress was bringing in a laden plate covered with a white cloth.

'Listen to me, going on,' the hotelier's wife smiled indulgently, 'and forgetting to mention that I have ordered freshly made scones with a wee bit of butter for you both.'

The waitress put down the plate on the low table and removed the cloth.

'This is too kind of you,' Maud said. Her stomach rumbled, reminding her she hadn't eaten any luncheon. 'You are spoiling us.'

'It's something I like to do for all my guests. And I'm never too busy to stop for a blether and a fine piece.'

Maud and Daisy each picked up a warm scone with melting butter.

Daisy took a bite. 'This is awfa good.' Crumbs dropped onto her lap.

Mrs Wallace smiled, looking pleased with Daisy's comment, and resumed her knitting. 'Now, tell me who else was on your train.'

It was Maud's turn to smile. In a different life, perhaps the hotelier's wife would herself have been a private detective.

Maud swallowed a morsel of scone, removed a trickle of butter from her chin and licked her finger. 'I can't answer that, but I do know there were three others in our compartment.'

'Yes?' Mrs Wallace glanced up, her eyes alight with interest.

'Miss Bisset, who identified her father.'

'So I heard. The poor lass,' murmured Mrs Wallace.

'There was also the schoolteacher.'

'Nicely dressed with dark hair going grey? Aye, that was the dominie, Mr Shepherd. He lost his wife some years ago and they had no children. He is quite lost without her.' She sighed.

Maud nodded to herself, pleased to have deduced correctly the profession of Mr Shepherd.

'Anyone else?' went on Mrs Wallace.

Goodness, Maud thought, Mrs Wallace was making a good job of interviewing her and Daisy, when it should be the other way round. Then Maud realised how much the pair of them were learning from her.

'The third passenger was a young man, but that's really all I can tell you about him.'

Mrs Wallace looked disappointed. 'I wonder who that can be?' She knitted and considered her own question.

'What about Mr Bisset?' put in Daisy. 'You havena told us about him.'

The hotelier's wife put down her knitting and looked first at Daisy and then Maud. 'Good riddance to the man, is all I can say.'

Maud was so surprised by the sudden change in the kindly woman that she almost choked on the last piece of her scone. She swallowed the crumb. 'Why do you say that?'

'Norman Bisset was a loud-mouthed brawler and a bully. The family – that's him, his wife and their daughter – haven't been here long, and yet Mr Wallace had already had to throw

him out of the lounge bar. Not once, but twice. Such behaviour
is more suited to the public bar of a lesser establishment. On the
second occasion, my husband told him if it happened again, at
the very least he'd be banned from drinking in either bar in the
hotel.'

'And he bullied his wife and daughter?' Daisy asked.

Mrs Wallace gave a short laugh. 'The girl, Lilias they call
her, looks to be following in her father's footsteps in terms of
temperament. And don't be feeling sorry for the wife either,'
she added. 'It's Mrs Bisset who rules the roost.' She sighed.
'They are rather vulgar people.'

'If nae his family, who did Mr Bisset bully?'

'Just about all the tradesmen hereabouts.' She lowered her
voice, although they were the only people in the parlour. 'He
had them doing repairs on Woodend and he didn't pay them
until they'd asked him more than once for their money. He
liked to see these men – good, fine, hard-working souls –
humiliate themselves by almost begging for what was rightly
theirs.' Her mouth drew into a tight line to hold in her
emotions.

'Who are these tradesmen?' Maud asked.

'That's not for me to say, lass. What I will say, though, is
that there's no one here who'll be sorry Norman Bisset has
gone.'

'Nae even his wife and daughter?'

'Not even them.' Mrs Wallace gave a firm nod.

'When she identified her father's body,' Maud said, 'the
young woman seemed genuinely upset.'

'Well, she would be – to start with.' Mrs Wallace fixed them
with a pointed look. 'That might not still be the case.'

'I wonder if I should pay Mrs Bisset a call?' Seeing the
surprised look on Mrs Wallace's face, Maud added, 'She might
like to talk to someone who was present when her husband was
found.'

Mrs Wallace nodded. 'Aye, that's a kind thought. I will speak to her and let you know what she says.'

Mrs Wallace took a scone from the plate and bit into it with obvious pleasure. She chewed and sighed and made appreciative noises, as Maud chatted on about how shocking it was to be involved in something so tragic. It was warm and cosy and the tea and scones were excellent, but the afternoon slipped away without Maud learning anything else of use to either case.

As soon as Mrs Wallace had replaced her knitting in the tapestry bag and left the parlour, Daisy turned to Maud. 'I thought we werena investigating Bisset's death?'

'We're not. I merely thought it would be interesting to meet Mrs Bisset.'

Daisy raised an eyebrow. 'To add to our knowledge of human behaviour?'

'Just so,' said Maud, smiling.

Maud began her day as usual with a few Indian club swings, followed by half a dozen *sautés*. She had just landed back on her feet when there was a knock on her bedroom door.

'Come in,' she called breathlessly.

The door opened and Daisy entered, looking smart in a black blouse with pink spots and a black skirt. 'I thought that was you doing your *sautés* when I heard the thumping.'

'Merely engaging my leg muscles,' Maud told her, catching her breath. 'You go ahead. I'll be down for breakfast shortly.'

She put away the clubs and slipped off the dressing gown, dressed in her serviceable tweed walking costume and joined Daisy downstairs.

They spent a pleasant morning wandering around Braemar, like the tourists they professed to be. They began with a visit to the site of Kindrochit Castle in the heart of the village and close by the River Clunie.

'*Madainn mhath!*' called a woman passing with a shopping bag over her arm.

'*Madainn mhath!*' Maud called back, as she and Daisy clambered over the ruins. She was getting used to wishing people good morning and good afternoon in Gaelic.

She knew her accent gave away that she was not a native speaker and was not surprised when the woman stopped to tell them about the castle.

'There's not much to see now,' she said, 'but it must have been something in its time. The castle was built by King Malcolm sometime in the eleventh century. But when the Great Plague broke out in the castle in the 1600s, the folk of the village barricaded it, and cannons were used to destroy the castle with all its inhabitants inside.'

'A wee bit like Mary King's Close in the Old Town,' put in Daisy.

The woman frowned. 'The Old Town?'

'In Edinburgh,' said Daisy. 'In Mary King's Close, the richest lived at the top of the buildings and the poorest at the bottom. The alleyway was so narrow that down at the bottom you were in near darkness and next to the sewage-covered streets. When the folk of Mary King's Close caught the plague, the alley was sealed off and those living below were trapped and left to die.'

'The Edinburgh story might not be entirely true, Daisy,' Maud cautioned.

'Either way, there have been plenty of stories of hauntings since,' Daisy said firmly.

'Kindrochit has its own ghostly tale,' added the woman, fixing Daisy with her eyes. 'In 1746, after the Jacobites lost on Culloden Moor, a Hanoverian soldier was lowered into one of the ruined vaults in search of treasure, but he fled when he found a ghostly company seated around a table piled with skulls.'

Goodness, thought Maud; the two of them seemed to be engaged in some sort of competitive tale of the worst atrocity.

'Thank you so much for the information,' Maud said hastily to the woman. 'It is always interesting to learn about places one is visiting.'

The woman looked mollified. 'We may be a small village, but there are many places worth seeing. Braemar Castle, which was burned by the Jacobites to prevent it falling into government hands, and the site of the raising of the standard for the 1715 Jacobite Rebellion, and...'

'Nae bad for a small village,' Daisy conceded, but Maud could see the gleam in her eye and knew she was about to give voice to her further thoughts.

Maud took hold of her friend's arm and, with a nod at the woman, hurried her away.

'Really, Daisy, there's no need to make an enemy of a villager.'

Daisy looked a little chastened. 'It was just that I couldna stand by and let Edinburgh be thought second-best.'

'The poor woman was hardly suggesting that. And you must admit that this little Highland village does have an impressive history.' She released Daisy's arm. 'Now, where would you like to visit next?'

Daisy grinned. 'Well, there's Braemar Castle, burned by the Jacobites...'

'I think it's been rebuilt since then, judging by what we could see of its condition from the train.'

'It's a pity we're too late for the Highland Games.' Daisy sounded wistful. 'Then we would have seen the King and Queen and their family. Royals have attended every Braemar Games since Queen Victoria's reign, you know.'

'We'll just have to keep our fingers crossed for an invitation to tea at Balmoral. Meanwhile, this afternoon we'll pay a visit to Mr McGonagall, to discover if he's the mystery forger.'

'And what about the body on the train case? I'm nae happy about Bisset.'

'Nor were a lot of other people, by the sound of it. Let's see what his widow has to say when Mrs Wallace has secured our invitation.'

EIGHT

After a light luncheon of mutton broth and a bowl of plums, Maud dressed in her raspberry linen costume with a high lacy collar and matching cuffs, and she and Daisy strolled to Mr McGonagall's cottage.

They found it easily enough, past the Anderson house and another they did not know, until they came to the last dwelling in the village. The remarks made by the manageress in the tea shop hadn't prepared Maud for anything with such an air of depressing neglect. The downstairs windows needed cleaning and in places the original white harling, the roughcast finish put on the walls to protect it from the weather, had peeled off, leaving the rough stone exposed.

As Maud's gaze travelled up to the windows on the first floor, she noticed there was an attic above, with two small dormer windows. This glass up there sparkled in the sunshine. Was that the artist's studio? Clearly a good light was needed in which to paint. Not that she painted. Maud had been happy to give up her attempts from about the age of six.

Làrach Cottage was in an isolated position, with a thick belt of trees on either side of the dwelling and a little copse on the opposite side of the road. Maud rapped with her knuckles on the blistered panels of the front door.

'I hope he's nae blootered again,' Daisy said under her breath.

'He wants to make a good impression in order that I buy a painting, so I doubt he'll be drunk today,' Maud whispered back.

After a few moments, Maud heard approaching footsteps and a bolt being drawn, and the door was flung open by Mr McGonagall. Sure enough, he'd obviously made an effort with his appearance and he looked not only sober, but also clean and tidy in a brown sack suit. The suit, like his boots, had clearly seen better days.

'Ah,' he said. 'Two ladies. Even better – perhaps two sales?'

Maud had to disabuse him of that notion straightaway. 'This is my friend, Miss Cameron. She has a very good eye for art, so she can advise me.'

He looked at Daisy with fresh interest and nodded. 'Come inside.'

One step forward and they were inside, for the front door led directly into a room which served to function as both sitting room and dining room.

A most unpleasant odour immediately caught Maud's nostrils. Daisy had also noticed the odour and was screwing up her face. She opened her mouth to speak.

'It's very kind of you to allow us to visit today, Mr McGo-nagall,' said Maud quickly, sending her friend a warning glance.

He had noticed their response to the smell. 'I will open the window a little. I should have done so earlier.'

Mr McGonagall moved hastily to open the casement window above a chest on which was scattered all sorts of artists' paraphernalia. He turned back to them. 'And now, you must take tea with me as a preliminary to our negotiations. I will make it immediately. The kettle is already on the stove. I don't keep a maid, so you will excuse me?'

'Certainly,' Maud said. 'And while you're making tea, perhaps we can have a look at your work?'

He made a gesture with his arm around the little room. 'Before you, ladies, you see my finest work.'

Maud gazed around them. Open sketchbooks were propped against the walls. Some looked to be no more than splashes of colour, others a riot of lines and cubes, one or two just about recognisable as landscapes.

'Take your time, all the better to appreciate what is before you.'

Maud smiled politely. He disappeared through a door which she could see led to a tiny scullery built out at the back of the cottage.

'I ken that mingin smell,' Daisy whispered to Maud. 'Linseed oil.'

'It certainly has a strange, heavy odour. What is it used for?'

'It was used in your faither's house to clean the boots.'

Maud and Daisy were now able to take stock of their surroundings. At the front of the room were the casement window and door through which they'd entered. On a side wall an inset staircase led to the upper storey, and on the opposite side wall was a fireplace, its grate empty. Years of cobwebs had formed between the oak beams in the low ceiling. A dirty rug lay across the wooden floor. There were two chairs, a table and, half facing the window, an easel on which was pinned a blank sheet of paper. Under the window itself, as Maud had seen a short while ago, stood a wooden chest which was covered with pastel sticks, a tightly rolled stump of what looked like paper, rags, a partly open brown paper package and an earthenware jar holding a selection of paint brushes.

'No sign of any copies of great works of art,' whispered Daisy.

'No.' Maud kept her voice as low as Daisy's. 'There are no cupboards and I daren't risk removing this paraphernalia on the chest to look inside before he comes back. Besides, although the paintings Rose described were small, I don't think anything that precious would be stored in this chest. You noticed when we were outside that there's an attic floor?'

Daisy nodded. 'But we can hardly ask to keek in his bedroom and the next storey, can we?'

'We'd better start looking at these pictures.' Maud lifted a sketchbook from the floor and began to leaf through it.

'I wonder if the stink is coming from those cloots.' Daisy indicated the cloths lying on the chest.

Maud glanced up as Daisy went over and lifted one of the rags to her nose.

'It's got a fruity smell...'

Mr McGonagall reappeared, carrying the tea tray. He stopped in the doorway, staring at Daisy.

'What are you doing?'

'Och, I had a wee spot on my coat and thought I could use this to get it off.'

His gaze dropped to Daisy's spotless moss green walking costume.

'Dinna worry, I got it off,' she went on blithely. 'Is it turpentine on this cloot? It smells like it.'

Mr McGonagall frowned. 'I keep turpentine as a balm for cuts and abrasions.'

'I dinna realise painting was such a dangerous activity.' Daisy looked like butter wouldn't melt in her mouth.

'It is when you climb down riverbanks as I do.' His voice was terse.

Daisy dropped the rag back onto the chest, as Mr McGonagall set the tea tray on the table. 'You have looked at my pictures? I work in the modern style with lines and shapes.'

'Right enough you've got the line and shapes,' said Daisy.

He nodded, pleased. 'I can explain to you what I've tried to express in them.'

'Please do,' Maud said. 'I can see that they are full of ideas.'

No further encouragement was needed. Maud and Daisy sat on the wooden chairs and drank tea, while he stood by the easel and talked volubly until Maud's head reeled.

'The pastel sticks you are using,' she said, when at last he paused for breath. 'I don't think I've seen a picture drawn with those before.'

'They are versatile tools. Soft pastels can be used on a wide range of surfaces including card and canvas, but they look best when used on textured paper.' He turned the easel into the room and pointed to the sheet of thick, coarse paper pinned to it. 'Not only that, the flat sides of the sticks can be used to make broad strokes, the edged ends are ideal for bold lines and the pointed corners are perfect for achieving fine details. The torchon' – he indicated the tight roll of paper on the chest and Maud saw now that the end had been formed into a pointed tip – 'is used to blend the pastels.'

'And the brushes?' Daisy nodded at the selection in the earthenware jar.

'They are also useful for blending the pastels.'

Was it Maud's imagination or did his cheeks flush?

'There are some who think pastels are not what a *real* artist should be using,' Mr McGonagall hastened on, 'but the French are way ahead of the rest of the world. Degas works in soft pastels as well as oils.'

'It is a great pity,' Maud said in a sympathetic tone, 'that your work is not widely recognised.'

'Yes, it is. But that day will come. And until then I shall enjoy my revenge on the stuffy art world in Scotland.'

In his excitement, he jerked an arm and the package lying on the chest fell onto the floor. Maud saw a soft metal tube, which could only have contained oil paint, protrude from the brown paper. Mr McGonagall swooped down, snatched up the package and placed it back on the chest. The tube of paint was no longer visible.

'But, come,' he said, 'and tell me which picture you have chosen.'

Maud rose, followed by Daisy, and they turned to the pictures. After consulting with her friend, Maud chose what she took to be a study of trees by the side of the river. Mr McGonagall seemed disappointed that she had chosen the least futuristic of his works, but he began to roll up the image.

'Is this where you also paint?' Maud said, glancing round the room.

'What?' He looked up quickly, the picture half-rolled.

'I asked if this is where you do your painting.' She gave him an innocent smile. 'You said that Degas did both pastel drawings and oil paintings, so I wondered if you did too.'

'Oh. No, I have no interest in oil. I do all my work here, as you see, with the easel facing the window for the best light.'

He finished rolling up the drawing Maud had chosen and slid it into a cardboard tube lying on a side table, then waited as she pulled her cheque book and pen from her bag. She wrote out the cheque and handed it to him. He gave her the picture.

'Thank you,' she said. 'I must find a… place for it, to show it to its best advantage.'

Mr McGonagall held up her cheque. 'The day will come, Miss McIntyre, when you will congratulate yourself that you were once able to buy a picture by Adam McGonagall for such a small price.'

Maud doubted this as she shook his hand and tucked the tube under her arm.

'I hope you'll display it where a great number of people can enjoy it.'

'I have the perfect place in mind.' Maud smiled.

She and Daisy took their leave.

'Did you spot what was in the parcel he knocked onto the floor?' Maud said, as soon as they had rounded the corner along the footpath.

'Aye, a tube of paint, and the fact that he didna want us to see it.'

'Was there anything else that caught your attention?'

'Apart from when he went red, you mean?'

'He did colour up when you asked him about the brushes in the jar on the kist. He said he did all his pictures in that room.'

'And then he started talking about how he'd enjoy his revenge on Scotland's stuck-up art world once he got to Paris.'

Maud nodded. Daisy was shaping up nicely as a detective. 'You don't believe that room is also his studio?' she went on.

'I dinna. It's got naewhere near enough light, to start with. I might not ken much about painting, but I do ken you need a lot of light. The windows were clean on the attic floor, so I reckon that's where he works.'

'As to that tube he dropped, it must have contained oil paint, and yet he said he didn't use oils.'

'And there was the turpentine. The smell evaporates quickly, so he must have used it nae long ago. I recognised it because the stuff is useful for getting oil stains out of silk, satin and velvet.'

'It's probably reasonable to assume he didn't have it for that reason. He might use it for cuts as he said, but it seems more likely its purpose is to clean oil paint from the brushes.'

'Those Zubaroos were oil paintings.'

'Zurbaráns,' Maud corrected absentmindedly. 'Then there was the smell of linseed oil.'

'Having seen Mr McG's boots, I dinna think he's been cleaning them.'

Maud nodded. 'The artist needs further investigation.'

'You saw his boots: brown and scuffed, as Rose said?'

'I did, but that fact alone doesn't make him guilty.'

'Well,' Daisy said, after a short silence, 'I dinna think I've ever seen a green sky. Or grey grass. The other way round now, I have nae problem seeing that.'

'Where shall we hang this picture?'

'In the cludgie.'

Maud smiled at her friend. 'Exactly what I had been thinking. The colours will go nicely in the water closet.'

'The drawing is dreich.' Daisy sighed. 'Och well, if anyone comments, you can say you're supporting modern art.'

Maud's smile widened. 'Perhaps we can donate it to the Scottish National Gallery. I rather like the idea of presenting a work of art to the nation.'

Mrs Wallace was at the hall desk when Maud and Daisy returned to the hotel. She smiled broadly.

'I have an invitation for the three of us to take tea with Mrs Bisset the day after tomorrow.'

'Thank you so much, Mrs Wallace,' Maud said. 'I hope I can answer any questions the poor lady has about finding her husband's body at the station.'

But more importantly, Maud thought, she hoped Mrs Bisset would provide some answers to her own.

NINE

A short while later, they were drinking tea in the parlour when a man in an expensively cut grey suit with the barest hint of a stripe entered the room. Maud recognised him immediately, as she had observed him through the window of the gallery.

The son's resemblance to his father was there in that both men were heavily built, but as he approached them, Maud noted that Mr Anderson the younger didn't move with the same easy grace as his father and, unlike the hirsute older man, the son's hair was thin and lacklustre.

'Miss McIntyre?' he said.

Maud inclined her head. 'I am she.'

'The owner of the M. McIntyre Agency? How do you do.' He glanced towards Daisy and gave a slight frown. 'May I join you, ladies?'

Had he recognised Daisy from the previous day? Red hair was not unusual in the Highlands, but the gallery must have few enough customers to make Daisy memorable. Maud shot her a look and saw that Daisy had assumed a guileless expression.

'You may, Mr...?'

'Anderson,' he said, taking a seat opposite them. 'David Anderson.'

Maud folded her hands neatly in her lap and concealed her satisfaction by giving the man a polite smile. 'How can we help you, Mr Anderson?'

He lowered himself into one of the armchairs placed by the glowing fire. 'I understand from my father that you're investigating some sales I recently made.'

Maud inclined her head. 'A question has been raised.'

'By whom?'

'I'm afraid I'm not at liberty to say.'

'Oh, come now,' he said in a jovial tone and crossing his legs to show how comfortable he intended to make himself. 'You can surely tell me that.'

'My client wishes to remain anonymous.'

'It will be one of two customers.'

'Then it's up to you to work it out,' said Daisy, no trace of the Morningside accent she'd adopted when she'd visited his shop.

He sent Daisy a thoughtful look, his eyes lingering slightly too long to make the exchange comfortable. For a moment, Maud was afraid he would make the decision to contact the two customers, which was to be avoided at all costs.

'Mr Anderson,' Maud said, drawing his attention away from Daisy, 'what can you tell us about the pictures: their provenance, where you bought them and so forth?'

'Nothing.' He uncrossed his legs and leaned forward, closer to Maud. 'Think of it as a dealer's privilege.'

'I'm not sure if calling on a *dealer's privilege* will carry any weight with the law.'

'Miss McIntyre, I believe someone has taken it in their head that there are some shady goings-on at my gallery, but it simply isn't true.' He leaned back in his seat and smiled. 'It's a rumour started by one of my competitors. There will be more than one person in the world of art dealing who is envious of my success.'

'You might very well think that. I couldn't possibly comment.'

It was Maud's turn to smile.

The following morning, rather bored with ballet exercises and Indian clubs, Maud felt in need of an invigorating walk. When an investigation was proving difficult, she thought it sensible to leave her thoughts to work on the problem while she did something else entirely.

'Mrs Wallace,' she said, as the hotelier's wife supervised the serving of breakfasts of poached eggs on thick brown bread, 'where do you recommend as a long walk to see the glorious views of this part of the country?'

'A long walk just for the scenery, you say?' She looked dubious. 'Are you sure, Miss McIntyre?'

Maud smiled. 'Yes, I'm sure.'

'I'm nae so sure.' Daisy pulled a face.

'Well, there's Loch Callater. That's bonnie. A high loch surrounded by mountains.'

'It sounds perfect. How do I get there?'

Mrs Wallace's frown deepened. 'It's a wee bit under two miles before you get to the start of the walk and then it'll be quite a distance before you reach the loch.'

Maud nodded.

'She's awfa keen to maintain her fitness—'

'Thank you for imparting that information to Mrs Wallace, Daisy, but I'm sure she didn't really want to know. Loch Callater sounds delightful, Mrs Wallace, thank you. That will do very well.' Once she got into a good stride, she could swing her arms and enjoy the views at the same time.

'You'll be passing the house where Robert Louis Stevenson

and his family stayed in the summer that he wrote one of his most famous books,' said Mrs Wallace, with a degree of pride. 'Yes, he wrote the first sixteen chapters of *Treasure Island* right here in Braemar.'

'Really?' Maud was surprised. 'And yet the village is miles from the sea.'

'Aye, but Mr Stevenson and his stepson drew a map of an imaginary island and that gave them the idea for the novel.'

'How wonderful!'

'And his characters' names were based on some of the villagers. Long John Silver came from the miller, John Silver. Mr Stevenson used other local family names. There's a Morgan, one of the pirates; a Hunter, who is a manservant of Squire Trelawney; and an Anderson – he's the boatswain on the pirate ship.'

'I didna ken that,' said Daisy, shooting Maud a glance.

Maud gave her a slight nod. Had the father or son Anderson been involved in illicit dealings like their fictional counterparts?

'Och, anyone around here could tell you that,' went on Mrs Wallace. 'It's common knowledge. Aye, this is an area rich in brigands and rebels, castles and tales of buried treasure. Now here's a wee bit of gossip for you.'

Mrs Wallace lowered her voice, although it was hardly necessary with the clatter of crockery coming from the kitchen, and the bustle of waiters and waitresses moving through the dining room carrying trays laden with plates of eggs, bowls of porridge and pots of tea.

'After a while Mr Stevenson had enough of villagers calling and disturbing his writing, so he turned the garden shed into his study and put a sign marked *Edinburgh* above the door. So that when folk came to chat, the servants could say quite honestly that he was in Edinburgh.'

Maud laughed. 'What a wonderful story.'

Mrs Wallace beamed. 'Let me make you a wee picnic to

take with you. All that exercise will make you hungry and thirsty. Just for yourself then, Miss McIntyre, and not you, Miss Cameron?'

'I'll bide here and visit the sites, thank you,' Daisy said with a smile. 'I'm awfa keen to see Braemar Castle and the site of the Raising of the Standard—'

'A sandwich and a bottle of ginger beer would be very welcome, Mrs Wallace,' Maud said firmly.

Before long she was walking south, the canvas knapsack containing the piece box Mrs Wallace had given her over one shoulder. It was a glorious day with a slight nip in the early morning air, reminding her that autumn was stealing in. The colours of the trees were spectacular in the sunlight. The Highland cattle on the green, their red coats almost glowing, looked up as she passed and, still chewing, watched her for a moment or two before they returned to their grazing.

Following Mrs Wallace's excellent directions, Maud passed the house where Robert Louis Stevenson had stayed. An attractive, two-storey, double-fronted dwelling built in stone, it sat close to the pavement. How sad that he had died. It would have been wonderful to have seen him walk out of his gate and to pass the time of day with him.

Very soon she had left the village behind and was on the country road. Birds sang with the joy of a new morning and Maud felt like doing the same.

A stout cob pulling an open cart filled with milk churns trundled up the road behind her, drew past a little way and stopped.

'Would you like a hurl, lassie?' the driver called down, his pipe clamped in the side of his mouth.

Maud walked towards him and looked up at the man. A young fellow dressed in a dark jacket in heavy wool, a belt pulled tight to hold up his trousers and wearing a flat cap, she felt he looked trustworthy. In Edinburgh, she would never accept a lift from a stranger, but she was a country lass at heart.

'Thank you.' Maud accepted his hand and held on to her straw boater as he pulled her up onto the seat next to him.

'Where are you off to?' he said, as the horse ambled along.

'To Loch Callater.' Maud placed the knapsack between them on the wooden bench and arranged her tweed skirts.

'You'll be taking Jock's Road then.'

'Jock's Road?'

'Aye. The mountain path that goes all the way to Glen Doll.'

'Didn't hundreds of Highlanders escape to the hills around there after fighting at Culloden?'

'That's what my father told me. That, and cattle thieves and whisky smugglers were fond of using Jock's Road too.'

Maud smiled. 'It sounds like the area has quite a history.'

He returned her smile. 'It's safe today, don't worry. And we can still use it,' he added with a frown. 'When Duncan Macpherson bought the estate, he tried to stop folk from crossing his land.'

'So what happened?'

'Nothing. It's an old drover's path, used for years to drive sheep to the market at the foot of Glen Clova, and the Scottish Rights of Way Society wasn't going to let him get away with that sort of nonsense. They took Macpherson to court, and it went all the way up to the House of Lords.' He nodded with satisfaction.

'When was this?' Maud hadn't heard of it.

'Nae so long ago,' said the driver. 'Somewhere around eighteen ninety. Maybe a year or two earlier. All I know for sure is that it was afore I was born.'

'And the laird lost the case?'

'Aye, and he was made bankrupt. The pity of it was, so was

the Society.' He was silent for a moment, no doubt thinking, as was Maud, of the cost of going to law.

'Who owns the estate now?' she asked.

'The King. Glen Doll borders Balmoral.' He glanced at her. 'I take it you're here on holiday since you're out seeing the sights, such as they are.'

'Yes, a friend and I are staying at the inn.' Maud gazed about at the fields and trees. 'It's so beautiful up here.'

'I suppose it is, right enough. Maybe it takes a city dweller to notice it. Where are you from then?'

'Edinburgh.'

'A big city dweller then!'

Maud laughed. 'I was brought up in the country, so not really. And to be honest, there are times when I truly miss it.'

'Perhaps not in the winter if it fares as badly as we do here, though. We can be cut off for weeks with the snow.'

His words brought a smile to her face, as she remembered fondly the snowball fights with her brothers and building a snowman with them, until one by one over the years they had grown old enough to go away to boarding school. Without her noisy playmates, the white landscape was still breathtaking, but less exciting. Maud glanced at the young man flicking the reins to keep the horse moving as the road became a little steeper, and she felt abashed. She dashed away her longing for winters past and thought of the young man and others like him; for those who had to work in temperatures below freezing for weeks on end, the depth of winter would be wretched.

'The royal family have brought business to the area, mind,' he went on, 'and we're grateful for that. The King is at Balmoral now, as it happens. He enjoys coming up here for the shooting season.'

'What does he shoot – pheasant?'

'Grouse mainly, and partridge. It's a wee bit too early for pheasant.'

Maud's father had never been interested in the slaughter of birds for sport, for which she was thankful, but it wasn't possible to grow up in the country without knowing those who enjoyed the sport. She had a mental image of the beating party, moving in a straight line and at the right pace, to flush out the birds from the undergrowth and into the path of the guns.

Her thoughts were broken into by the unmistakable sound of squealing and a high-pitched shouting. Alarmed, Maud looked around for the source. A young woman seated backwards astride a large ginger pig bounced into view through the bracken.

'*Madainn mhath*, Mistress Lisa,' Maud's driver called.

The young woman returned his greeting and gave a cheery wave, fell off the pig and landed in a heap in the bracken.

'We must stop!' Maud cried, clutching the young man's arm. 'She might be hurt.'

'Not her,' he said with a smile. 'She's from the north of England, and folk there are as hardy as we are.'

The horse ambled on.

'I—' Maud turned in her seat and was relieved to see the young woman get to her feet, brush down her long skirts and march over to where the pig was now contentedly grazing.

'Those Tams are good pigs, but they do keep escaping,' he went on.

'But why on earth was she *riding* it?' Maud demanded, turning back to look at him.

He laughed. 'She wouldn't have been riding it on purpose, poor lass, but trying to chase it back into the field. They push their long narrow body between your legs and before you know where you are, they're up and running with you on their back. So if you see one walking along the road—'

'I'll make sure to walk in the other direction.'

The young man laughed and snapped the reins to chivvy the horse on. They continued in silence for a good half a mile, the only sounds to be heard the plodding of horse hooves on the dry ground and the mewing of a young buzzard riding the thermals of the wide blue sky.

Eventually, her driver slowed the horse.

'This is the Callater Burn we're coming up to. I'll take you across and let you off. It's the nearest I can go, as the track's not fit for a cart.'

'Thank you, Mr...?'

'Geddes, Rabbie Geddes.' He brought the horse to a halt. 'That's where you start your walk.' He pointed to a track that ran beside a farmhouse on the other side of the road. 'Go through the glen, following the course of the burn, and that'll take you to the loch. If you're lucky, you might even get to see the little folk.'

'Little folk?'

'Aye. A professor about fifty years ago reported that a man had seen fairies dancing on a hillock with a piper playing to them.' The young man grinned.

'A professor, you say?' Maud smiled and gathered up her knapsack.

'Aye. No local folk have ever claimed to see them, so the village is convinced either he or the other man must have taken a wee dram or three.'

She laughed and climbed from the seat down onto the road. 'Thank you again, Mr Geddes. You have been very kind.' She hesitated for only a moment. That he was not well-heeled was evident. 'My name is Miss Maud McIntyre. I'm a private detective and if you ever find yourself in need of one, ask for me through Mrs Wallace at the hotel.'

The young man's eyes widened, then he touched his cap, shook the horse's reins and resumed his journey.

Maud pushed her arms through the straps of the knapsack and settled it comfortably on her back as she watched them go. Crossing the road, she followed the track up the glen.

TEN

It wasn't long before the ground levelled and she was striding along, the wide Callater Burn on her left sparkling as it rushed over the bed of stones. It was a perfect early autumn day. The purple heather was past its best, but it still bloomed all around her in the wide valley as she made her way along the track, her skirts brushing the heather. Hills rose steeply around the glen, and she looked, only half seriously, for the hillock inhabited by the little folk. Maud laughed at herself. Myth and magic breed easily in lonely straths.

She crossed a wooden bridge and caught sight of a golden eagle as it swooped in the clear blue sky, watching for prey. By now, the day was growing warm, and once she was back on the grass, she kneeled down by the burn, cupped her hands and eagerly drank the cool, fresh water.

She glanced around. There was no one in sight, so she unbuttoned and slipped off her blue tweed coat. But now what to do with it? It was too warm to carry the garment and no trees to hang it on. She decided to leave it on one of the many flat rocks dotted through the heather alongside the track near the bridge. As she folded it neatly and placed it on a rock, Maud laughed to herself. If she had attempted to do something similar in the city, her jacket would be gone in no time. Hoisting the knapsack back in position, on she went, delighting in the sweet, fresh air.

High up on the hillside, a large red deer appeared. A lone male with huge antlers. It raised its head and looked straight at her before bounding away.

Maud strode on. And then ahead of her she saw the loch, shimmering blue in the sunshine, surrounded by snow-capped mountains. A small stone building sat near the lochside, a ghillie's lodge, she supposed. She stopped for a moment and breathed deeply, filling her lungs with the pure mountain air. It was all so perfect. Why would anyone ever wish to be anywhere else? She knew why the King chose here for his holidays. She'd also be back to visit the Highlands in the summer, when the days were warm and the nights only four hours long.

She walked on until she reached the loch. There was another of the large, flat stones by the side of the water and she determined to sit there for a while and eat her picnic luncheon before she would turn and retrace her steps to the village.

The stone was beautifully warm as Maud lowered her derrière onto it, arranged her skirts and made herself comfortable. She was sorely tempted to kick off her boots, undo the garters attached to her corset and roll down her cotton stockings. But decency triumphed.

From the knapsack, Maud unpacked the piece box containing the sandwich of crumbly local cheese that Mrs Wallace had made for her. She gazed at the sparkling loch, the majestic mountains, the gulls squawking and diving over the surface of the water. The warm sun shone and a bee buzzed by, rather too close for Maud's liking.

She paused, the bread halfway to her mouth. The buzzing grew louder.

Maud swatted it away. Its buzzing became distinctly peevish. She waved her free hand in a more pointed manner. It buzzed to within an inch of the hand holding her luncheon. She snatched the sandwich away, but one of its chums joined it.

She gave a foolish little scream and jumped up, the box of sandwiches slipping from her lap, and ran towards the shelter of the lodge. Before she'd reached it, Maud stumbled on a loose stone and went flying. She landed on her hands and knees.

'Allow me to help you, madam.'

Maud looked slowly up. A bearded man of middle years in a homburg hat had appeared out of nowhere. He was too large for one of the fairie folk, but with that sculpted beard and sparkling eyes, he seemed familiar. Not a tall man, but he looked imposing as he stood over her in his belted tweed jacket and knickerbockers, his hand held out. A short way behind him a group of men stood in similar attire. She'd passed no one on her walk here. It must be a shooting party from the Glen Doll estate. Presumably they had been at the other side of the small lodge, enjoying their own picnic luncheon.

The man had removed his hat. The hand extended to assist her was that of His Majesty, King George V.

Maud caught her breath. Who would have believed it: Maud Constance McIntyre was on her hands and knees in front of His Majesty!

Her face flushed with shame; she reached up and clasped his hand with a new-found strength thanks to the Indian clubs. The King's eyes went from her face to her hand, his eyebrows lifting in surprise as he helped her to her feet, a little more vigorously than he also had expected by the look on his face. Maud lost her footing and managed to draw back just before their foreheads clashed.

'I seemed to be attempting to rescue you, and then to knock you out.' He smiled.

'Your Majesty.' Maud curtsied, grateful that her years of ballet practice enabled her to do so without wobbling.

But her embarrassment was not yet over. When she straightened, she was looking down at him. The King was a few inches shorter.

'Miss...?' He looked enquiringly at Maud.

'McIntyre, sir.'

'There was no need to curtsy, Miss McIntyre. We pride ourselves on being informal when out on a shoot. And' – he smiled again as he replaced his homburg – 'it is no longer necessary that I be approached on hands and knees.'

He looked towards the scattered contents of her box of bread, cheese and an apple, and frowned. 'You have dropped your luncheon. It is beyond eating. You must join us.' He indicated the other men standing back a little way.

It was then that she spotted Lord Urquhart detaching himself from the group. Maud's heart picked up speed and she chastised herself. Ordinarily, she took no notice of men, except as obstacles in her path, which in her experience appeared to be their primary function.

With a look of enquiry, he walked towards them. How could a man wearing such ridiculous knickerbockers look so... manly?

'I couldn't possibly intrude on a private party, Your Majesty,' Maud said quickly, preparing to turn and retrace her steps, and thanking the gods that her face couldn't get any hotter, no matter how deeply embarrassing her situation threatened to become.

'Nonsense. I insist.' The King spoke in a voice that brooked no dissention. 'We have plenty and you have none.'

'Miss McIntyre.' Lord Urquhart raised his tweed cap to her as he reached them. 'Are you hurt?'

'You know the lady, Hamish?' It was the King's turn to look surprised.

'Indeed I do, sir. Miss Maud McIntyre and I are, dare I say, old friends.' Lord Urquhart smiled at her, his eyes flashing in amusement.

Maud glared at him. Their relationship, if indeed their acquaintance could be called that, was one of detective and client. She would not be put off by Lord Urquhart, she decided. She was hungry and very much wanted to eat before the long walk back. Besides, she felt sure Daisy would never forgive her if she refused an opportunity to talk to the King.

She flashed a disapproving look towards Lord Urquhart before accepting the King's invitation. 'If you are certain, sir, I would be honoured to join you for luncheon.'

'That's settled then.' He called to one of his retinue to pack up and collect her knapsack, and she followed him. One of the other men brought forward three folding chairs and a small round table which he set a little apart from the others. Maud was grateful, for lunching with more than a dozen men by herself was not something she would have relished.

The King indicated to his man that Maud should be seated first. My goodness, she thought as the King took another seat, he really doesn't want to stand on ceremony when he's out shooting. As Lord Urquhart the remaining one, she couldn't help but smile when the wooden chair squeaked under his large, powerful frame.

'Remind the ghillie to bring a more substantial chair for you tomorrow, Hamish.'

A deer-horn drinking cup was filled with lemonade and passed to her. Soon she and the King were eating and chatting – not at the same time; her father had brought her up correctly. She was having luncheon with the King!

Not only that, but the plate of smoked salmon was wonderful.

'You are here on holiday?' His Majesty asked.

'I am, sir.'

'Are you staying at the Braemar Arms?' he went on. 'I

mention it only because, in gratitude for an excellent luncheon my party and I recently enjoyed there, yesterday I had one of my aides deliver to the hotel a rather fine *Lophophanes cristatus*.'

Maud tried to look as though she knew what such a thing was. An ingredient for a meal, perhaps?

She clearly didn't succeed for the King went on politely, 'It is of course the *Scottish* crested tit to which I refer.'

Ah, Maud thought, a bird. Thank goodness she hadn't responded to his comment on a rather fine *Lophophanes cristatus* by remarking, 'Delicious.'

'It will be an excellent addition to the inn's display of stuffed birds,' he added. 'Although not as colourful as some other tits, the black and white crest on the top of its head coupled with its black and white speckled forehead and black marking round the eyes makes for a most distinctive member of its species.'

'I will make a point of visiting the display on my return to the hotel.'

As Maud and the King chatted on for a while, she was aware that Lord Urquhart was watching her.

'You're unusually quiet, Hamish,' the King said, glancing at him after a while.

Lord Urquhart inclined his head graciously. 'Merely not wishing to impose myself on the conversation, sir. Miss McIntyre and I can resume our friendship at a more convenient time.'

Maud was swallowing the last portion of her salmon and almost choked in the process. Lord Urquhart reached out and patted her back.

'I should now rejoin my friends,' said the King, getting to his feet. 'Goodbye, Miss McIntyre. It has been most pleasant talking to you.'

'Goodbye, Your Majesty. And thank you, sir, for your timely rescue and for luncheon.'

'Lord Urquhart.' Maud nodded at him, picked up her knapsack, directed a deep curtsy to the King and marched away. She was furious with him for claiming a close friendship.

She had first met him when he walked into her office with his case involving stolen compromising letters, and then on finding the agency was run by a woman he had promptly walked out. Meeting him again at Duddingston House only days later, another case she and Daisy had solved, did not constitute a friendship, no matter how *friendly* he had been.

Maud coloured as she realised how close she had come just a short while ago to removing her stockings. Imagine if she had given Lord Urquhart – or, much worse, the King – a glimpse of her garters, no matter how attractively they were trimmed in white lace.

She strode back along the rough path she had followed to the shooting lodge, until she reached the bridge. Plucking her jacket from where she'd left it, she walked on. When she gained the small incline that led back to the road, Maud pulled on her jacket and buttoned it as high as it would go. Half an hour to reach the village, she thought, then she'd be back at the Braemar Arms and would seek out the crested tit.

Meanwhile, she would return to her usual controlled self by concentrating on the few clues she and Daisy had in their current investigations. In the art case: a forger with brown scuffed boots who kept late hours. In the Bisset case: a murderer in tradesmen's clothing who knew little about the position of spent cartridges.

A dreadful thought struck and her heart hammered. What if it were not a painter and decorator with paint on his trousers, but an artist? When she'd spoken to Mr McGonagall at the Linn of Dee, was there paint on his clothing? To her shame, she hadn't noticed and had only made a point of looking at his boots. But, she told herself, breathing deeply now to slow her heart rate, surely the fact that she hadn't noticed meant that his

trousers were free of paint. *She* might have got the stuff everywhere, but an artist would be too experienced to do so and too
careful with the expensive materials.

No, whatever else Mr McGonagall might have done, she
was sure he was not Norman Bisset's murderer.

Pushing open the door to the hotel, Maud entered the hall. The
hotelier was reading a newspaper at the desk. He looked up.

'*Feasgar math*, Miss McIntyre. Have you had an enjoyable
walk? My wife tells me you were going to Loch Callater.'

'Yes, thank you, Mr Wallace. It turned out to be quite an
experience. I met the King—'

'The King?' Mr Wallace smiled. 'Such a gracious gentleman. He dined here with a small party just the other day.'

'Yes, I know. He told me while we were eating luncheon.'

'You had *luncheon* with His Majesty?'

'Yes, and he told me he had presented you with a delightful
specimen for your stuffed bird cabinet. I would very much like
to see the bird, if I may.'

Mr Wallace beamed. 'Of course, of course. Do come this
way.'

He walked round from the desk and was about to lead
Maud to the room, when the hotel door opened and an elderly
couple dressed in city attire entered.

'Will you excuse me a moment while I see to our new
guests?' he said to Maud.

'If you would direct me, I can make my own way.'

Mr Wallace hesitated, clearly torn between his responsibility as hotelier and his desire to show off the King's gift. The
elderly couple reached the desk where Maud and Mr Wallace
stood. He made up his mind.

'If you go through the lounge bar,' he said, gesturing to the
door in the opposite direction to the parlour, 'you will come to

the room housing the cabinets.' He turned to greet the new arrivals.

Maud opened the door he had indicated. Silence fell as the eyes of the three male patrons turned towards her.

Maud nodded at them. '*Feasgar math*, gentlemen.'

She wasn't surprised to see the little group's bemusement at the sight of an unaccompanied woman in the bar, but she was on a mission. Keeping that thought in her head, Maud looked straight ahead as she marched towards the archway at the far end of the room.

Two steps up and, drawing aside the thick red curtain, she entered a small room. Two glass cabinets met her gaze, a small one on a table in the centre, and against the right-hand wall a large floor-to-ceiling display case. The wall in front of her held the fireplace with a merrily burning blaze and the usual two stuffed armchairs by it. The chairs, and indeed room, were empty. There were no disapproving glares turned towards her here, only a multitude of glass eyes that glittered in the firelight.

The tall cabinet on the side wall housed the large birds. A distinctive huge black capercaillies, a golden-headed eagle, various species of owls. She turned to the small birds in the glass case on the table in the centre of the room.

The Scottish crested tit had been perched on the branch of a section of tree. Attached to the trunk was a card written in beautiful copperplate proclaiming the *Lophophanes cristatus* a gift from King George V. Mr Wallace was right to be proud of such an exhibit. The cream and brown bird was small – small enough, Maud judged, to fit into a person's hand – but it was arresting. A black and white crest stuck up on top of its head, its forehead was speckled, and around its eyes was a black line, looking like some sort of strange new cosmetic. Around its throat was a thin black marking like a collar.

Maud's gaze moved on to the bird next to it on the branch.

It was larger than the crested tit and had attractive markings in black, brown, cream and grey with yellow legs.

She straightened. Fascinating as all this was, time was getting on.

Maud left the trophy room, marched back through the bar to the accompaniment of sudden silence once again and emerged into the hall. Mr Wallace was arranging for the new guests' luggage to be taken up to their rooms, so Maud gave him a brief nod and climbed the stairs.

She would first go to Daisy's room and see if her assistant had learned anything of interest to their investigations.

ELEVEN

'I went for my stravaig,' said Daisy, comfortably propped up on her bed.

Maud sat on the end of the mattress. 'Did you meet anyone? Hear anything of interest?'

'Maybe. I was strolling along a lane and who should I meet but that meddling besom we met at the ruins.'

'She was hardly meddling, Daisy, but interested in telling us some of the local history.'

Daisy huffed. 'Be that as it may, she was standing in the front garden of a cottage talking to a man there. She waved me over and you ken me, friendly to a fault. I felt I couldna ignore her. It turns out that the mannie is her neighbour and he sorts out her garden for her once a week.'

'What a kind neighbour.'

'That's nae the important bit!'

'Go on.'

'Well, we got talking and guess what?'

'Daisy.' Maud's tone was decidedly cool.

'The important bit is he'd done some gardening and handyman work for Bisset. And when the wifie went into her house, I had a chat with Mr Buston. He – John Buston, that is – had been engaged to work at the Bissets'. He was supposed to be paid at the end of each week, but he stopped going after a while when Bisset hadna paid him anything.'

'Hmm,' Maud said. 'That fits in with what we've heard about Mr Bisset. Was John Buston eventually paid?'

Daisy shook her head. 'He called at the house three times, cap in hand almost. It seems that old man Bisset really did like to see people humiliated.'

'What Mrs Wallace told us wasn't an exaggeration.' Maud frowned. 'He made a number of tradesmen wait before he paid them.'

'But they eventually got their money, so it doesna make sense that John Buston should have killed him and not wait to be paid. Could a person be so black-affronted that all reason goes and he strikes out?'

'Perhaps we should have a chat with Mr Buston.'

'And you, Maud, did you find out anything on your walk?'

'Oh, well.' Maud looked down at the cream candlewick cover on Daisy's bed and smoothed it with her hand. 'Nothing that is of use to our forgery case or the murder. But I must confess the day was a bit of a surprise.'

'What happened?'

'I met the King.'

Daisy sat up abruptly. 'You never did!'

'He was at Loch Callater with a small shooting party.'

Daisy swung her legs off the bed. 'I dinna believe it!'

'It's true. He was charming and shared his luncheon with me.'

'I've aye wanted to meet a member of the royal family.' Daisy let out a long sigh.

'I'm sorry, Daisy.'

'It's nae fault of yours. I should have come with you on that walk.'

'I met someone else too,' Maud went on.

'Nae Prince Edward?'

Maud laughed. 'No.'

'Then who?'

Maud rose from the bed, walked over to the dressing table and began to rearrange Daisy's hairbrush and pins.

'Lord Urquhart.'

'The Baron of Hearts,' Daisy scoffed.

Maud glanced up and met her friend's gaze in the looking glass. 'That was a silly title used in a society magazine.' She turned around and sat on the stool.

'Dinna tell me he's come up here to offer his help with our investigation?'

'Perish the thought.' Maud shuddered. 'He was surprised to see me, although not as surprised as I was to see him.'

'That's a relief. Last time we were in hot pursuit, he seemed to think a male brain, namely his, would be an advantage.'

'Two heads are better than one, but—'

'You can't beat two *female* brains?'

Maud had to agree. Men were apt to be single-minded and stubborn when it came to overriding female logic. A lot of time can be wasted by men going down the wrong route.

'So what was his lordship doing there?' Daisy said.

'He was on the shoot with His Majesty.'

'Of course he was. Then do you think his lordship is staying at Balmoral?'

'I suppose so.' Maud smiled at Daisy. 'But that's no concern of ours. Shall we finally admit that we're going to investigate Bisset's murder? We're in the village already, so it's not as if we have any extra expenses. And we seem to have been skirting round the matter ever since we found his body.'

'I think we should, and as I've nae been long back, let's see if Mr Buston is still working in the garden.'

Maud waited while Daisy pinned on her hat, and the two of them left the hotel and went out into the still-warm afternoon.

It was only a short walk, taking them past the tea shop to the short row of pretty cottages. They were in luck – John Buston was digging over a plot of earth in his front garden. A man in his mid-thirties, Maud guessed, his skin brown from working outdoors, he had a cheerful countenance. He nodded his recognition at Daisy as they stopped by the front gate.

'You're still at it, Mr Buston?'

'Aye.'

'You clearly have green fingers.' Maud gazed over the low wooden gate at a border filled with bright helichrysums. 'I hope you don't mind my coming to have a look. My friend Miss Cameron admired your flowers so much. I am Miss McIntyre, by the way.'

He dug the garden fork into the soil and rested a forearm on the handle. 'Pleased to meet you.'

'I'm afraid we are interrupting your work...'

He pulled a large, earth-coloured handkerchief from his trouser pocket and wiped his face. ''Tis hard work, so I'm glad of a breather.'

'It must have been especially hard, working in the heat we've had this summer,' Maud went on.

'It was, right enough.' A scowl crossed his cheerful face. 'Especially when some folks don't pay for the work you've done. I told the young lady earlier.'

'Yes, Miss Cameron did mention that. It must have been hard for you.'

'Aye. Bisset stomped about his garden, making himself as unpleasant as possible, ordering me about, telling me where to put things, when he had no idea about the right place for plants and didn't like it when I told him.'

'Such foolishness to treat a man of your knowledge in that way.'

The gardener's face darkened. 'He knew I needed the money to pay for new tools. I've sharpened the blade on my scythe that many times that now there's mickle left of the blade. A man's only as good as his tools. Work will dry up if I can't do it properly. I've never put anything on the slate before, but now I've had to, thanks to that man.' He turned his head and spat on the earth before pushing the grubby handkerchief back into his pocket and taking hold of the spade again.

'I'm not the kind of man who would wish harm to any soul, but I'll say this. I don't condemn the person who did it, and now it's happened I'm glad he's dead.'

'Do you think we should put the gardener on our list of suspects in the Bisset case?' Daisy asked, as she and Maud walked back towards the hotel.

'We haven't actually got a list of suspects yet,' Maud reminded her.

'Then let's have a cup of tea and draw one up.'

They continued past the hotel and entered the village tea shop, took a table by the window and ordered a pot of tea for two. There were only two other ladies drinking tea, both young and engrossed in whatever it was they were talking about. Maud and Daisy chatted about inconsequential things until their tea arrived.

'Now let us examine what we know.' Maud began ticking off items on the fingers of her right hand. 'One.'

She paused as Daisy took her notebook from her bag, opened it at a fresh page and headed it *Bisset Investigation*.

'One,' Maud continued. 'Mr Bisset was on the train that left Braemar at one twenty and arrived at Ballater at two o'clock on Tuesday.'

Daisy nodded. 'We dinna ken exactly when he was killed, but somewhere between Braemar and Bridge of Gairn.'

It was Maud's turn to nod. 'We can be reasonably certain that his murderer didn't get off at Ballater as he, or she,' Maud added, striving as usual for fairness, 'would have been seen.

'Two. At Bridge of Gairn the stationmaster *did* see someone alight from the train. He described this person as having pale unkempt whiskers and wearing trousers that were splashed with brown paint. The fact that he hurried away was put down by the police sergeant as being in trouble with his wife.'

Daisy snorted.

'Three. The train reached Bridge of Gairn at...' She frowned as she tried to remember.

'Just a minute. I wrote down the train times.' Daisy turned back to the relevant entry in her notebook. 'One fifty.'

'Thank you, Daisy. Now, if the assailant was the man with the whiskers, we can assume by this time Bisset was dead. Four,' she went on, as Daisy returned to her list. 'We must, therefore, assume that the killer got on the train at Braemar. Not only that, given they were in the same compartment, he could have boarded *with* Bisset.'

'Then, five,' Daisy said, nodding at Maud's fingers, 'the two must have known each other.'

'Not necessarily. If the train was busy—'

'But that wasna the case, as the stationmaster saw no one on the train when it left Bridge of Gairn and we ken there was no one on it, apart from the body, when it reached Ballater.'

'True. Another possibility to consider on the subject of whether or not killer and victim knew each other, is that the killer arrived late at Braemar station and may simply have jumped on the train just as the whistle blew. Mr Bisset was found in the last compartment, after all.'

'But that would mean the murder hadna been planned, and yet the killer had taken a gun on the train.'

'Hmm, you're right. We should assume they knew each other.'

Daisy nodded.

'Six.' Maud moved on to the fingers on her left hand. 'As far as we know, no money was taken. This suggests that the murderer was interested only in bringing about the death of his victim.'

Maud stopped and took a sip of her tea.

'We ken more than we thought,' Daisy said. 'Next is number seven.'

'Seven. Now we come to suspects. We know that Mr Buston the gardener hated him, but an unpaid account seems insufficient reason for murder.'

'People can be driven to kill by the most unlikely thing.'

'I'm sure you're correct, Daisy, but... well, Mr Buston seems such a pleasant man.'

'Nae doubt people thought Amelia Dyer in England was a kind-hearted soul looking after all those unwanted bairns,' Daisy said darkly.

'I don't think we can put the gardener and a convicted child-murderer in the same category.'

'Maybe not,' Daisy conceded, 'but he should be on our list, don't you think?'

'Very well. So, Mr Buston the gardener. We've not yet met Mrs Bisset, but it appears by all accounts that she's not exactly a grieving widow.'

'And the dochter,' Daisy put in. 'I'll put her on the list too.'

'Daisy, she was on the train with us and so cannot have killed her father.'

Daisy shrugged. 'She might have paid someone to do it.'

'Why on earth would she do that?'

'I dinna ken, but there's something about that family. According to Mrs Wallace, they aye hated each other.'

'She didn't actually say that. But very well. Who else should be on the list?'

'What about Mr Wallace? His wife said he'd thrown Bisset

out of the bar on more than one occasion for getting into a rammle and that Mr Wallace had warned him if it happened again, Bisset would be banned at the very least.'

'Put him on the list too. Now, where are we?'

Daisy looked back down at her notes. 'Under number seven, Suspects, we've got Mr Buston, Mrs Bisset and Miss Bisset. That's three.' She added Mr Wallace to the list. 'Now we've got four.' She looked up again. 'What do you think Mr Wallace meant when he said Bisset would be banned *at the very least?*'

'I can't believe Mr Wallace meant that he would murder Mr Bisset. What about the young man on the train? There's something about the way the Bisset girl spoke to him when he got into the argument with the schoolteacher, and he then immediately behaved himself.'

'Nae to mention his giving her a bosie when she found out it was her faither lying there deid,' said Daisy. 'It looked like she knew the crabbit young fellow.'

'I agree, but it's strange that he disappeared as soon as we reached Braemar station.'

'Aye. Why did he come here? And where is he now?'

'There's certainly something suspicious about that young man,' Maud agreed. 'Although he was also on the train with us, which should exclude him from our list. But if Miss Bisset *had* arranged the murder of her father – which I'm not convinced about, Daisy – then the young man could be involved in it with her.'

Daisy added the further name to her list. 'That's *five* possible suspects, but aye weak.'

'Weak is a bit of an understatement, but we have to start somewhere.'

'It's nae much to go on, is it? Like the case with yon lassie under the art dealer's roof.'

'You're right. We have nothing but a hunch to go on in that case, and it's not even our hunch!'

'Anything else to go on the list?' Daisy said, nodding at Maud's fingers. 'That's seven points.'

'Not that I can think of.'

'It would be braw to have a round number.'

'What about,' Maud said doubtfully, 'at number eight: is there a connection to our art forgery case and if so what?'

Daisy frowned. 'I canna see how. Are you beginning to wish we hadna taken on Rose's case?'

'No. Nor can I see how any of it can fit together, but I've got this feeling.'

'Isna that just another way of saying you have a hunch?'

'Maybe, but we need to do something. Rose must be thinking we've given up with the investigation.'

'Anyway, that's two points: is there a connection and if so what? That means we're left with an odd number again.'

'Not necessarily. We can put them together at number eight.'

Daisy laughed. 'Aye, we can!'

Maud smiled and went on. 'And now we need a plan of action.'

Daisy grinned. 'An eight-point plan?'

'If at all possible. It's always preferable to have a sheet that balances.'

Despite their best endeavours, they came up with only two points. One, take tea with Mrs Bisset tomorrow afternoon, and two, carry out a search of Mr McGonagall's cottage as soon as possible.

TWELVE

Maud and Daisy were crossing the hall on their way to breakfast the following morning when Mr Wallace rushed distractedly through the doors of the lounge bar.

'Mr Wallace,' said Maud, alarmed, 'is everything quite all right?'

'There's been a theft!' he cried, before hurriedly composing himself. 'My apologies, ladies. I should not have told you that. It does not inspire confidence among the guests.'

The three of them glanced around. There was no one else there.

'What has been taken?' she asked.

'A bird...'

Maud blinked in surprise.

'From the display case,' he went on.

'Nae the crested tit – the *King's* gift?' Daisy paled.

'No,' Mr Wallace said. 'The one next to it. A merlin.'

'How strange,' Maud said. 'Has it really been stolen?'

'It canna have flown away,' Daisy muttered.

Mr Wallace ran a hand through what remained of his hair.

'I visit the King's bird every morning and evening, and the merlin was there yesterday. Now it's not.'

'Are you absolutely sure?'

'Of course I'm sure!' He threw up his arms in agitation. 'I noticed the door of the display case wasn't quite shut and then I saw the merlin was no longer on its perch!'

'Could it have fallen to the—'

'Floor of the cabinet? No, I've checked. To think it might easily have been the King's gift that was taken.' He sank into a chair. 'It's dreadful, dreadful.'

'It *is* dreadful,' Maud said thoughtfully, 'but don't you think a bird a strange item to take? When the hotel must contain any number of valuable items, not least amongst the guests' belongings.'

Mr Wallace shook his head. 'It doesn't make sense.'

Unless, thought Maud, the wrong bird was taken... 'What if the thief's real target was the crested tit? That would be more understandable.'

A look of alarm shot across Mr Wallace's features. 'But who would take such a thing? Many people would want to possess a gift from the King, but the thief wouldn't be able to show it to anyone else as then he would have to explain how he had come by it.'

'Perhaps he wanted it for his own private collection?' put in Daisy.

Mr Wallace looked horrified. 'Then once he realises he's taken the wrong bird, he might come back for the tit.'

Daisy shrugged. 'Aye, it's possible.'

The hotelier turned towards the desk. 'Then I must inform the police at once!'

Daisy put her hand reassuringly on his arm. 'Nae need to be so hasty, Mr Wallace. It just so happens that Miss McIntyre and I are private detectives. Here for a holiday,' she added, shooting Maud a glance, 'but we'd be happy to take on your case.'

'Private detectives?' He turned back and frowned. 'Two young ladies such as yourselves dealing with the criminal element in society?'

'And as luck would have it for you, we're rather good at the job.' Maud smiled at his astonishment.

'I can't say I've ever heard of such a thing.'

'Which works in our favour,' Daisy said.

'I would have to pay.'

'Aye, but isna that better than all and sundry knowing what's happened? Guests will think their belongings are nae safe here and, as you pointed out, that would be bad for business.' She gave him an encouraging smile. 'Our fees are reasonable.'

Oh well done, Daisy, thought Maud.

'I saw the exhibit myself yesterday,' Maud said. 'You know of course that I met the King and his shooting party in the hills above Loch Callater and that His Majesty told me about the crested tit.'

'Didna you say he seemed awfa proud of the bird, Maud?'

Daisy was clearly pressing her advantage.

Mr Wallace groaned.

'It's quite a small thing, the other bird, I seem to remember?' Maud continued.

'A little more than four and a half inches.'

'Then could it have been taken on the spur of the moment? If the cabinet door had been left even slightly ajar by, say, a cleaner?' Although Maud was certain the door had been shut tight yesterday.

'Impossible. The case is kept locked, and I am the only one who has the keys. Oh, what shall I do? If His Majesty discovers...' Mr Wallace's face was the colour of porridge.

'There is no reason for him to find out if you don't inform the police,' Maud said. 'And who is to know if none of us speak of it? Come, Mr Wallace, we can help you.'

Mr Wallace took a breath to calm himself. 'You are correct. I've made up my mind. I would like you ladies to investigate.'

Daisy smiled. 'You've made the right decision.'

Although she and Daisy hadn't done well in their investigations so far, Maud thought: the art forgery, Mr Bisset's murder...

'We will do our very best to find the thief and the bird,' she told him, with more confidence than she felt.

Mr Wallace looked hopeful. 'All the guests who stay in this hotel are honest. That's always been the case. It must be a stranger in the area.' A thought struck him. 'A fellow has been seen about acting suspiciously. He might be any kind of criminal.' The hotelier paused, fixing a stern eye on Maud and Daisy. 'I've heard he travelled to Braemar on the same train as you.'

Maud could see why Mr Wallace was suspicious of the bad-tempered youth in their compartment, given the report he must have heard from the teacher, but she could not simply march up to the young fellow and demand to ask his whereabouts last night. And even if she could, she would have to find him first.

'In what way acting suspiciously?' she asked.

'Hardly anyone has seen him since he arrived and that's not easy to do in a place this size. He's not staying here or at Bessie Baxter's bed and breakfast, and there's nowhere else so he must be sleeping like a common vagabond. He's been spotted in the village once, buying provisions. What is he up to, I'd like to know.'

Maud raised an eyebrow. 'But doesn't the area attract those who enjoy the hills, such as His Majesty?'

Mr Wallace frowned. 'That is different.'

'I don't think it's right to assume that a man is a thief without any proof.' Maud pushed aside the thought that she and Daisy had put him on their suspect list for murder.

'That is why I require you to find proof.' Mr Wallace's gaze searched Maud's face. 'One exhibit has been stolen and the

King's bird might be next. Will you take on this case or not, Miss McIntyre?'

She inclined her head. 'Please lead us to the display cabinet.'

'This way, ladies.'

They followed the hotelier through the door, across the bar and into the small room beyond. He indicated the glass cabinet on the table in front of them, where Maud had examined the King's crested tit the previous day. Now the door to the case stood open and the section of tree on which the merlin had been placed was without its avian appendage. She looked for the card stating the missing exhibit's provenance.

'The card,' she said, indicating the empty space.

Mr Wallace nodded glumly. 'That also has been taken. Whoever snatched the two items does not know birds or understand Latin. I should have placed it immediately under the crested tit.'

'Cheer up,' said Daisy, smiling. 'If the card had been closer, then the thief would have got away with the King's bird.'

The hotelier's face showed no sign of cheering up.

'That the card was taken,' Maud went on, 'leads me to suppose the thief, although he took the wrong feathered creature, was particularly interested in the bird's provenance.'

'I believe you are correct, Miss McIntyre,' Mr Wallace said. 'Whether the culprit wanted the exhibit to sell or to keep for himself, he needed the card.'

'Let us now examine the cabinet door.' Maud bent to get a closer look at the lock and indicated for Daisy to do the same. The brass plate around the key hole had a small number of scratch marks, where the thief had clumsily attempted to insert a sharp object into the lock itself.

'At least we can be reasonably sure that no one has used your keys, Mr Wallace,' Maud said, straightening. 'The lock has been picked.'

He drew in his breath sharply. 'It's that fellow from the train, I'm sure. Ladies, I'd like you to follow him.'

Daisy stood. 'We have nae reason to think he's the thief.'

'It was someone,' Mr Wallace said, his tone sharp.

'Well, we like to keep an open mind,' Daisy said.

Mr Wallace shuddered. 'Just find the guilty person – before he comes back for the King's gift.'

THIRTEEN

For afternoon tea with Mrs Bisset, Maud had dressed in a purple organdie gown with white embroidered collar and cuffs. This seemed to be the most suitable dress for this afternoon, from the small number of garments she had packed for the trip. Seated at the dressing table, she slipped on her low-heeled ivory-coloured shoes and buttoned the three straps across each foot.

Maud gazed in the mirror and considered her hair. She would fashion it into a cottage loaf pompadour. Gathering her tresses loosely on to the top of her head, she twisted them into a bun. The difficulty was getting the ensemble to stay in place long enough for her to secure it in position.

'Come in!' she called through a mouthful of pins, at the knock on the door.

Daisy entered and saw Maud's predicament. 'Here, let me do that.'

As Maud passed her each pin in turn, Daisy pinned her hair into the classic style.

'There now.' Daisy stood back to admire her handiwork.

'Very bonnie.' She considered further. 'Have you ever thought about getting your hair cut short, Maud?'

'In what I believe is called a bob?' Maud turned on the stool to look at her friend. 'I understand some women in America are following this fad. What do you think, Daisy?'

She flushed. 'Nae cutting it short. I did think of trying a Marcel wave...'

'But?'

'But a friend had one and it singed her hair, so I changed my mind.'

'Oh dear.'

'Aye.'

'Well, you're looking very smart.'

Daisy had pinned her own hair in swirls and she wore a pale green chiffon blouse with a dark green skirt.

They met Mrs Wallace in the hall downstairs and the three of them made their way out of the hotel and along the footpath. Within a short time, they passed through the open wrought-iron gates of the driveway leading to the Bissets' house. Woodend stood between the artist's cottage and the Anderson home.

'Mrs Wallace,' Maud asked, 'what does the name of the Anderson house, An Taigh Mòr, mean?'

'It's Gaelic for The Big House.'

'That's nae surprise.'

'This house is almost as imposing,' Maud said, as they drew near to Woodend, a large edifice built in grey stone.

Mrs Wallace pulled up the high cream collar of her dress. 'It is also well-known for being draughty and uncomfortable, which is why the laird has trouble letting it.'

They rang the bell, were shown into the drawing room, and Maud's eye was immediately taken with the ornate cornicing on the high ceiling. Mrs Bisset and her daughter seemed dwarfed as they rose to greet their guests. After the usual preliminaries, they all took their seats.

Maud had seen Lilias Bisset before, so now she regarded the mother, a petite woman with sharp features, her hair presumably once fair but now turning white, her eyes a pale blue. She wore a grey dress with a lot of fussy tucks and lace, and buttons from its high waist down to the hem.

'I do not have a black costume, as black does not suit me,' Mrs Bisset told her guests. 'And my daughter Lilias is far too young to own a frock in such a colour. We will have to make a journey into Aberdeen for suitable clothing for the funeral.'

What an extraordinary conversation opening, Maud thought.

Mrs Wallace rallied. 'Do you know when the funeral will be, Mrs Bisset?'

Mrs Bisset sighed. 'Not yet. It seems there must be a post-mortem to establish the cause of his death. Yet it must be obvious to the authorities that he shot himself.'

Maud blinked. Goodness, the woman really was not the grieving widow. 'It isn't obvious, Mrs Bisset.'

The older woman glared at her, but failed to ask Maud what she meant by that comment. Lilias Bisset for her part took a cigarette from her slim silver case and placed it between her lips. The girl lifted a long-barrelled pistol, raised it to the cigarette's tip and pulled the trigger. As she bent her head to the flame, Maud could see the words Ronson Pist-O-Liter picked out in white on the handle. It was the same lighter the girl had used on the train, but now it showed a shocking lack of sensitivity.

Miss Bisset drew in the vapour and expelled it through her nostrils. With her other hand, she wafted away the smoke and gazed out of the window.

After a pause, Mrs Wallace continued. 'Miss McIntyre and Miss Cameron were present when your husband's body was found, Mrs Bisset, and they would be pleased to answer any questions you might have.'

Mrs Bisset turned a gimlet gaze on them. 'What did you see?'

What a strange way to phrase the question, Maud thought. 'Not very much, I'm afraid.' Did the women's features relax a little at that reply? 'I opened the door to the compartment and...' – she softened her voice in sympathy – 'your husband was there, already dead. I am so sorry.'

Mrs Bisset nodded. 'And there was no one else in the compartment?'

'Just your man,' Daisy said.

'My man?' The words burst from Mrs Bisset. 'You make it sound as if he were a loving, supportive spouse.' She gave a harsh laugh. 'He was an inconsiderate husband and a bully. I'm happy he's gone.'

Daisy raised an eyebrow almost to the brim of her straw hat.

'When we first met,' Mrs Bisset went on, 'he used his family's wealth to impress me. And like a fool I fell for it. I was young, impressionable, flattered by his attention. When he proposed to me, I accepted.' She shook her head. 'Marry in haste, they say, and repent at leisure. Well, I certainly had plenty of time for that. We had nothing in common. He never loved me. The man was obsessed with one thing only: himself. He'd delight in telling me about some victory he'd had over another person, always someone with less power and money. It was all about him, his image, his perception of how others saw him.'

Was that the reason he'd moved his family to the village? To live like a laird?

There was silence for a moment before Maud asked gently, 'Do you think it likely that he would kill himself?'

Mrs Bisset shrugged. 'It's possible. He wasn't content to be a small fish in a big pond, which was the case where we used to stay. He wanted somewhere new, to be seen as a gentleman. Well, it didn't work. How he thought we could be accepted here, or anywhere, with his uncouth ways, I cannot imagine.' She sent a glance at her daughter. 'Neither I nor Lilias wanted to move here. I was perfectly happy in our house in Inverness and Lilias – well, she misses her friends, and girls of her age yearn for the bright lights of Edinburgh, not a backwater village.'

Maud took a sharp breath at the insult to the village and the people who made their lives there, including Mrs Wallace.

She had a question she needed to ask, and it seemed there would be no natural opening for it. 'Was your husband right- or left-handed, Mrs Bisset?'

'Right.' The other woman frowned. 'Why?'

'Only that I was thinking of where the gun was found in the compartment.'

'And?'

'It was on the correct side for a right-handed man.'

Mrs Bisset looked satisfied with the reply.

Maud turned her attention to the young woman. Today, Lilias Bisset wore a pale blue dress with white facings, but otherwise she was as Maud remembered her. A handsome girl, dark-haired and full-lipped, but with a sulky droop to her mouth.

'I suppose we are a close-knit little place,' Mrs Wallace was saying, her usually kind face void of expression although her colour was high.

'No doubt you think it a charming village.' Mrs Bisset's voice was bitter.

'Braemar is sleepy and keeps itself to itself,' Mrs Wallace admitted.

'I don't know if we will stay here or not, now he's gone.' The widow looked doubtfully at her daughter. 'I suppose I will if Lilias meets a nice young laird and marries him and settles here. Securing her future is my only ambition now.'

'A very suitable ambition, no doubt,' agreed Mrs Wallace.

Lilias Bisset spoke suddenly. '*Is* there a nice young laird hiding somewhere around here?'

Mrs Wallace looked thoughtful. 'There's the laird of Kindrochit. He's unmarried.'

Her mother's face lit up. 'Our landlord. How *convenient* that would be. The tenancy was agreed with his agent, so I have not met the laird himself, although I have noticed Kindrochit House out on the road towards Aberdeen.'

Noticed? Maud thought. Noted, more likely, and in particular its size, as it must be the mansion she had seen from the train window on their approach to Braemar.

'Tell me,' went on Mrs Bisset, 'what is the laird like?'

Clearly realising the only other information Mrs Bisset wanted, Mrs Wallace said, 'He'll not be what you would call young.'

'How old is he?' demanded Lilias Bisset, still staring out of the window at the trees beyond.

'He must be sixty, if he's a day.'

'I'd kill myself first.'

She was as shockingly rude as Maud remembered.

Miss Bisset turned back to face the room. 'You see, Mother, there's no one *suitable* in this dump.'

Mrs Wallace drew a sharp breath.

'Don't be so impolite, darling.' Mrs Bisset seemed to perk up at a fresh notion. 'The laird has no wife to be the chief lady of the village? Perhaps I can assume that role, if I do my duty as the occupier of one of the largest houses in Braemar and immerse myself in good works.'

Oh dear, thought Maud. The woman had been complaining about her husband's self-obsessed behaviour and yet she showed no sense of self-awareness. A cold silence crept over the room. A physical chill too, as the room was of noble proportions and it needed more heating than the low fire Mrs Bisset provided.

'Where is that wretched girl with the tea?' She rang the bell violently.

'Alice,' Mrs Bisset said in a peevish tone when the maid entered almost immediately with a tray laden with the tea things, 'there you are. Why did you take so long?'

Alice said nothing, but put the tray down with some force.

'Be careful, girl!' snapped Mrs Bisset. 'You will break the china.'

Alice marched out of the room.

'You see what I have to suffer,' said Mrs Bisset with exasperation.

'Well,' Mrs Wallace went on as soon as she'd recovered her speech, 'I do hope that we'll be seeing you in church. The kirk brings all together and—'

'I'm afraid I have no intention of attending.' Mrs Bisset poured tea from the beautiful silver pot.

'Perhaps you are not Church of Scotland, but Episcopalian or of the Roman faith?'

'I'm an atheist.'

'Oh dear,' Mrs Wallace said, shaking her head.

'When we lived in Inverness, I had a full social life and church attendance was not a deciding factor to be invited into the best houses.' Mrs Bisset handed a cup to Mrs Wallace. 'Here, I have few calls on my time,' she paused as a thought struck her, 'so perhaps I will come to church and so will my daughter – if there is cause to stay on in Braemar.'

Lilias Bisset muttered something under her breath that sounded to Maud like, 'How tiresome,' and the girl yawned.

Her mother passed Maud and then Daisy a cup of tea. 'I expect I will come to think that Braemar is a marvellous place to live eventually.'

'More like a marvellous place to be *buried* in,' Lilias Bisset said in a bitter voice.

Daisy looked at Maud and Maud saw her own shock

reflected in her friend's face. Neither of them dared glance at Mrs Wallace to see her reaction.

Unaware of the effect her words had on their visitors, Mrs Bisset poured tea for her daughter and herself. There was a pause while all sipped, a very weak blend of China, Maud noticed. It would have been better if Mrs Bisset had let the tea draw for a little longer.

Eventually, the widow spoke again. 'I have had a lifetime of living on a farm – well, some years,' she added, rearranging her skirts, 'I am not of course so *very* old. In fact,' she went on, warming to her theme, 'men often express their surprise when they meet Lilias, as they cannot believe I am old enough to have a daughter of her age.'

Their surprise may not be related so much to the girl's age as to her appearance, Maud thought, but smiled politely at Mrs Bisset.

'There is to be a ceilidh at the village hall next Saturday,' put in Mrs Wallace. 'It's in aid of church funds and as such would not be improper if you wore black for the occasion. Your daughter could wear a black ribbon, if you think her too young to be dressed in black. The hotel's kitchen is doing the catering, and there'll be a band coming from Ballater. I'm sure you will find that enjoyable, Miss Bisset.'

'Damn the ceilidh,' the girl cried. 'I don't intend to spend my life in this place. I want adventure!'

'Don't talk such silly nonsense,' said her mother. 'Drink your tea. That will make you feel better.' She turned back to Maud and Daisy. 'Mr Wallace has told me that you have been asked to investigate a theft at the hotel.'

Mrs Wallace spluttered into her tea.

Maud felt equally surprised and didn't attempt to hide it. 'I understood that Mr Wallace didn't want anyone else to know about the theft.'

Mrs Bisset smiled. 'He said it was only me that he told. It is odd, don't you think, that the stranger some people have been talking about seems to have disappeared?'

What on earth made the hotelier confide in this ghastly woman? 'Why do you think it odd? Isn't a man on his holiday free to go about as he wishes?'

Mrs Bisset shrugged. 'I only mean that, if it is found that my husband was murdered, this young man may be the culprit.'

'A disreputable-looking fellow arrives in the village, an item is stolen and suddenly the stranger cannot be found. I'm inclined to disagree with you on your assumption,' Maud said. 'The evidence is so clearly against him that it is doubtful he did it. There is nothing more deceptive than an obvious fact.'

That last sentence was an observation by Sherlock Holmes in *The Boscombe Valley Mystery* and one Maud agreed with.

'I still think it was him.' Mrs Bisset's voice was firm.

There was a hissing sound and Maud turned to see Lilias Bisset dousing the remains of her cigarette in her full teacup.

'Lilias?'

Wrenching the soggy remains from the cup, the girl shot her mother an angry look and rose. 'You talk such rot, Mother.' She left the room swiftly, banging the door behind her.

Mrs Bisset sighed, a smile fixed unconvincingly on her pale face. 'Young people...'

Yes, Maud wanted to say, what about them? Not all have such bad manners as your daughter, or indeed your maid.

'Let us talk about more interesting matters,' Mrs Bisset went on. 'I have been admiring your tortoiseshell hat pin, Mrs Wallace. Where did you purchase it, if I may ask?'

Mrs Wallace touched the pin in her hat. The frown that had been on her face since Mrs Bisset had mentioned the stolen bird now disappeared.

'From the travelling salesman. When he next comes, I could ask him to call here, if you wish.'

'Would you? I've had to throw away my favourite silver filigree hat pin. It got bent, you see, although I have no idea how that happened. I only know that *I* didn't do it. When I asked my maid, the silly girl said she knew nothing about it. I'm not convinced she was telling the truth. I would have given her notice, but I wasn't sure how easy it would be to replace her. I can't think what she could have been doing with it to bend the thing.'

Maud caught Daisy's eye and knew they were having the same thought. She glanced discreetly at the marble clock on the mantlepiece. It was too soon to take their leave without causing offence.

'May I ask a favour of you, Mrs Bisset?' Mrs Wallace was saying.

Mrs Bisset inclined her head.

'Every year the parish church school has a wee poetry recitation competition for the bairns and Mr Shepherd the dominie, knowing I was taking tea with you this afternoon, wanted me to ask if you would be the judge.'

It was clear to Maud that the village's opinion was very reserved and not interested in a display of the interloper's wealth. But the request had come from the headmaster, who perhaps thought this was an opportunity to bring Mrs Bisset into the fold. If she became involved in local interests, then perhaps all would be well now her bullying husband was soon to be in his grave.

Mrs Bisset frowned and drew back. 'Oh, I don't think that would be for me. I know nothing about poetry.'

'The pupils are merely reciting a poem they have learned. All you have to do is listen to them and chose the child you judge to be speaking with the most feeling.'

Mrs Bisset shuddered. She didn't actually say she couldn't think of anything worse than listening to small children recite poetry with feeling, but she didn't need to. To make the matter even clearer, she shook her head firmly.

'I'm sorry, Mrs Wallace, but my diary would not allow it at present. I have a funeral to arrange.' She looked pointedly at the mantlepiece clock.

'Then we mustn't be keeping you.' Mrs Wallace rose.

They all followed suit and Mrs Bisset rang for the maid. They stood in uncomfortable silence until the girl arrived and showed them out.

'Well!' Daisy exploded, as soon as the front door was closed behind them. 'What a crabbit wifie. Nae to mention her dochter.'

'I'm sure Mrs Bisset didn't *mean* to be ill-tempered,' Maud said. 'I don't like her, but I can't help feeling sorry for her. She must be at least a little upset by the death of her husband, even though it may not seem that way.'

Daisy snorted. 'Oh aye, awfa upset.' She imitated the other woman's voice. '"I'm happy he's gone." Nae, she probably didn't *mean* to be crabbit. Like the dochter, it just comes naturally to her.'

'She thinks she can come to the kirk just to curry favour,' spluttered Mrs Wallace. 'And the house has belonged to the laird's estate for generations, yet she acts as if she's one of the family. And I don't believe my husband told her about the stolen bird. *And*,' she went on, 'the woman says she wants to help in any way she can and the first thing I ask her to do she refuses.'

'I'm happy to listen to the poetry reading, Mrs Wallace,' Maud said, as the three of them walked back down the drive. 'If Mr Shepherd allows it, that is.'

'That's very kind of you, lass.' She beamed at Maud. 'I must confess that you were the dominie's first choice. It's a good idea to have a judge unconnected with the school. That way there'll not be any accusations of favouritism. I asked that foolish woman only because Mr Shepherd and I felt sorry for her, and

we thought she might wish to be involved in the affairs of the
village now her husband has passed.'

'No matter, Mrs Wallace. I'm sure it will be a joy.'

She looked doubtful. 'It's "The Sair Finger" by Walter
Wingate. Do you know it?'

Maud murmured that she didn't, but her mind was on
another matter entirely. Something had stirred in her brain, and
in Daisy's too, she was sure, when Mrs Bisset had mentioned
her bent hat pin. She thought about the scratches on that
circular piece of brass. A hat pin would make a very good implement with which to pick a lock.

FOURTEEN

'It looks like it was her that did it,' said Daisy, when they had arrived back at the hotel and Mrs Wallace had gone in search of her husband.

'You think Mrs Bisset killed her husband?' Maud asked. 'What happened to, "Well, we like to keep an open mind"?'

'That was with regards to the case of the stuffed bird,' Daisy scoffed. 'The murder investigation seems more straightforward to me.'

'Why do you think she did it?'

'She hated him, that's obvious, and all those years on a farm she must have learned how to shoot.'

'That's true, but wouldn't she then have realised about the position of the spent cartridge?'

'Nae if she panicked after she'd shot him.'

'Hmm. Although I'm not sure she's the type to walk fifteen miles back to Braemar.'

'Aye.' Daisy sighed.

Maud knew Daisy would agree with what she proposed to do next. 'I have an idea I would like to try, Daisy.'

'Is it the hat pin?'

'It is. One of the reasons women make superior detectives, Daisy, is because, unlike men, they do not fail to recognise domestic clues.' This was why Lady Molly of Scotland Yard succeeded. Baroness Orczy's collection of short stories might not be as famous as her *Scarlet Pimpernel* novels, but to Maud's mind Molly Robertson-Kirk was as formidable as Sir Percy Blakeney.

She strode through the deserted bar, her purple skirts swishing about her legs, Daisy following. On reaching the small room, thankfully once again empty, Maud first made sure the case had been locked since she and Daisy had examined it that morning. It had. She slid the long pin from her boater.

Maud handed her hat to Daisy, then bent and peered at the brass lock. Yes, it looked entirely possible that the scratches had been made by a hat pin.

She inserted her pin into the lock. Unlike the thief, she could take her time and so not damage the escutcheon any further. She twisted it around inside the keyhole until she felt the mechanism. The pin had to be pushed in quite far, confirming her opinion that the original lock-picking implement had to be long, as well as thin and sharp, pliable yet strong. There was resistance from the tumbler at first, but after a few minutes' persistence, she heard a click, felt the lock release and the cabinet door opened. She straightened, pin in hand, and smiled at Daisy.

'Michty me,' said Daisy with a grin, just as a flustered Mr Wallace appeared on the threshold of the room.

'Miss McIntyre, Miss Cameron.' Relief was evident in his voice. 'When the bartender told me he'd heard sound coming from this room, I feared the thief had returned.' The hotelier's eyes went from Maud's face to the open cabinet door and his eyebrows shot up. 'How did you manage that? I know I made sure the case was locked.'

'We can tell you, but you must swear not to reveal this to another.' Daisy gave him a severe look.

'I would not.'

Maud held up her hat pin.

'It's a hat pin.' He looked confused.

'It is, Mr Wallace, and I have just opened the cabinet with it.'

'I— How did you manage that?'

'Never mind my skills, Mr Wallace,' said Maud, fixing him with her steely eye. 'Mrs Bisset has said that you told her about the break-in.'

He flushed a dark red. 'I can assure you, ladies, that I did no such thing.'

Daisy raised an eyebrow. 'Then how did she ken?'

Mr Wallace shrugged. 'Perhaps one of the chambermaids or a waitress, friends with that maid of Mrs Bisset's, overheard my telling you or my wife. This village can spread gossip in next to no time.'

'Which is why you were to tell no one.'

'Surely I can tell my wife?'

'Mrs Wallace could have been told later. Secrecy is of the utmost importance. We must be sure of having all the evidence before we can reveal the culprit.'

His eyes immediately lit up. 'You have caught that scoundrel already?'

'I earlier said we shouldn't conclude that the man you refer to is the guilty party. Some people might argue that nowadays stealing might almost be a gentleman's profession.'

'The bankers, you mean?'

'No, Mr Wallace, I mean that people read stories about characters such as Raffles and imagine they are based on a real person. The thought that there might be a man-about-town, who is invited into all the best houses but proves to be a thief, is a thrilling one for some people. Admittedly, Raffles is a thief

with a conscience – of sorts – for he never steals from his hosts
and he helps old friends in trouble. He might be a fictional character, but some think there is no smoke without fire, as the
expression goes.'

Her thoughts moved seamlessly to Lord Urquhart. When
she first met him, she had thought him to be such a person and
had suspected him of stealing valuable jewellery from country
houses. Her belief was nothing to do with reading too many
Raffles' stories, but had come about because of his suspicious
behaviour at Duddingston House, where she and Daisy had
been employed undercover. The fact that Lord Urquhart hadn't
been the jewel thief was neither here nor there – he *might* have
been. And now here he was again, staying in the area. Admittedly as a guest of the King, but...

'Circumstantial evidence points to him,' Mr Wallace
suddenly said.

Maud started. Did the hotelier suspect Lord Urquhart of
stealing the crested tit? But then Mr Wallace's gaze dropped to
the hat pin in her hand and Maud's common sense prevailed –
of course he wasn't referring to Lord Urquhart.

'Precisely,' she said. 'The evidence is only circumstantial. It
does not directly prove a fact. Miss Cameron and I have learned
that the young man to whom you refer had travelled from Inverness. I doubt someone would journey a distance of some eighty
miles to steal a stuffed bird from a locked case. Even,' – she
went on quickly, seeing Mr Wallace open his mouth and
guessing what he was about to say – 'even if it was a gift from
His Majesty. Which the fellow could hardly have known about
until he arrived here.'

'A moment!' Mr Wallace was animated. 'I see it all now. No
doubt he found out – all thieves have means of finding things
out – came here and took the bird to distract my attention. He
may return and steal valuable items from guests' rooms.'

Daisy shook her head. 'Nae, I dinna think so. He would

expect the hotel to be hoatching with police by now, and if he came back to pinch anything more costly, he'd be spotted at once.'

Maud reclaimed her hat from Daisy, returned it to her head and worked her bent hat pin into place as best she could. She closed the cabinet door and stood aside.

'Mr Wallace, would you please lock the cabinet?'

'Most certainly.' He pulled the key from a pocket in his waistcoat. 'What is your plan now, Miss McIntyre? I assure you I will tell no one, not even my good lady.'

'Then can we speak somewhere more private?'

'Certainly.'

He ushered Maud and Daisy through the entrance hall and into his office at the back of the hotel. An old golden Labrador, curled up on a blanket on the floor, wagged its tail as they entered and got to its feet with arthritic back legs. It hobbled over to them.

'Oh, how delightful!' Maud bent to stroke the dog's head. 'My father always had Labradors when my brothers and I were growing up.'

'This is Bonnie,' said Mr Wallace.

At the sound of her name, the dog's tail wagged harder.

Maud smiled. 'Hello, Bonnie.'

Daisy fondled the dog's ear. 'I aye think a yellow Labrador's ears look like they've been lightly toasted.'

Bonnie grinned.

Mr Wallace bid Maud and Daisy take the two armchairs. The old dog ambled with her awkward gait back to her blanket and settled down again.

Mr Wallace sat in his chair at the desk and threw Maud an enquiring look.

'I didn't know you had a dog,' she said, glancing at Bonnie. 'Does she sleep in here at night?'

'She does. And if you're wondering why she didn't bark

when she heard the intruder in the middle of the night, that's because she's almost entirely deaf. She only heard her name just now because we were standing so close.'

'And is your night porter also deaf?' enquired Maud.

'No,' Mr Wallace answered ruefully. 'I allow him to sit in this office once the hotel has officially closed for the evening. The thief must have been very quiet.'

'Yet it seems that something disturbed the culprit, for he seems to have stolen a bird without taking care to ensure he had the correct one.'

'I suppose he might have wanted to snatch it and get away quickly.'

'Perhaps someone who hasna done any stealing before?' suggested Daisy.

Maud nodded. 'It's possible the thief has been watching the hotel since he realised he had taken the wrong bird, noticed that there are no police about and will try his hand again.'

Mr Wallace looked alarmed. 'What should I do?'

'You need do naething,' Daisy said with a smile. 'Miss McIntyre and I will keep watch on the bird cabinet.'

'And when will you do that?'

'Tonight,' Maud told him firmly. 'And every night until he puts in an appearance.'

Mr Wallace's jaw dropped. 'I'm not certain it's safe work for ladies,' he said awkwardly. 'Let me ask one of the menservants. If it's the money you are thinking of, don't worry, I will still pay your fee.'

'Not at all. It's kind of you to suggest such a thing, but Miss Cameron and I are determined to see the job through, and to be candid, we prefer to work alone. We will catch the thief. It's a matter of pride in our work.'

'What time do you close the hotel?' Daisy asked.

'We do not lock the main doors in case a late guest should

arrive, in which case there is a bell at the reception desk to call for the night porter. Officially, the hotel closes at eleven o'clock.'

'Very good,' said Maud. 'We will be in the parlour at half past ten.'

Back in Maud's bedchamber, Daisy dropped into an armchair.

'Mrs Bisset is the culprit. Her or her maid.'

'I don't think it can be Mrs Bisset, as she would hardly draw our attention to her bent hat pin...' Maud murmured.

'What if it's a double bluff?'

Maud sat down on the edge of her bed. 'It might be.'

'If it's not her or the maid, then it must be the daughter.' Daisy was adamant.

'Perhaps, but I think our best course of action is to find that young man from the train. I'm certain he has at the very least a close acquaintance with Miss Bisset. With luck he may be able to shed some light on both the missing bird and the dead man.'

Daisy grinned. 'And the art forgery?'

'Who knows?' Maud smiled. 'It's not impossible. There are more things in heaven and earth, Horatio, than are dreamt of in your philosophy.' Seeing Daisy's frown, she added, 'Hamlet and his scientific friend Horatio go up to the castle battlements and see the ghost of Hamlet's father.'

Daisy shivered. 'I hope we see nae bogles tonight...'

FIFTEEN

Maud and Daisy changed their afternoon costumes for warm cardigan jackets and tweed skirts. The hotelier met them in the parlour at a half past ten as arranged. There was no one else there at this hour, but voices in the entrance hall reminded Maud that some guests were still around.

She kept her voice low. 'Please ask the waiter bring us some strong black coffee,' she said to Mr Wallace. She and Daisy would need to stay awake. 'Then everyone should go about their business as normal. It is best that as few people as possible know we are here. Ensure the night porter is aware of our presence and that, save him of course, you are the last person to retire.'

'I always am, Miss McIntyre.'

She nodded. 'And Miss Cameron and I will remain quietly here in comfortable chairs in the corner of the darkened room.'

'And then?'

'And then we will see what happens.'

They chose armchairs with wingbacks and half turned them towards the thickly curtained windows. Should anyone peer into the parlour, the pair would not easily be noticed. Only one oil lamp still burned. Maud lifted the lamp from the central table where it sat and carried it over to the low table between their two chairs. Making themselves comfortable, they sat and waited.

'Make a mental note of the placement of furniture, Daisy,' Maud murmured. 'It wouldn't do, once the light is extinguished, to crash into anything as we creep after our quarry.'

Daisy nodded, her gaze going round the room.

A waiter brought them each a cup of coffee, placed it on the table by the lamp and bid them goodnight. Daisy blew on her coffee to cool it and drank it.

'I'm just going to rest my eyes.' She closed them.

She herself must stay awake, Maud thought, so she rose quietly and browsed the small bookshelf in the dimly lit parlour.

A title immediately caught her eye. *The Experiences of Loveday Brooke: Lady Detective* by Catherine Louisa Pirkis. This looked promising. A female heroine created by a female author. Maud opened the book. The content was presented in casebook form. Excellent; exactly what she enjoyed reading. She returned to her seat and began to read the first story, *The Black Bag Left on a Door-Step*.

Gradually, the hotel settled for the night and grew quiet. The grandfather clock in the hall struck eleven and as the last chime faded away, Mr Wallace softly entered the parlour, nodded at Maud when she looked up, and withdrew, leaving the door ajar. Maud turned down the wick of the lamp, leaving just the faintest light to read by.

Her coffee was long finished when she closed her book, wishing she could solve crimes as quickly as did Loveday Brooke. Every now and again Daisy had opened her eyes to indicate to Maud she was not asleep. Maud cupped her hands above the glass chimney of the oil lamp and blew to extinguish the flame.

She peered into the darkness. All was quiet. Nothing moved. The wood fire had burned low.

It's a funny thing, Maud thought, but the idea of surveillance is a lot more exciting than the actual experience. Take *The Adventure of the Speckled Band*, for example, when Holmes and Watson kept a silent vigil in the room where one young woman had mysteriously died and the same fate would certainly have befallen her sister without the duo's intervention.

Maud yawned. After a while, she fell to meditating.

Had a chambermaid or waitress discovered the bird had been stolen and gossiped about it to Mrs Bisset's maid? It was entirely possible. Or was Mr Wallace not telling the truth when he denied revealing the theft to Mrs Bisset? He had flushed a dark red when Daisy accused him of this. But did it mean he was embarrassed at being caught out in a lie or he was angry at Mrs Bisset for making such a claim?

She moved on to other thoughts troubling her. The art forgery. They didn't have enough information on the techniques of oil painting to be able to make an assessment of Mr McGonagall in this respect. At the very least, a visit to the public library would be required.

As to the case of Mr Bisset, she had a strange feeling that if the mystery of the stolen bird could be solved, then that would provide a lead to his murderer. Though why this should be, she couldn't fathom – only that the bird, the beastly fellow on the train and the Bissets were all somehow connected...

Her thoughts slid on to Lord Urquhart. During their time together at Duddingston House, he had expressed a wish to assist with her detective work. Later, when he had bumped into her at a tea shop in Edinburgh – had that really been by chance? – he had repeated that offer, to no avail of course. It seemed to her that he had appeared with some regularity in her life. And here he was again. The fact that he was one of the King's guests at Balmoral was only a coincidence, wasn't it? Of course it was;

what was she thinking? It was plain to Maud that the life he was leading was an aimless one and doing him no good.

She couldn't say that her heart bled for him, for he was a man of wealth and standing and could pass the time as he wished, but that was exactly it. He was simply passing his time. It was distressing to see the manner in which he seemed to hang about. Maud was sure, for all his faults, he had a degree of intelligence.

But her concern had its limits. He must find his own path.

The clock in the hall had chimed a quarter to the hour a short while ago. It was almost midnight. If the thief was to strike tonight, it must surely be soon. All remained quiet.

But wait – was that a soft click coming from the main door? Leaving Daisy still resting her eyes, Maud crept to the ajar door of the parlour, treading carefully in the darkness around the memorised furniture plan. Just inside the doorway she stopped and listened.

Yes, now she was sure she could hear muffled footsteps crossing the hall. She peered round the door, just in time to see the outline of a slim figure in a long coat and a fedora enter the lounge bar. Was this the thief on his way to the trophy room? Better get Daisy.

Moving silently but swiftly, Maud stepped back into the room, the blood pumping in her ears, and gently shook her friend. Daisy's eyes opened immediately. Maud gestured to follow her and the pair moved stealthily into the hall, after the dark figure, and into the bar. Their quarry was fortunate, as were they, that the floor was carpeted and the table and chairs were not arranged in some artistic fashion, pleasing to the eye perhaps but not suited to a midnight excursion. They were placed in nice, neat positions, with the result that the thief and his furtive followers made progress unhindered by such obstacles.

He reached the threshold of the small room, misplaced his

footing on the steps and stumbled. He swore softly into the darkness. Thank goodness her father was not here to witness that, Maud thought; he would have been horrified to know she'd heard such a vulgar word.

There was something familiar about the voice that uttered that oath...

The thief regained his footing and paused at the entrance to the trophy room. By common consent, Maud and Daisy also halted. They needed to catch the culprit red-handed.

He was on the move again. As soon as he had pulled back the curtain at the entrance and disappeared into the room, Maud stole forward, Daisy on her heels. The curtain had fallen back across the entrance. They waited at the top of the steps and listened. Through the curtain she heard the thief's nervous breathing as in the dark he worked to pick the lock of the cabinet containing the small birds. A sigh of satisfaction and the cabinet door creaked open.

Maud stepped up to the threshold and drew the curtain sharply back. 'Good evening.'

He spun round. The hall clock began to chime midnight. Taking advantage of Maud and Daisy's brief distraction, the thief went to push past them. Maud grabbed at him and clung to his coat. They toppled, cannoned down the steps together and landed at the bottom. The thief's hat fell off. Winded, they lay there for a second or two, gathering their wits. Maud was the first to recover. As Maud got to her feet, Daisy stepped forward and with the side of her hand, she chopped smartly at the fellow's throat.

He let out an '*Oof!*' and fell silent.

The night porter appeared, holding aloft a lamp, with the old Labrador plodding behind. 'You've caught the thief then, lassies?'

'Miss McIntyre and Miss Cameron, if you please,' Maud

said primly, brushing down her skirts. 'A detective always gets her man.'

'Hold the lamp closer,' Daisy instructed. 'Let's see who the thief is.'

Lilias Bisset.

She struggled to sit up, her hand to her throat. 'That hurt,' she croaked.

'It would have hurt even more if you'd been a mannie with an Adam's apple,' Daisy pointed out.

Miss Bisset looked at them. 'You two are detectives?'

From the tone of her voice, Maud was sure the young woman would have laughed if her vocal chords had been up to it.

'Why did you steal the birds, Miss Bisset?' asked Maud.

She glared at Maud. 'It's none of your business.'

Now Mr Wallace arrived in his pyjamas and a velvet dressing gown. Whether he had been contacted by the night porter or, sleeping lightly, had been woken by the sound of Miss Bisset and herself crashing down the stairs, Maud knew not. What she did know was that they had solved another case.

Mr Wallace helped Lilias Bisset to her feet. He picked up the fedora from the floor and frowned at it.

'My father's,' she said in a sulky voice.

He handed her the hat and addressed her in no uncertain terms. 'Miss Bisset, I am beyond words.' He paused, giving himself time to think of some. 'If it were solely up to me, I would march you to the police office immediately, wake up Constable Oliphant and hand you over to the full majesty of the law.' He seemed now to notice that although the girl's chin was tilted in a defiant manner, there was also a look of shame on her face. Shame over her actions or shame at getting caught?

'However,' Mr Wallace went on, 'I am conscious of this hotel's reputation and I have no wish for you to sully it. I am also aware that you have recently lost your father, so I will take that into account.'

'Mr Wallace,' Maud said, 'there is something protruding from Miss Bisset's pocket. It looks very much like the beak of a small bird.'

'Please see what it is.'

Maud reached into the pocket of the young woman's long coat and pulled out a squashed mass of brown and cream feathers.

They all, apart from Miss Bisset, drew in a breath.

'Poor wee bird,' Daisy said, taking it from Maud and quite forgetting for the moment that it was already dead and stuffed. Now the stuffing had been knocked out of it.

'It's the King's Scottish crested tit,' said Mr Wallace. 'It is a pity she had enough time to push it into her pocket before you accosted her. Had you ladies been a bit quicker, it might still be intact.'

'So much for his horror over two young ladies dealing with the criminal element,' Daisy whispered into Maud's ear.

Mr Wallace turned to Miss Bisset and spoke coldly. 'If I ever learn that you have entered this hotel for any reason what-soever in the future, then the police will be notified of what has happened here tonight.' He took hold of her arm.

'Lead the way to the front door,' he said to the night porter.

They all trooped forward. The porter pulled open the main door of the hotel. Mr Wallace released Miss Bisset into the cold night air.

'Off you go, before I throw you out, the same way I did your father.'

Miss Bisset replaced the fedora tightly onto her head and marched down the road. The porter closed the door behind her.

'Well, that is the end of that,' added Mr Wallace, dusting off his hands.

'Let us hope so,' Maud said, and she meant it. She was left

with a feeling of disappointment, of an anticlimax. Detectives like a tidy end to a case and this felt to her unsatisfactory. It was the decision of the hotelier and she appreciated his reasoning, but Maud had felt sure that if she caught the culprit and discovered the motive for the thefts, she would know who killed Mr Bisset.

Mr Wallace took the bird from Daisy and gently stroked it with his fingers. 'I will find a taxidermist to get this wee fellow back into shape.' He looked up. 'My apologies for being a little short with you both just now. I was shocked that a young lady had proved to be the villain.'

'Fair enough,' Daisy said.

'Thank you for preventing the theft and finding the thief so quickly.'

'Our pleasure.' Maud smiled. 'The account will be sent to you once we are back in Edinburgh.' She liked to do these things properly, typed on the agency's headed paper. 'And now we will bid you goodnight.'

As she and Daisy mounted the stairs to their rooms, Maud said quietly, 'Don't you think that stealing birds is a strange thing for the young woman to do?'

'She canna have wanted them for herself, so I think she was going to sell the King's gift.'

Which means Miss Bisset wanted money, Maud thought. But why?

SIXTEEN

'It's awfa bonnie to solve a case,' Daisy said brightly, when they met at the breakfast table the following morning.

'Although we still have two unsolved cases,' Maud reminded her in a low voice. With a start, she realised that, as it was Sunday, they had been here for five days already and had made little progress.

'Glass half-empty,' Daisy said with a grin.

It was Maud's turn to smile. 'You are right.' She lifted a forkful of haddock to her mouth and let her taste buds savour it. 'I think we need to find that young fellow from the train.'

'Aye, catching the bird thief didna give us anything to help in the murder case. I'm sure Lilias Bisset kens more than she's letting on.'

'Especially about the young man. I believe he's linked in some way to Miss Bisset, whose behaviour last night was extraordinary, and I still think that relationship might be relevant to her father's death.'

'You really think she had something to do with killing her faither?' Daisy paused in the act of adding a large dose of salt to her porridge.

'Ssh,' Maud whispered, glancing around at the other occupied tables, 'keep your voice down.'

Daisy spooned some of the porridge into her mouth.

'No, I don't think so,' Maud continued, 'only that there's some sort of connection and we won't find out until we can speak to him.'

'We could try to ask Miss Bisset.'

'We could, but I'm not sure she would talk to us or how honest her answer might be. She wasn't exactly forthcoming last night. I'd rather find that young fellow first.'

Daisy nodded. 'So how do we go about it? No one in the village kens where he is, according to Mr Wallace.'

'If he's sleeping rough in the hills, as Mr Wallace seems to think, then I suggest after church we walk into the hills.'

Daisy shuddered. 'That's nae for me.'

Maud laughed. 'Daisy, will I never be able to convince you that vigorous exercise and fresh country air are essential to good health?'

'I dinna think so. Edinburgh air is plenty good enough for me. There's nae a fairer city with the clean air blowing in from the river Forth.'

'Have it your way. I'm happy to look in the hills.'

'It'll be like looking for a needle in a haystook, but one of us has to give it a try.'

'What would you like to do? Work on the art forgery case?'

'Aye, but I havena a clue where to start.'

'Hmm, that is the difficulty. It's Sunday which means the public library will be closed, otherwise you could have done some research on the old masters' methods of working.'

'I'll try and speak to Rose, to let her know how we're getting on and to see if there's been any more developments.'

'Good idea, Daisy.'

'And perhaps see if I can have a wee word with that Miss Bisset.'

Maud nodded. 'I may be gone all day, so let's say we'll meet here for dinner this evening.'

Mrs Wallace appeared at their breakfast table, dressed once again in her professional costume of royal blue silk day dress with cream lace on the bodice.

'*Madainn mhath.*' She smiled. 'I hear from my husband that last night went very well. I can't thank you both enough. It's a huge relief to have an end to the matter.'

'Our pleasure, Mrs Wallace,' Maud said.

'Now, Miss McIntyre, I just wanted to say that the dominie was delighted you accepted the offer to judge the bairns' poetry recitation. It's to be held at the school on Friday afternoon. Will that be suiting you? I realise I should have consulted you before.'

'Friday?' Given their progress on the two cases, it looked very much as if she and Daisy would still be here in five days' time. 'Yes, that will be convenient. My time is pretty much my own. I look forward to it.'

Mrs Wallace's face expressed a degree of doubt, which Maud chose to overlook. How difficult could it be to listen to a handful of youngsters take it in turns to recite a poem?

'And where will you be off to today?' Mrs Wallace asked brightly.

'After church, I thought I would go for a walk in the hills and Miss Cameron has chosen to stay in the village.'

The older woman glanced at Daisy approvingly and turned to Maud. 'You could do worse than walk up Morrone.'

'Morrone?'

'It's the hill that dominates the village. Some say it's the model for Spy-Glass Hill in *Treasure Island.*' Mrs Wallace smiled. 'Be that as it may, there's a beautiful ancient birchwood on the lower slopes and a delightful view about halfway up Morrone. You'll have an excellent view of Beinn a' Bhuird, the table mountain.'

'I like the sound of a table mountain.'

'Would you both like to hear the legend of The Laird's Tablecloth?'

'Aye, we would,' Daisy said.

'The snow on Beinn a' Bhuird lies unmelted all year round. It's said that once upon a time the laird of Kindrochit had to produce a bucket of snow whenever the king demanded it. If the laird couldn't, then the family would lose their centuries-old lands.'

'And has His Majesty asked recently?' Maud asked with a smile.

Mrs Wallace shook her head.

'Just as well, though,' said Daisy, 'that the hill's still got snaw on it.'

'The walk sounds perfect. How do I get there?' Maud asked.

'Take the road towards Linn of Dee, but when you get to the crossroads instead of continuing ahead, turn left up Chapel Brae. You'll pass a small lochan at the top of the brae and from there you'll be seeing a bonnie view of Morrone. It's only a hill, mind, but it is part of the Grampian Mountains. Then you follow the track up through the woods.'

Maud smiled. There was nothing she liked more than an invigorating walk. That is, almost nothing more... investigating a case was something she liked even more.

The bell rang summoning people to church. She and Daisy hastened across the road and down the lane leading to the little parish kirk. What it lacked in size on the ground, it made up for in height with a very tall, slender spire. And in grandeur with its splendid Gothic-style architecture.

Being visitors to the village, they were not on the kirk elder's round and so had no tokens to allow them to take Holy Communion, but they could attend the service. They squeezed into one of the crowded pews. With the rest of the congregation, they sang the old, well-known hymns, listenened to the minister's sermon delivered in English and Gaelic on the importance of living in hope, and came out into the clean sharp air.

The snow-capped hills gleamed in the sun. Maud breathed a small sigh of contentment. This feeling of peace could not last, not while murderers had to be uncovered, but she would enjoy it while she could. Leaving Daisy chatting to some of the other members of the congregation, Maud hastened back to the hotel. As she changed from her dark Sunday morning suit into her blue country tweeds, she resolved to live in hope that she and Daisy would solve their two cases before the end of the fortnight. Their money wouldn't stretch any further than that.

Anywhere beyond Braemar was off the map as far as local transport was concerned. Maud already knew there was no omnibus service. And of course, after the train deposited its passengers, it returned to Ballater. If anyone wanted to go beyond the village any further west and had no horse, bicycle or motor car, he or she simply walked. That suited her. It was a fine day and the country around Braemar was glorious in its rural seclusion.

Before long Maud was striding up Chapel Brae, swinging her arms as she went and taking deep breaths of the fresh country air.

She reached the lochan, where three mallards paddled contentedly, and saw rising ahead the magnificent Morrone. The road was now a track and it wound uphill into the birch-woods, as Mrs Wallace had said.

The silver birch trees were draped heavily in lichen, evidence of clear air, Maud knew, and of the great age of the woods. Beneath the trees lay a dense carpet of juniper. The track climbed higher, past a farmhouse, where the farmer's wife, pegging out washing on a line strung between two trees, gave her a cheerful wave.

Maud walked higher and turned to look back. Below she saw the sparkling Dee as it looped round the little village nestling peacefully in the valley. She began the gentle climb again, the path narrowing and leading into open moorland covered with the fading purple heather.

This seemed to be the viewing point Mrs Wallace had mentioned, and Maud stopped to rest for a while. She imagined Mr Stevenson pausing at this spot almost thirty years ago and deciding it would make a perfect Spy-Glass Hill in his new novel.

There was a breeze up here and she put her hand to her straw hat. She could see why people talked of feeling small and insignificant on mountains. From here the village could not be seen at all. Away in the distance she could see the laird's table-cloth on top of Beinn a' Bhuird. She smiled to herself. Should the King ask for a bucket of snow today, the laird of Kindrochit's lands would be safe.

Behind her the track continued to wind up Morrone, but Maud decided the walk had been pleasant and now she should make her way back down. There had been no sign of a camp as far as she could see, so rather than retrace her steps she would return by a different path in the hope of spotting the mystery man.

She began to make her way downhill, her boots skittering over loose stones. From here, she could see across moorland and over the birches to a vast carpet of fields and the rooftops of Braemar, and above her the snow-capped hills of the Cairngorms.

Maud reached a burn and was about to cross on the stepping stones when something caught her eye. A large piece of dark green cloth between the trees to her right. She entered the woods, treading softly through the undergrowth. She drew closer. Yes, it was a tent of sorts, the cloth draped over low-hanging branches between two trees. The blackened remains of a fire pit lay nearby. This could well be the young man's camp.

She paused and listened. There seemed to be no one at home. She edged nearer to the roughly constructed tent and called softly. 'Hello?'

No reply. Maud walked up to the camp and peered inside the tent.

On the ground lay a rolled-up blanket, a tin of sardines and another of biscuits. Someone was definitely camping here and with luck it was the man she sought. There was a knapsack that looked very much like the one he had used on the train. But then, didn't all knapsacks look the same? There was only one way to learn more.

Maud crawled into the tent and opened the knapsack. Inside was what she supposed was a change of undergarments. She had no wish to examine those items. More interestingly, there was an envelope which had been torn open. She pulled it out, sat back on her heels and looked at the name and address.

Lt. Conrad Elliot, Queen's Own Cameron Highlanders, Cameron Barracks, Inverness-shire.

Conrad Elliot. Maud smiled. Now she had a name for him. He was a soldier, a man used to a degree of discomfort in his living conditions, which accounted for the rough camp.

Maud considered what she wanted to do next. She wasn't about to steal or destroy any letter inside, but simply *reading* it wasn't a crime, she was sure. She pulled out the letter. Her glance went to the top of the sheet of paper. It was dated over a week ago.

Darling Conrad,

I miss you terribly. We are still living in this ridiculously quaint village where my father is attempting to lord it over everyone. I will be in Aberdeen Tuesday as we agreed. I really do want to run away with you, but can we give him one more chance to accept we are in love and want to marry? We can catch the same train back to Braemar, but from Ballater we should sit in different compartments so that we're not seen together before you speak to him. The people here are unbearably nosy, nothing else to do in their little lives I suppose, and he would be furious if they worked out what was going on before he's told.

All my love forever,

Lili.

Maud slid the letter back in the envelope. As she did so, she heard the snap of a twig breaking underfoot and quickly replaced her find in the knapsack. The sound of the approaching footsteps grew closer. The person was making no attempt to be quiet, so it must be Mr Elliot himself. Hastily, she crawled out of the tent.

She was on her feet and had moved a couple of steps away from the tent when Lilias Bisset said, 'How funny our meeting like this.'

Hilarious, Maud thought, brushing soil and leaves from her tweed skirt. 'Indeed.'

Dressed in a dark blue spotted dress with a cameo brooch at her throat and a small round hat with a band in the same dark blue, Miss Bisset was clearly not out for a country walk.

The young woman set down the shopping basket she carried. 'What are you doing here?'

'I was out for a walk and came across this campsite.' That was true. To an extent.

Miss Bisset glanced from Maud to the tent and back again. 'As you're brushing leaves from your skirt, you must have been rummaging through his things.'

Maud tried to look as innocent as she could and opened her mouth to smooth the situation over when Miss Bisset spoke again.

'Don't try to deny it, Miss McIntyre. No self-respecting detective would pass up the chance, if detective novels are anything to go by. I assume you know all about Mr Elliot and myself. The question is, what do you intend to do with that information?'

There was nothing to be gained by pretending ignorance. 'You know that his behaviour on the train has made the village think the worst of him?'

'I do know.' She gazed down as she twisted a laced Oxford shoe in the earth. 'He'd had a whisky and then, well, another. He'd done it for Dutch courage as he was going to speak to my father that same evening, but then of course it wasn't possible...' Her voice trailed off.

Maud let a sympathetic pause hang in the air for a moment.

'You and Mr Elliot had done your best not to look like a couple,' she couldn't help saying, 'but of course that was the objective.'

Lilias Bisset looked up. 'Yes, but then I had to intervene because of the way he was speaking to the schoolteacher. I was afraid I'd given the game away.'

Hardly, considering the sharp tone she'd used on her beloved.

'I was furious with Conrad too,' the girl added.

Ah, thought Maud, that might explain her angry look when the teacher assisted her from the train at Ballater.

'I didn't see Mr Elliot leave the train at Braemar,' Maud said. 'Where did he go?'

'When we arrived, he thought it best he disappeared quickly to sober up. The last thing either of us wanted was for him to be questioned by the local policeman. As it turned out, it was probably the worst thing to do, as now everyone in the village thinks he killed my father.'

Probably not *everyone*. This deplorable habit of exaggerating that all young people had nowadays. *Some* young people, Maud amended; she mustn't exaggerate.

'For a while it was thought Mr Elliot was the person who stole the bird from the hotel,' Maud added.

'Well, he didn't,' Lilias Bisset said in a sullen tone.

'I know that now.' Maud looked at the young woman, whose cheeks had flushed. 'So why did you do it?'

'Because I wanted to sell the King's gift and use the money to fund our elopement.' Her colour deepened. 'I'm going to marry Conrad, no matter what my mother thinks.'

Maud wasn't sure it was a good idea if the girl had no means to make a living, or if Conrad didn't have enough money to support a wife. It might be 1911, but until women had the vote, there would be no true road to independence for most. Maud felt a sudden flush of gratitude towards her father who'd encouraged her to open the agency as soon as she'd told him of her plan.

'Congratulations.' Maud failed to make the statement sound convincing.

Miss Bisset sensed it and obviously felt something was required in her beau's defence. 'He's in the Queen's Own Cameron Highlanders, you know,' she said with pride. 'He's stationed just outside Inverness and has got a few weeks' leave.'

'How did you meet?'

'It was at a house in Inverness. A friend threw a Saturday-to-Monday party and he was there.' Her voice grew dreamy. 'I'll never forget that evening in the garden, with the moon beginning to rise—' She broke off, embarrassed. 'We got engaged and I returned home to tell my parents.'

'And they weren't happy?'

'No. They said they had no intention of allowing me to

marry a soldier – at least, not a junior officer.'

'But he surely won't be junior forever.'

She shrugged. 'That made no difference to them.'

'So that was the end of your engagement?'

'Officially, yes. Unofficially, no. We're secretly engaged. And if my mother doesn't accept it this time, then we're going to elope.'

Maud glanced at the shopping basket at Miss Bisset's feet. 'Meanwhile, you bring him provisions?'

Lilias Bisset nodded. She sent Maud a grin and in that moment looked very young. 'There's only so much raw rabbit a man can eat.' She became serious again. 'The problem is, he's only a subaltern and my parents want me to make a big match.'

Maud noticed that she spoke of her father in the present tense. That was a sign, surely, that she at least wasn't guilty of his murder?

'Has your mother met Mr Elliot?' Maud asked.

'No.'

'They may get along splendidly.'

'They may,' she replied, but her dispirited tone seemed to suggest otherwise. 'What I'm hoping is that, even if she doesn't agree to our marrying at once, she will at least like Conrad well enough to accept our engagement.'

It was possible, but unlikely, Maud thought.

Miss Bisset must have seen the slight frown on Maud's face, for she said vehemently, 'I love him and he loves me and that's all that matters.'

Maud inclined her head in a non-committal way. She didn't think it was *all* that mattered; there were a number of other things that were quite important...

'You won't tell my mother I come here, will you?'

Once again the girl sounded young and unsure. Only a few years separated them, but Lilias Bisset had been brought up in a very different way to Maud.

'It's not for me to inform your mother.' Maud had no wish to see the woman again.

'In fact,' added Miss Bisset, 'that's where Conrad is now, telling my mother that we wish to marry!'

A rustling through the undergrowth indicated a further person was coming, and the young man himself stepped into view.

SEVENTEEN

Unlike the last time Maud had seen him, he looked sober. No doubt by necessity, he wore the same loose wool jacket, collarless shirt and flat cap. He cast a surprised glance at Maud.

'It's all right,' Miss Bisset said. 'Miss McIntyre knows all. Now, tell me what happened.'

'I saw your mother...' His brows drew together.

'Yes?'

'And I told her of our engagement. Then she told me in no uncertain terms that she had no intention of letting me have your hand or any other part of you for that matter.'

Lilias Bisset drew in a deep breath through her nose, then let it slowly out. 'And then?'

'Then we exchanged a few short words and I left.'

'What sort of words?' Lilias asked.

Not a wise question, in Maud's opinion. It seemed that the delicate thing would be for Maud to withdraw, so they could discuss the matter privately.

'I must go. Miss Bisset, don't forget to return the merlin to the hotel.'

'I'm not allowed in.'

'I expect you'll think of something. Perhaps your maid's waitress or waiter friend can return it on your behalf.'

'Who?' She didn't meet Maud's eye.

'The one who furnished you with information about the King's gift to Mr Wallace.' With that, Maud set off back through the woods.

She had just reached the track when she heard Lilias Bisset call after her.

'Miss McIntyre! Wait, please!'

Reluctantly, Maud turned. This girl was proving most tiresome.

'Yes, Miss Bisset?' she said wearily.

'Please help us, Miss McIntyre,' the girl burst out.

'I'm a detective, Miss Bisset, not a marriage broker,' Maud said dryly.

'But it's your detective skills we're in need of.'

Maud was alarmed. Had something else happened?

'I'm sorry that I'm being a nuisance, but we don't know who else to turn to.'

The poor girl was so wretched that Maud waited until she had composed herself.

'My mother says she is sure that Conrad killed my father, but he honestly didn't. He couldn't have. He was on the train with me when it happened. You know that; you saw us.'

'Then he has nothing to fear. He cannot be accused of your father's murder, Miss Bisset.'

'You don't understand! My mother dislikes Conrad as he has no wealth or position. She is accusing him so that he will be arrested and that will give her another reason for refusing to let me marry him.'

'How old are you, Miss Bisset?'

She drew herself up. 'I am twenty.'

'As you are over twelve, your mother's consent is not required in Scots law.' Maud softened her tone. She felt some sympathy for Lilias Bisset, who clearly hoped for her mother's approval to the marriage. 'I don't see what I can do about it.'

'I want you to clear his name.'

Maud frowned. 'I'm sorry, but I cannot prove a negative.'

'Find the man who did kill my father.' Miss Bisset picked at a thread in her skirt and looked up again at Maud. 'Conrad is good and kind, and he has prospects. In a year or two he will rise from a junior to a senior lieutenant and then a couple of years after that he'll be a captain.'

At least she knew the correct order of ranking. In fact, she was beginning to impress Maud that she might possibly be a sensible girl, after all.

'On the day we were travelling in the same compartment,' Maud pointed out, 'Mr Elliot was not good and kind that day.'

Miss Bisset flushed at the challenge but stood her ground. 'He rarely drinks because it does not agree with him. Conrad was ashamed of his behaviour afterwards and he's apologised to me. When all this has been cleared up – that is, when my father's murderer has been found – he will apologise to Mr Shepherd. We hadn't expected you or the teacher to be sharing our compartment,' she went on. 'Conrad and I had arranged to meet at Aberdeen station and travel together as far as Ballater. We'd thought – foolishly, I see now – that we would be the only passengers. And then the plan was that we'd separate at Ballater and he would travel in a separate compartment so that we wouldn't be seen arriving together.'

'And then he made camp up here?'

'Yes. We meet whenever I can get away from my mother. It's very quiet in the hills, you know, and,' she cast her eyes downward, 'very private, especially in the heather.'

It was Maud's turn to look embarrassed, when for some extraordinary reason her mind went immediately to Lord Urquhart.

'There is absolutely no need to go into detail,' Maud said,

her cheeks flushed and her voice not as steady as she would wish.

'I'm only telling you so you can understand that we are very much in *love*.' She lifted her head and held Maud's gaze. 'That is why, Miss McIntyre, I beg you to clear Conrad's name.'

'I will do my best to find out the truth,' Maud promised, and she meant it.

EIGHTEEN

Maud made her way down the track back to the village. The breeze had become quite chilly. Glancing up, she saw an ominous cloud making its way across the sky. She pulled her straw boater lower on her head and strode on.

She reached the crossroads. A cream Sunbeam, its hood raised against the coming rain, was drawn up by the side of the road, facing towards the village. Its owner, in a Norfolk suit, stood by the four-seater and was looking about him with interest. She stopped short and her heart skidded to a stop as well, then started again. It was too soon after her mental image of him reclining in the sun-warmed heather, wearing only a...

Maud faltered. Then she took a deep breath and walked on. Heat washed through her in waves. What was Lord Urquhart doing in the village, if not to try and impose himself on her and Daisy's investigations? Then she realised he was unlikely to know of their latest cases. Although might he reasonably assume an investigation was the reason they were here?

He had not seen her yet, or anyway he appeared not to have, so she studied him as her feet took her closer to where he stood. With his dark eyebrows over dark eyes, straight strong nose and sensuous mouth, it was a face that could have looked out from the frame of a family portrait, as no doubt it did. He certainly had a very noble *profile*, but did he have noble *qualities*?

As if sensing her approach, Lord Urquhart turned from his contemplation of the landscape and smiled.

'Good evening, Miss McIntyre,' he said in his deep, familiar voice, raising his cap. 'I wonder, can you direct me to Balmoral? I have rather lost my way and there's no signpost.'

He was laughing at her, she was sure, and she fixed him with a gimlet stare. 'You are facing in the right direction. Continue through the village and take the road that curves to the left. It is less than ten miles to Balmoral. You cannot miss it.'

'Why do people giving directions always end by saying, "You cannot miss it", when it seems to me that it's entirely possible to do so,' he said, smiling. He didn't seem at all disconcerted by her chilly reply.

'On this occasion it is the correct response. Balmoral Castle is, I'm told, large and rather grand.'

She made to move on, but then stopped. This couldn't be ignored. 'Lord Urquhart, what exactly are you doing here?'

'I like to look around an area when I am staying nearby, to get a sense of the place.' He looked at her with surprised interest. 'I'm curious, Miss McIntyre, as to what motives you are attributing to my presence.'

'I think you know very well why I am asking you. It can't be a coincidence that you have chosen to visit this delightful but secluded village at the same time I am here.'

He opened his eyes wide and no doubt was about to make some amusing comment when he thought better of it. 'I wanted to have a look at the paintings in the art gallery.'

'It was open on a Sunday?'

'I was fortunate that it was this afternoon. I wondered if there was anything interesting to buy.'

Her pulse picked up speed. 'And was there?'

'A rather fine still life in oil by a Spanish artist, which I am considering.'

Thoughts jostled for Maud's attention. David Anderson had lied about having sold the supposed Zurbarán and was displaying it again. Was Lord Urquhart seriously interested in buying a painting or had he heard about possible forgeries? Was that why he'd visited the gallery, to see if it was genuine? Was he testing her, to see what she knew? If he was genuinely unaware of the possible provenance of the picture, should she tell him of her suspicions?

Lord Urquhart was looking curiously at her. Realising his stare was making her uncomfortable, he directed his gaze up at the low drift of dark cloud now overhead. He turned up the collar of his driving coat.

'If you're going in the direction of the village,' he said in a matter-of-fact sort of way, 'jump in and I will drive you. It looks like it's about to rain.'

'No, thank you. I am enjoying my walk.'

'Very well. Then I wish you a good day and hope you make it before the rain starts to fall.'

'I'm sure I shall.'

At that moment, the cloud burst.

'It looks like it's set to become quite a downpour,' he said.

Maud looked at his car. It was certainly tempting. The rain was already stinging her cheeks and soaking her straw bonnet and tweed jacket.

'No, thank you. I like walking in the rain.'

She set off at a brisk pace with a resolute air through the downpour. She stepped into a puddle and gasped as the cold water splashed over her ankle and inside her boot. Really, she thought, how could the weather change so quickly? Glancing over her shoulder, she saw that he was still standing there in the rain, looking after her.

The late afternoon was growing dark as the black cloud spread. It was an obvious observation, but without the benefit of streetlights, the country was always so much darker than the city. Not that she was afraid of the dark, having been brought up on her father's country estate.

The rain hit her like a waterspout. She marched back to the crossroads.

'Very well. I accept your offer of a lift.'

'Let's get in, shall we?' he said cheerfully.

He assisted her into the motor car and returned to the front, where the starting handle was already in position. On the second rotation the engine sprang into life. Almost immediately the hiss and splash of the rain began to lessen.

He jumped into the driver's seat. 'You must be very cold.'

Maud wasn't sure where that sentence might be leading, but through chattering teeth she replied, 'Not at all.'

He smiled. 'Where exactly are you staying? I'll drive you there.'

'There's no need. I think I can get out now the storm is passing.'

He sighed. 'Well, if you'd rather.' He got out and again walked round the motor, opened the door for her and offered his hand.

'Thank you.' Maud took it and climbed out. She nodded and walked on towards the village.

Within a minute or two, she heard him drive off. Good, she thought, preparing to look in the other direction as he passed. But he drew up alongside her. She felt herself grow warm with anger, which was no bad thing as she really had been very cold.

To make matters worse, the rain was beginning again and the brim of her boater was collapsing.

It was Maud's turn to sigh. She climbed back into the Sunbeam.

'That's better.' He put the engine into gear and they set off.

'Please don't be angry with me,' he said. 'I know you think I'm a bit of a cad, but I'm respectable enough really and it's not acceptable to allow you to walk to the village in this weather when I am driving through it.'

'It is kind of you,' Maud said in her most prim voice.

He smiled.

'I very much enjoyed your column in *The Edinburgh Times*,' he added. 'Most informative.'

She frowned. 'But you are already aware of such matters.'

'Of course, but it was informative to learn your opinions.'

What was she supposed to make of that?

Before she could ask, they were round the bend in the road and lamps glowed in windows. They drove slowly past the scattering of houses and shops.

'There is the hotel,' she pointed to it, 'where Miss Cameron and I are staying.'

He nodded, pulled over and parked. The gleam of the lamp outside the hotel shed a welcoming ray out into the wet darkness. It also illuminated and sent shadows over Lord Urquhart's features.

Good manners are hard to ignore when one has been used to employing them all one's life, so Maud said, 'Thank you again, Lord Urquhart. Won't you come in and have some tea with me and Miss Cameron?'

'It is very kind of you,' he said, employing his own good manners, 'but I should probably return to Balmoral. I would like to bathe before dressing for dinner.'

Oh dear, that image again.

'But perhaps I could call on you tomorrow?'

'I'm afraid that Miss Cameron and I are working...' The words had been out of her mouth before she realised. Well, she supposed she should give him some warning, no matter how oblique.

'About the painting you admired in the gallery...'

He gave her a quick look.

'Was it by Zurbarán?' she ventured.

Lord Urquhart raised an eyebrow. 'I had no idea you were so knowledgeable about seventeenth-century artists.'

'One hears things,' she said airily.

He looked at her, but the shadows on his face made it difficult for her to discern his thoughts.

'No, I saw no Zurbaráns.'

'Oh.' Either David Anderson had indeed sold the forged painting or he had removed it from display after Daisy's visit.

Lord Urquhart must have heard the disappointment in her voice, for he went on carefully, 'I know only a little about oil paintings, but I will try to answer any questions you may have on the matter.'

She nodded. 'Did these artists use turpentine – again, just for example?'

'Yes. It was – and still is – used to clean oil paint from brushes.'

She nodded again. 'As I thought.'

'I believe another use is to thin the oils so they dry more quickly.'

'Oh – how quickly?'

'Weeks, rather than months.'

'I see.' This was promising. 'And did they use linseed oil?'

'That I do not know, I'm afraid. Is there anything else you wish to ask me?'

'Not that I can think of. Thank you, Lord Urquhart.' She waited.

He hopped out of the motor and opened her door. She climbed out. 'Goodbye.'

'Goodnight, surely. This village, and indeed Edinburgh, is sufficiently small that we must meet again.'

Maud walked up to the door of the hotel, stood on the step and turned. Perhaps her warning about the painting had been too oblique. Head down against the rain, she ran back to the Sunbeam, pulled open the driver's door and leaned into the dark interior.

'The Zurbarán might be a fake,' she whispered breathily. 'Please tell no one.'

He leaned towards her, gravely studying her mouth as she spoke. She felt his breath on her skin. Her lips parted. He leaned closer.

'You didn't listen to a word I said!' She pulled back and slammed the door shut.

Her blood boiled as she marched back to the hotel. It would serve him right if he bought the painting and lost a lot of money. When she reached the hotel entrance, she turned to watch his motor car drive over the bridge and disappear round the bend in the road.

NINETEEN

Maud's skirt felt uncomfortably damp and rivulets of water were running down the inside of the collar of her sturdy tweed jacket. She pushed open the door of the hotel, pulled off her soggy boater and stepped gratefully into the well-lit entrance hall.

'*Feasgar math*, Miss McIntyre,' said Mrs Wallace from behind the reception desk, as Maud closed the door, shutting out the rain. 'What a dreich afternoon it is. I was beginning to worry about you, away up on Morrone. The storm came on so sudden.'

'I was fortunate to be almost back when the heavens opened,' Maud gasped, peeling off her wet gloves.

The little hall was busy, with small groups of guests milling about and chatting to acquaintances about whatever activities they had enjoyed until the rainstorm.

'Your friend is in the parlour with a nice cup of tea. I expect you'll be wanting one too.'

Never mind tea, Maud thought. It was a hot toddy she needed.

Mrs Wallace frowned at Maud's drenched state. 'You poor

lass; you must be nigh on drowned. But there, no one could have imagined such rain after so many months of such hot and dry weather!'

As if on cue, it rattled against the glass and they both turned to look at the window.

'What you need,' Mrs Wallace said firmly, 'is whisky with hot water, honey and lemon. 'I'll make it myself. It won't take long. The kettle is already on the stove.'

'A hot toddy is exactly what I wish for, Mrs Wallace.'

Maud went through into the warm parlour, where Daisy looked up from writing in her notebook.

She leaped to her feet. 'Goodness, Maud, you look half-drowned.'

'I feel it.'

'I was getting feart, thinking of you up that mountain.'

'It was only a hill.'

'Here, let me help you.' Daisy took Maud's hat from her and set it on a table. 'I'm nae sure your bonnet will ever recover.' She eyed it askance.

'Perhaps I can buy another at the general store.'

'Aye, perhaps you can.' Daisy slipped Maud's sodden jacket from her shoulders and hung it on the back of a chair.

Maud flapped her heavy skirts in front of the fire.

'It'll never get it dry like that,' Daisy said. 'You need to change your clothes.'

'I'll have my hot toddy first.' Maud sank into the armchair by the hearth next to Daisy and held out her hands and boots towards the flames.

'You'll get chilblains,' warned Daisy.

Maud smiled as Daisy briefly slipped back into her old role of Maud's lady's maid. 'Only for a few minutes.'

Maud drew her feet away from the hearth as Mrs Wallace appeared and handed Maud a steaming cup.

'*Slàinte mhath.*' Maud lifted the cup.

Mrs Wallace smiled. 'Och, you do know some Gaelic.'

Maud returned her smile. 'Every Scot knows that expression.' She took a sip. The liquid trickled down her insides and sent a warm glow through her chilled body. 'Perfect.'

Mrs Wallace nodded, pleased. 'I'll make sure there's a nice fire going in your room.'

'I'd like a bath too, if there is hot water to spare.'

'I'll put the Occupied notice on the door, to make sure of it.'

'Thank you, Mrs Wallace.'

'Now,' said Daisy, when Mrs Wallace had left the parlour, 'what did you discover in the hills?'

'I came across the young man's camp. His name is Conrad Elliot, he's a soldier from Inverness, he and Miss Bisset are betrothed, both her parents were against the marriage and her mother still is. Miss Bisset was also there and told me she took the bird to sell it and fund their elopement.'

Daisy's mouth had fallen open as she took in the information. Now she closed it and swallowed. 'Michty me! You've nae had a wasted day.'

'They wanted to give the impression they didn't know each other when they travelled to Braemar, to allay any word reaching her parents before Mr Elliot had a chance to ask Mr Bisset for Lilias's hand in marriage.'

'And then we found the old mannie murdered.'

'Exactly,' Maud went on. 'He had one drink too many and became belligerent, and then hurried from the train to get some air to sober himself up.'

'But he ended up focusing suspicion on himself.'

Maud nodded.

'People in love can be awfa glaikit.' Daisy looked again at Maud's wet costume. 'And if you're nae going to be glaikit yourself, you shouldna sit around in those wet things for much longer.'

Maud took another sip of her hot toddy. 'First tell me of your afternoon.'

'I can tell you over dinner.'

'Tell me now, Daisy. I like to mull over problems in the bath.'

'Och, well, as you ken I couldna go to the library – but I did discover that Mr McGonagall likes to drink in the hotel's public bar most evenings.'

'Goodness, Daisy, you never would have learned that at the public library!'

'Nae, but I did get it from the librarian. I spoke to him after kirk. He's an awfa sweetiewife.'

Maud smiled. 'Men can be such gossips.'

Daisy laughed.

'And did you manage to see Rose?' Maud went on.

'I caught a glimpse of her in the kirk, but I couldna speak to her then. Once I guessed she was back at the Anderson house, I got a message to her via the kitchen, pretending to be a friend here on a short visit, and I waited for her in the tea shop. She didna have long, but I told her what we had learned so far and, although she was disappointed that we have no real answers yet, she said she understood.'

Maud sighed. 'We do need answers...'

'One interesting thing she did say, though, was that before coming to work for Mr David, she'd been employed for some years in the faither's house in Edinburgh.'

'Oh?' Maud set down her cup. 'Did she give a reason for the move?'

'She wanted a quieter life. Had enough of the hurly burly of the city, apparently.'

'Poor Rose. That's not worked out well for her so far. Now, I should check that Mrs Wallace managed to put that notice on the bathroom along the corridor and it's not being used by

anyone. I need to get out of these wet things and have a soak...'
Maud paused.

'What is it?' asked Daisy.

Maud gave a casual shrug. 'Only that I met Lord Urquhart on my way back to the village. I would have been even more drenched if he hadn't given me a lift to the hotel.' She got to her feet and gathered up her soaked boater and tweed jacket. 'I'll see you at dinner. Perhaps by then inspiration will have struck.'

'We'll return to Mr McGonagall's tonight, while he's drinking in the bar, and search his cottage,' Maud said to Daisy over a dinner of chicken casserole.

Daisy's face lit up, then immediately fell. 'We canna go in disguise, as we have none.'

Maud let out a frustrated breath. 'It is a pity we had no space in our bags for such things.'

'My bag is smaller than yours. You would have had room if you hadna packed those clubs,' Daisy muttered darkly.

'They took almost no space at all,' Maud lied. 'Besides, the time will come when I will be glad I kept up that exercise.'

'You ken, I quite fancied our being a couple of gentlemen, on their way home from their club. We'd each need,' Daisy mused, 'a white shirt, black trousers, white silk scarf and top hat. A monocle. And a swagger! Oh, what simple creatures are men.'

The agency having been in operation since the summer, Maud and Daisy were used to donning disguises. Maud's favourite so far had been the gypsy woman who told the fortune of Miss Angela Grant, friend to the absconding fiancée of Douglas Laing. Maud spared a brief thought for the disgraced advocate-depute and wondered how he was managing to cope with life in Calton Gaol, awaiting trial for robbery, murder and two counts of incitement to commit murder.

'Daisy, even if we did have man-about-town disguises, we'd hardly melt into the background here. It's likely that the nearest gentleman's club is back in Edinburgh.'

'Aye,' Daisy agreed sadly. 'I was just having a wee bit of a dwam.'

'Well, stop dreaming and think of a story to use if we are discovered tonight. I'm sure we'll need a gentleman's disguise one day,' Maud went on, 'but this evening we will have to be two lady tourists taking the night air before turning in.'

In her room Maud opened the wardrobe and eyed its contents. Her tweed suit was too damp to wear after the downpour and had been taken away by the chambermaid to dry elsewhere. Perhaps, Maud thought, it might have been better if she had left the Indian clubs behind and instead packed another item or two of clothing. But no, she had made the correct decision: it was important for a detective to maintain her physical fitness. She removed from the cupboard her cardigan jacket and the grey skirt with a little pleat at the back, and closed the door firmly.

The chambermaid had also taken away her boater, which looked unlikely to recover from its drenching. Once dressed and in need of a hat, Maud wound a clean white hand towel around her head in the style of a turban and secured it at the front with her white gold Krementz brooch. Maud thought it looked rather chic. She drew on her long woollen coat.

Maud knocked on Daisy's door and it was flung open. Daisy took one look at Maud's head covering and burst into laughter.

'What on earth have you got on, Maud?' she managed to ask when she'd regained breath.

'I believe Poiret has decreed the turban to be very fashionable,' Maud said with dignity.

Daisy sniggered. 'Aye, in Paris, maybe – but nae in Braemar.'

'Well, it's all I have to wear, now my boater is no more.'

'Come in.' Daisy held the door wide. 'I have something for you.'

Maud entered and saw on the bed a new straw boater with a pretty pink ribbon.

'Daisy! Where did you find that?'

'In the general store. I nipped out before dinner, while you were having your bath. It sells everything: food and clothes, household equipment, china, tourist souvenirs...'

'And hats.' Maud crossed to the bed and took the boater to the dressing table. She sat on the stool, unwound her temporary turban and tried on the hat in front of the mirror. 'It fits perfectly. Thank you so much, my dear friend.'

Daisy beamed.

Maud pinned her brooch to the lapel of her coat, while Daisy bundled herself up against a chilly evening. Then they stepped out into the corridor.

'We need to know that our man is in the bar,' Maud murmured, as they descended the stairs.

They paused in the hall. The night porter, a young fellow with a thin face and red hair, was at the desk. It wasn't the same man as last night, which was just as well as she didn't want their appearance to raise any suspicion.

'Good evening,' Maud said to him, as he looked up on their approach. 'It seems a fine night after this afternoon's storm.'

'It does, miss.' He looked doubtful. 'But the rain has brought the gloaming on early. Are you out for a walk?'

'We thought we'd take a short stroll. Is the hotel busy tonight?'

He nodded. 'New guests in the hotel, plus the regulars in the lounge and public bars, miss.'

Regulars? Did that include Mr McGonagall? Maud couldn't see how to phrase the question. They would have to watch the cottage for any activity inside and hope for the best. She took Daisy's arm and steered her out of the hotel.

Her friend paused on the step. 'Maud, we need to be as sure as we can that the artist isna in his cottage. Bide here, I have an idea.'

To Maud's astonishment, Daisy disappeared back inside the hotel. She waited. Just as she had decided to return inside and see what Daisy was up to, her friend reappeared looking pleased with herself.

'What was that all about, Daisy? You went off without telling me what you were going to do.'

Daisy gave Maud a cheeky smile. 'That's because I ken you'd have told me not to.'

Maud arched an eyebrow.

'Let's walk and I'll tell you,' Daisy said.

They strolled away from the hotel, in the direction of the cottage.

'I asked the night porter if he nae got much time off.'

'Heavens, Daisy, don't give him the wrong impression.'

Daisy continued. 'He smiled and said he didna have to work on Saturday nights and I said, "I'll keep that in mind, my braw lad." Then,' she added quickly, seeing Maud about to remonstrate, 'still in my capacity as detective's assistant, I moved on to say there were so many fascinating men in this village and I'd like to meet the local artist and was he here tonight?'

'Detective's assistant or not—'

'He told me he *thought* he'd seen Mr McGonagall go into the public bar not ten minutes ago.'

Maud was immediately interested. 'Only thought?'

'He was as sure as he could be.'

'Thank you for that, Daisy, but one of these days you are going to find yourself entangled with a man if you're not careful.'

'Then we'd both be in the same boat.' Daisy grinned.

Maud stopped walking. 'What on earth do you mean?'

'Keep walking, Maud, it's too cold to stand about.'

Maud moved forward again. 'You haven't answered my question.'

'I meant how was it that Lord Urquhart just happened to be about on your way back to the village earlier?'

'He told me he was looking round the area.'

Daisy widened her eyes. 'In the *rain?*'

'It probably wasn't raining when he started out.'

The storm had passed, but the evening was overcast. A waning moon shone fitfully through the clouds. They walked on in silence, passing only a gentleman taking his smooth-haired Collie for an evening stroll.

'Good evening, ladies.' He raised his hat to them.

Maud and Daisy nodded politely and continued. They passed the Anderson house and a few minutes later, treading softly, drew near to Làrach Cottage. When they had come before, Maud had noted the isolation of the little house, but now, in the fast-gathering darkness, she felt it even more.

Suddenly, Daisy gripped Maud's arm, startling her. They stopped dead.

'There's a light!' Daisy hissed under her breath.

The upper windows were in darkness, but there was a dim glow shining through the blind in the room downstairs.

'Shall we knock on the door first,' Maud whispered, 'in case your young man was mistaken and Mr McGonagall decided not to go out, after all?'

'He's nae *my* young man.'

Maud angled her wristwatch to catch what she could of the moonlight. 'It's almost half past nine. If Mr McGonagall is out, we should have a while to search his cottage before he leaves the hotel bar.'

'Aye,' Daisy whispered, looking at the downstairs window,

'but we canna tell if he's in there, or if he's in the bar and has left a light burning for his return.'

'Well, we can't stand here. If anyone came along, we'd be very obvious whenever the moon emerged from behind a cloud. Let's wait in the shadow of the trees over there for a while.'

Daisy nodded and followed Maud across the road to the copse. They stood under the wet branches, the silence broken only by the hoot of a distant owl.

Daisy shivered. 'That sound's a bad omen.' She kept her voice low.

'It's nothing more than superstition, Daisy.'

'You ken the hoot of an owl is supposed to foretell a death?' Daisy shot Maud a glance.

'If someone died every time an owl hooted, there would be a lot of deaths in the world.'

'Aye,' Daisy said with grim satisfaction.

Silence again fell. Not quite silence; there were tiny noises around them – intermittent dripping from the leaves, scufflings from small animals – but nothing from the cottage across the road.

After some five minutes, Daisy spoke again. 'All this waiting about is making my back ache. Nae to mention the trees dripping cold water down my neck. I dinna think he's in.' She took a step forward. 'I'm going to try and have a keek inside.'

'No, Daisy.' Maud put out a hand to stop her. 'He might be there and catch you looking through his window.'

'That's what I'll have to find out, won't I?'

Daisy was right. Standing here was achieving nothing, apart from making them cold and damp. Maud dropped her hand and Daisy crept forward, across the road and down the short garden path. She peered through the ground floor window at the side of the door before returning to where Maud waited.

'I canna hear anything, but there's a light on in there, right enough. Come and see for yourself.'

Maud followed her friend as she retraced her steps. They inched along the wall of the cottage until they reached the window and stood listening intently. It was just as Daisy had said. Not the slightest sound came from the room on the other side of the glass.

'I think you're right. He's either in the hotel bar as the night porter believes, or he's indoors and asleep.'

Maud made up her mind, raised her hand and knocked smartly on the door. 'We need to find out the truth and there's no time like the present.' She knocked again.

They waited. Again there was only silence.

'He must be out.' Daisy stepped back to the window and set her eye to the dirty pane. 'This glass is boggin, but at least the blind isna quite down.' She drew in a sharp breath. 'Maud, look! There's something I canna quite make out.'

Maud bent and put her face to the pane. A glimmer of light showed through the slight gap where the blind didn't meet the windowsill.

'The room looks as I remember it. Oh, but wait! I think I can see an arm. Yes, I recognise Mr McGonagall's jacket. Then he must be sitting there! Bother this blind.'

She stared harder. Someone was definitely seated in the chair at the table. In the lamp light Maud could make out an arm in an old tweed sleeve. Below the cuff a hand hung. She tried to see more, but the gap was too narrow. The hand didn't move and the silence remained.

'There's something wrong, Daisy. Try the door.'

Daisy put her hand on the latch. 'It's bound to be snibbed.'

But the latch lifted. Daisy eased the door open and they peered in. 'Oh my Lord.'

There, in the centre of the sad little room, Mr McGonagall was slumped horribly in a chair, a bloody gash on his head and looking quite dead.

TWENTY

His mouth hung open, as if in the middle of expressing surprise, and the whites of his eyes gaped vacantly in the dim glow from the lamp.

Daisy's hand fell from the latch of the door. 'I think I'm going to boke.'

'Don't you dare.'

Maud went up to the body, averting her gaze from the blood glistening in the dark hair and on the shoulder of the jacket. She touched one of the drooping hands. It still felt warm to the touch. She quickly drew back her hand and placed her cheek close to his open mouth. There was no breath.

'Dead,' she said. 'Poor fellow.'

'The night porter got that wrong,' Daisy said. 'There's nae way Mr McGonagall could have left the bar and got back here before we did.'

She was looking around the room and Maud's gaze followed. A single dirty plate with a knife and fork sat on the table, suggesting the killer arrived shortly after Mr McGonagall had finished eating. Or perhaps it was just Maud who liked to have used plates removed in a timely fashion. There was no sign of a struggle having taken place, so the killer must have been known to him.

'Murder?' Daisy instinctively lowered her voice.

'I've never heard of anyone clubbing themselves to death.'

Daisy nodded. 'Can you see the murder weapon?'

'The killer might have it.'

Daisy jumped and looked around. 'You dinna think he's still here?'

Maud glanced at the fireplace. Was the grate still as empty as it had been when they visited two days ago? In Poe's story, *The Murders in the Rue Morgue*, traces of soot led the neighbours and the policemen to look up the chimney, where they found the bloodied corpse of Mademoiselle Camille. Could Mr McGonagall's murderer be hiding up this chimney, having heard her and Daisy at the door of the cottage?

Reason reasserted itself. 'No. He's not been dead for long by the warmth of his skin, but we saw and heard nothing outside all the time we waited, so I doubt the killer is still here.'

Her gaze fell on the chest under the window and stopped on the earthenware receptacle for paint brushes. 'Surely that had been a plain brown jar?'

Daisy moved forward. 'And now it seems to be decorated in a red colour...' She peered at it.

Maud joined her and they looked at each other.

'I think we've found the murder weapon,' Daisy said.

'This is a matter for the police, Daisy. We can't do anything here. We must return to the hotel and telephone the police office.'

Daisy glanced at the staircase. Maud knew what she was thinking and it was tempting, but they could not.

'The police won't thank us for interfering.'

'I willna be long.' Daisy sprinted across the room and disappeared up the steep wooden stairs.

'Daisy!' Maud hastened after her, then stopped at the bottom of the staircase.

If anyone should come and find them, they would be instant suspects. She should keep watch on the bottom step. Her heart pounding, she strained to listen to Daisy's footsteps. Her friend was small and light, but the floorboards were old and they creaked. She followed Daisy's progress by ear. After a few minutes, Maud heard her clattering up a second flight of stairs.

What if she were wrong and the killer was hiding upstairs? It didn't bear thinking about.

'I'm coming up!' she called after her.

As she ran up the staircase, Daisy reappeared at the very top. 'It's all there.' She grinned.

Maud stepped back down and waited for Daisy to join her.

'What did you find?'

'Everything! Linseed oil, turpentine, varnish, oil paints, one of those wooden palette things where you mix paints and with a hole for the thumb, and the easel set with a canvas.'

'Anything painted on the canvas?'

Daisy shook her head.

'All those items are convincing,' said Maud, 'but not exactly proof of forging paintings.'

Daisy turned back to the body of Mr McGonagall. 'What are we going to do with him? We canna leave him here alone. It doesna seem... right.'

'We certainly can't move him and we mustn't. Come on, let's get out of here.'

Daisy followed her outside and Maud shut the door. She was glad to be out of that dreadful room. They set off at a brisk pace in the direction of the hotel.

'Wait,' Maud said suddenly, coming to a halt. 'I have an idea.'

Daisy sent her a questioning look.

'We will get to the Anderson house before the hotel. Let us call there and ask to use their telephone.'

Daisy nodded. 'And at the same time we can learn if Mr Anderson the younger has been at home all evening.'

'Exactly. The two are involved in a business relationship and to my mind David Anderson is a plausible suspect for McGonagall's death.'

They hurried on towards An Taigh Mòr. The place was in darkness, but Maud pressed the bell and heard it ring somewhere inside. After a short interval the door was opened and Rose's startled face looked out.

'We need to use the telephone, Rose,' Maud said in a low voice. 'It's urgent.'

'What's happened?' Clutching her woollen dressing gown to her body, she stood back from the door so that Maud and Daisy could enter.

'The artist is dead,' Daisy whispered to her.

'*Dead*!'

'Wheesh.' Daisy sent her a quick look. 'Remember you dinna know us from Adam.'

'Where is the telephone?' Maud asked.

'I'll show you, but I don't know that Mr Anderson...'

'Havers!' Daisy's voice was back to its normal pitch. 'He canna mind our using his telephone. Where is he?'

'Mr Anderson is away at present. Mr David retired to bed some time ago.'

'There's nae much else to do in the country,' Daisy muttered.

Rose led the way down the passage to where the instrument stood on the hall table. She cast a worried look at them. 'I'll rouse Mr David at once.' She went off towards the back of the house.

Maud lifted the receiver for the operator and asked for the

police office. When the line was connected, she heard the sleepy constable at the other end.

'Good evening. This is Miss Maud McIntyre speaking. You must go to Mr McGonagall's cottage at once. There's been an... incident. I'm afraid it looks like murder... Yes, Làrach Cottage. We'll meet you there. Goodbye.'

She hung up the receiver and turned to Daisy. 'The constable is coming straightaway...'

She broke off, staring past Daisy as David Anderson came into view at the top of the staircase.

'Sorry to keep you waiting, ladies, but I deemed it proper that I put on some clothes. The maid said you wanted to use the telephone urgently. What is the problem?'

He came down the stairs, a look of anxiety on his face.

'It's Mr McGonagall,' Maud said. 'We've just been to his cottage and... well... he's dead.'

David Anderson had reached the hall and he stopped abruptly. 'McGonagall is *dead*? Are you sure?' He gave a small laugh. 'Perhaps he's in an alcoholic stupor.'

'He's dead, right enough,' said Daisy. 'We found him with a dunt in his heid.'

David Anderson drew in a sharp breath. 'You mean someone has killed him?'

'It certainly looks like it,' Maud said.

David Anderson turned to her. 'You have telephoned the police?'

'I have. I don't suppose you heard anything, Mr Anderson, given your house is close to the dead man's cottage?'

He stiffened. 'I went out earlier for a quick drink in the hotel's lounge bar, but otherwise I have been here all evening. I heard nothing untoward coming from the man's hovel. If I had, you can be sure I would have called for the police myself.'

Maud nodded. 'Miss Cameron and I have to go back now to his cottage and meet the policeman there.'

'Of course. Can I offer you a stiff drink before you go – brandy perhaps? It must have upset you both, finding him like that.'

'Nae a bonny sight.'

'We have no time for a drink, Mr Anderson,' Maud told him. 'Come, Daisy.'

'Dead,' he repeated, following them back along the passage and to the front door of the house. 'My God, I can't believe it.'

They paused at the door and waited for him to open it.

'I've sent my maid back to bed.' Mr Anderson put his hand on the doorknob. 'Let me come with you, ladies. You will feel happier with a male escort.'

Maud sent Daisy a look and drew herself up. 'Thank you, Mr Anderson, but we came here without one and we can just as easily return without one.'

They took their leave.

'We need a reason to tell the officer for being out late at night,' Daisy said, as they hastened towards the cottage. 'I'm nae sure saying we went for a stroll would work. What about saying we have been working amongst the fallen women in the area?'

'Are there any?'

'Bound to be, given how few chances there are for women to earn money.' Daisy pulled a face. 'Don't you just hate that term, fallen?' She smiled mischievously. 'It might be more fun if we could work with fallen men.'

'Why did we enter the cottage?' Maud said, hurrying on.

'Because we were concerned about the light burning inside and the door ajar?'

'Except that it wasn't, was it? Ajar?'

TWENTY-ONE

As they approached Làrach Cottage, the police officer bicycled towards them. They waited outside for him to join them. A tall, thin man with a huge white moustache, he dismounted and, leaving the lamp switched on, propped his bicycle against the wall.

'I'm Constable Oliphant,' he said briskly. 'Now, which of you young ladies is Miss Maud McIntyre?'

'I am she, constable. And this lady is... my friend, Miss Daisy Cameron.' Maud had been on the point of saying her assistant, but she felt the less the man knew of their involvement in the case, the better.

'You say the man is dead, miss?'

'Aye,' said Daisy. 'Nae doubt about that.'

'And you are sure that he is the artist, Mr McGonagall?'

Maud nodded. 'We are. Miss Cameron and I came here to buy a picture from him only the other day.'

Constable Oliphant produced a notebook and pencil from the top pocket of his uniform, and looked at them. 'Before we enter, if you would like to tell me what happened here this evening. To the best of your knowledge, that is.'

'Certainly, constable. Miss Cameron and I were taking an evening stroll. We are visiting from Edinburgh and it is so beautiful here that we wanted to make the most of our time in the village.'

The policeman nodded and smiled, pleased at her compliment. By the lamp of his bicycle, he noted a few comments in his book.

'We were on our way back to the Braemar Arms, where we are staying, when we noticed there was a light inside the artist's cottage and the door' – she cleared her throat – 'ajar.'

'Feart for him on a cold night, leaving the door ajar,' continued Daisy, 'especially as we've heard he gets blootered, we thought to close the door for him. We called out, gave the door a wee push and...' She pulled a handkerchief from the sleeve of her coat and held it to her eyes.

'There now, miss,' said the constable in a kindly voice. 'And after you found the body... found the gentleman... you telephoned the police office from where exactly?'

Maud gave him David Anderson's name, keeping her suspicions to herself. The constable added their Edinburgh address to the notes in his book. 'Now, I shall have to ask you young ladies to come inside with me. I hope you don't mind.'

Maud nodded.

Daisy put away her handkerchief and once again they entered the cottage, this time following the constable. He wrote in his notebook again, his gaze lifting from time to time to note what was in the room. It didn't take him long.

'Does the room look as it did when you entered this evening?'

'As far as I can tell, yes,' Maud said and Daisy agreed.

'Could you say if anything is missing?'

'You think the motive might have been robbery and that Mr McGonagall disturbed the thief?'

'It's possible.'

'But not very likely,' Maud couldn't help pointing out. 'The door hasn't been forced and there are no obvious signs of a struggle.'

The constable stared at her in surprise. 'Very observant, miss, if I may say so.'

Was she really going to have to do his job for him? 'I'm afraid I cannot say if any items have been stolen, as we have been in this room only once before and then only for a short time. But there is an addition to what was in the room.'

'Yes?' He looked hopefully at Maud.

'Blood on the jar holding the paint brushes.' She gestured to the object.

The constable approached the chest cautiously. He reached out a hand and touched the glistening streak with the tip of a finger. 'Still sticky.' He lifted the finger to his nose and sniffed. 'Not paint. Definitely blood.'

Pulling a large white handkerchief from his trouser pocket, he wiped the blood from his fingertip.

'Perhaps something has been taken from upstairs,' said Daisy, starting forward. 'Shall we go up and see if there's any sign of a search?'

'Miss!' The police officer called her back. 'You can't go up there.' He gave her a stern look.

'Sorry.' Daisy managed to sound contrite. 'It must be the smell of the linseed oil that's gone to my heid.'

He spoke kindly again. 'It's not very pleasant for you two ladies and so I shan't keep you long.'

'Good evening, Constable Oliphant.' A short, plump man in a brown suit with a watch and chain across his waistcoat appeared in the doorway. He indicated the body slumped in the chair. 'What have you for me?'

'Dr Simpson. Pleased to see you, sir. The gentleman is Mr McGonagall, found by these two ladies a short while ago, bludgeoned to death.'

The doctor nodded to Maud and Daisy, walked over to the chair and bent to examine the wound on Mr McGonagall's head.

'Quite a mess. Have you found the weapon?'

'It looks like the killer used the jar holding the fellow's paint brushes. It's got blood on it.'

The doctor straightened, followed the police officer's gaze and nodded. 'Aye, very likely that's the weapon.' He glanced down at the body. 'As soon as the handcart arrives, I'll get this away.'

'Now, ladies,' said Constable Oliphant, 'I don't think there's any need for me to keep you standing about here any longer.'

Maud didn't ask about the need for an investigation by the Procurator Fiscal, as she knew the answer. Besides, she didn't want to draw attention to her and Daisy's knowledge of such matters. The police officer would be the one gathering evidence. With a little help from two lady detectives of course, thought Maud.

'It's my opinion that this suspicious young man I've heard about,' the constable added, 'is behind this.'

Maud's heart sank. It was dispiriting to hear another unfounded accusation against Conrad Elliot. But she did not intend to reveal the reason for the young man being here, or his whereabouts. The policeman really would need her and Daisy's help to uncover the truth.

The doctor was speaking. 'I'll stay to supervise the moving of the body to the dead house.'

Daisy shivered at the use of the old-fashioned term for mortuary.

Seeing her reaction, the doctor said, 'I hope what you've seen won't keep you awake, miss.'

'Aye, so do I.'

It was not quite eleven o'clock when Maud and Daisy

returned to the hotel, the night porter still seated at the hall desk.

'I don't know about you, Daisy,' said Maud, as they made their way up the stairs, 'but I'm ready for bed.'

Daisy stifled a yawn. 'So am I. That was some walk.'

The dining room was busy when they went down for breakfast the next morning. There was a low hum of voices and Maud was certain she could detect the words 'murder', 'shocking' and 'artist'. In a small village, word of Mr McGonagall's violent death would spread very quickly. There were no curious looks directed at her and Daisy, so Maud guessed that the police officer had kept their identities quiet.

Over their scrambled eggs, the pair spoke in hushed tones.

'It's been exactly a week since we travelled here,' Maud said, 'and what a lot has happened since then.'

'Aye, and plenty still to do...' Daisy murmured in agreement.

Maud nodded. 'After sleeping on it, I still think that the most likely suspect for Mr McGonagall's murder is David Anderson.'

'If it's nae him, then it must be a complete stranger, which doesna make sense.'

'What about Conrad Elliot?'

'Maud, you didna think it was him last night and you still dinna think it's him. I trust your opinion.'

'I might be wrong.' Maud was touched by Daisy's loyalty. 'But I think we should start with David Anderson. Tell me, did anything strike you as suspicious about the fellow at his house yesterday evening?'

'Aye,' Daisy replied between mouthfuls of eggs. 'Two things.'

'Yes?' Maud lifted her cup and took a sip of tea.

'He was dressed as if he'd just got in and he offered us a drink.'

'Both of those struck me too. We need to consider the actions of Mr Anderson the younger if we're to get to the bottom of this case. Let's start with the first item. Rose said he had gone to bed a while ago, which could mean almost anything. But it must be possible for David Anderson to steal out of the house without her knowledge.'

'You mean he would know which stair treads creak and to avoid them?'

'That and the doors. Also, I doubt the maid's bedroom is anywhere near the young master's.'

Daisy nodded. 'You get used to your own doors and can close them quietly.' She spread butter on her slice of toast.

'And the second factor,' Maud went on. 'Offering us brandy was an extraordinary thing to do. He said it was because we had suffered a shock, but I don't believe that was his reason.'

'He wanted us to have alcohol on our breath, so as to make the policeman think we werena trustworthy.'

'And perhaps even to cast suspicion on us, as two women lacking sobriety and thus being possible murderers.'

'You dinna really think that?'

'Who knows what was going through David Anderson's mind? If he's guilty, he must have been in a panic when we arrived at his house and said we'd found Mr McGonagall's body. He probably thought no one would discover the murder until the next day at least.'

Daisy scowled. 'The deil.'

A devil indeed, if Mr Anderson were the murderer, Maud thought.

They continued with their breakfast in silence for a while.

'Perhaps David Anderson did go there, but only to say that he didna want to deal with any more fakes?'

Maud put her knife and fork onto her plate with a clatter.

'You might have something there, Daisy. What if the killer was Mr Anderson *senior?*'

Daisy stared at her. 'You mean maybe he'd discovered what his son was up to and went to tell the artist the business was over?' She thought for a moment. 'But Rose said the faither was away from home.'

'A person can return to his own house whenever he wishes.'

'I'm nae sure. There'd be a risk the faither would be spotted in the village and his arrival commented on.'

'You may be right, but let's bear in mind that Mr Anderson senior has almost as much to lose as his son if the truth came out about the forgeries. Apart from the shame of David being sent to prison, the father's reputation in the art world would be ruined.'

'Let's keep both the Andersons as suspects,' said Daisy. 'The artist could have tried to blackmail whichever Mr Anderson turned up.'

'He was certainly convinced he would soon be on his way to Paris, where fame and fortune awaited. A spot of blackmail would surely prove more lucrative than the occasional faked painting.'

'Mr Anderson – whichever one – might not have gone to the cottage with the intention to kill the artist, but once there and faced with blackmail...'

'Intention is of no matter to us.' Maud spread marmalade lavishly on her toast. 'Kill him someone undoubtedly did, and it could hardly have been an accident.'

'The artist must have been taken by surprise, since he didna try to defend himself. He probably let the person in and before he knew it, the other mannie had dunted his heid with the jug.'

'Mr McGonagall didn't look like a strong man, so even if he'd seen it coming, there was probably little he could have done to defend himself.'

'You know, Maud, we dinna actually ken if Mr McGonagall

could produce proper oil paintings. We saw the tubes of oil paint and so on, but there's a lot more to faking a masterpiece than the tools. The work we've seen of his is, well, nothing like the Zubaroos.'

'Zurbaráns.' Maud bit into her toast and marmalade.

'Aye. I dinna think I could do one.'

Maud swallowed. 'Nor I. But if Mr McGonagall wasn't forging the paintings, then who was?'

'I havena got the answer to that, any more than I have to who murdered him or Bisset.'

Like a bolt of lightning, a thought struck Maud. Could the murderer of Mr McGonagall also have killed Mr Bisset? She couldn't see an obvious connection between the two cases and yet was it likely there could be two killers in such a sleepy village?

Maud and Daisy had finished breakfast and were folding their napkins when Mrs Wallace came hurrying over to their table.

'Your father is on the telephone, Miss McIntyre,' she said in a low voice.

'My father?' Maud felt her pulse jump. He disliked using the telephone, so it must be something serious to cause him to use it. 'Thank you, Mrs Wallace.'

Daisy shot Maud a worried look, as Maud got to her feet and hastened after Mrs Wallace, through the hall and into the office, with Daisy close behind her. Mrs Wallace indicated the candlestick telephone on the desk before discreetly disappearing back into the hall.

Maud picked up the telephone and held the other piece to her ear.

'Hello, father?' She forced down her concerns and tried to sound normal. 'How are you?'

'I'm very well, my dear,' she heard his voice faint down the line, 'but I'm afraid I have some bad news for you.'

'Oh,' Maud said, and immediately her stomach tightened. 'What is it?' A chill went through her. 'Is one of my brothers ill? Or' – Heaven forbid, she thought – 'one of the children?'

'No. It's your Aunt Sophy. You know she has been unwell for a wee while?'

'Yes, but I thought it was simply a cold.'

'It was initially, but sadly it turned into pneumonia and she passed away yesterday afternoon.'

'Oh, father, I am so sorry.' Maud knew she hadn't visited her father's sister as often as she should have and she felt the guilt settling in the pit of her stomach.

'The service will be held at the Parish Church in Portobello and the interment at Piershill Cemetery tomorrow afternoon,' he went on.

'So soon?'

'She died in hospital and there was no need for a post-mortem.' His voice sounded anxious. 'Will you be able to attend?'

Her heart went out to him. 'Of course I will, darling. What time should I be at your house?'

'There's no need to come all the way out here, Maud, when you have quite a journey to get back to Edinburgh. I'll meet you at the kirk at two o'clock. Have a safe journey, my dear.'

Maud hung the earpiece back onto the telephone, replaced the instrument on the desk and sighed with relief. Her beloved father was well. But she was sad about Aunt Sophy, for all the old lady's sternness.

Daisy waited anxiously at her elbow. 'Is your faither all right?'

'He is well, thank you. It's my Aunt Sophy. She died yesterday.'

'That crabbit old thing.'

'Daisy, you mustn't speak ill of the dead.'

'I dinna know why not. I believe in calling a spurtle a spurtle.'

'Don't you mean a spade a spade?'

'I ken what I mean. She was like a wooden stick for stirring the porridge. She was probably a bad-tempered old lady even when she was young.'

Maud frowned. 'I didn't really know her. She lived abroad for so long that I've hardly met her. Even so...'

Maud pictured the forbidding elderly lady she had only ever seen dressed in black silk. Sophy had been widowed when still young. She and her husband had no children and perhaps that had eaten away at her aunt's temperament as the years passed. Maud, though, had been convinced that Sophy must have once been a brave and intrepid young woman, as she had stayed in India for many years after her husband's death.

'Will you go to the funeral?' Daisy asked, breaking into Maud's reminiscences.

'Yes. I must. If for no other reason than that's what my father would want.' Maud looked at Daisy. 'Would you like to come?'

'If you dinna mind, I won't. Funerals aye make me greet, even when I didna really know the person.'

'Of course I don't mind. She was my relative and not yours. What will you do?'

'I'll stay here. I might learn something of interest and it's good to have this wee break from the city.'

'Don't tell me you're enjoying the village? Are you feeling quite well? You've told me on more than one occasion since we moved to Edinburgh that you preferred the city to the country.'

'Living in the city is exciting, right enough, but there are times when you long for a bit of peace and quiet.'

Maud smiled. 'I'm not sure there's been much peace and quiet to enjoy in the village.'

'I'll bide here anyway.'

'I can't help but feel relieved. It's better that one of us remain, in case some new evidence turns up.'

Daisy nodded. 'What will you do about clothes? You canna wear that.'

Maud glanced down at her purple dress with its white collar and cuffs.

'And you havena got a suitable hat either.'

'I'll spend tonight at the apartment. My black taffeta is there.' The fabric was a little out-of-date, but the dress was entirely suitable for a funeral. 'And my black hat with black silk roses.'

Daisy nodded her approval. 'What train will you catch?'

'I'll speak to Mrs Wallace. She may have a Bradshaw. Even if she doesn't, she'll probably know the times of the trains.'

Mrs Wallace did. Within a short time, Maud had packed a few essentials and was boarding the ten o'clock train.

TWENTY-TWO

Maud found a corner seat in an empty compartment and placed the Gladstone on the floor by her feet, handy for her reading and her notebook. The capacious bag was only half-full, to allow for any disguises she might purchase while in Edinburgh.

The train pulled out of the station with a judder and a billowing of steam. From the window she saw again the fields and sheep, the river and woods.

Bridge of Gairn station brought a reminder of the Bisset case, but it wasn't until she got out to change trains at Ballater that she remembered a much earlier thought she'd had. It had been only a slight suspicion then, but now she felt an icy trickle run down her back. Was it a coincidence that the forged paintings and the Bissets' arrival in the village occurred about the same time?

Rose Gilmour reported that she had first observed the delivery of one of these paintings four months ago, and Mrs Wallace had told them the Bisset family took up residence a couple of months ago. Of course Rose had not been working in Braemar for long, but even in Edinburgh wouldn't she have been aware if there was even the smallest disquiet over sales

from the village gallery? Besides, when she and Daisy had
visited the father, he had mentioned his son's finding of two
Zurbaráns. Not that Maud suspected any of the Bissets of
forging the still lifes.

She boarded the train to Aberdeen and although two other
passengers joined her in her compartment, after nodding briefly
she was able to remain quiet and thoughtful. To her relief, they
were content to observe the passing scenery or read their news-
papers or journals.

At Aberdeen, she changed again. They were no longer travelling east, but south. The engine huffed, the iron wheels
clanked upon iron rails. The train rumbled on. Maud began to
feel weary; weary of the journey and weary of being jolted
about. She wanted a fire, a hot dinner and a warm bed. But as
she'd given Martha the time off while they were away, there
would be no meal waiting to be put in the oven.

She looked at her wristwatch. Another hour to go.

Her thoughts went round and round with the train wheels.
There must be a connection between the artist Mr McGonagall
and the retired farmer Mr Bisset, but what was it?

The gas lamp on each landing had been lit by the lamp lighter,
but Maud's apartment in Broughton Street was cold and
gloomy. It was interesting how a place so familiar to her could
very quickly become unwelcoming without her and Daisy to fill
it with their effects and busy lives. She thought then about the
Bissets; was this how Mrs Bisset had felt when the family
moved to Woodend? The large and draughty house must have
seemed unwelcoming to its reluctant new tenant.

The fire had been set in the sitting room. Maud put a match
to the kindlers and watched the flame catch the paper and thin
sticks of wood. Soon a few larger pieces of wood could be
added. Once the flames licked up and around them, Maud

lifted the tongs and carefully placed on top three pieces of coal. It didn't take long before the coals, too, were burning. She put her hands to the growing warmth for a few moments before lighting the oil lamp on the small table by the sofa. It gave a cosier effect than the gas lamps on the wall and Maud felt the need for comfort this evening.

Next was dinner. In the kitchen she filled the kettle with water, placed it on the hob and lit the gas. Rooting around in the cupboard, she found some cheese and an apple. That would have to do.

She spooned tea leaves into the pot and placed the stone pig hot water bottle next to it. As soon as the kettle had boiled, she poured water into the tea pot, then filled the hot water bottle, screwed the neck closed and dried it with a cloth. Maud carried the bottle through to her bedroom and slid it between the sheets to warm the bed.

Yawning, she prepared her tray to carry back into the sitting room. It had been a long day. The theatrical outfitters was next on her list. She would go there in the morning.

After a good night's sleep and quick breakfast of more cheese and another apple – really, she should ensure her cupboard was better stocked in future – Maud did a few ballet exercises. Holding on to the back of a chair in the kitchen, she bent her knees in a basic *plié*, from first position to fifth, stretching every muscle in her legs. She moved into a *relevé*, raising her heels from the floor and rolling up onto the balls of her feet to strengthen her feet and ankles. Maud resisted the temptation to try a pirouette – she was too out of practice for that and it seemed too frivolous for the day of a funeral.

She dressed in her black taffeta, secured the large black hat on her head with a straight hat pin from her drawer and set off for Blair Street in the Old Town. It was less than a mile and she reached William Mutrie and Sons' premises in less than twenty minutes. Dim light filtered through the stained-glass window, showing the motes of dust disturbed by her entrance. The shop was crammed with fake weapons, masks and outfits of all types and colours; it never failed to give her a thrill.

William Mutrie himself had died some years past, but one of his sons had taken over the business. He now entered the shop from a room at the back, the workshop and heart of the establishment. Through the open doorway Maud caught a glimpse of a woman hand-sewing a red costume with sequins before the door closed again.

'Good morning, Miss McIntyre.' Mr Mutrie came forward, a welcoming smile on his face. He noticed her costume and at once became sombre. 'My commiserations on your loss. Is it...'– he hesitated – 'your father?'

'My aunt,' she said, 'my father's sister.'

He nodded gravely. 'How can I help you today?'

'I'd like a costume that is easy to pack, doesn't require too many accessories and can be worn by any female.'

'Let me see.' His gaze went around the shop. 'We could start with the hat. One that will not be easily crushed when packed into a bag.' His eye lit on a dark grey velvet bonnet which had collapsed on one side.

He crossed the floor, leaned over a pile of assorted boxes and lifted the hat.

'That's possible,' Maud said, 'but what would be the most suitable garment to wear with it?'

'A plain scarf tied at the neck,' he suggested, 'with a threadbare jacket, blouse and skirt. That would enable to wearer to look the part of a match girl.'

One thing was missing, she thought: a swollen face.

Maud's heart constricted with pity for the poor match girls. Exposed to white phosphorus during the manufacture of matches, most of the women suffered terrible toothache, loss of teeth, swelling of the gums and then the collapse of their jawbone, followed by death. The match girls had tried many times to improve their dreadful working conditions...

Maud realised Mr Mutrie was waiting for her decision.

'I was thinking of a more simple outfit.'

'More simple than a match girl?' He considered further. 'Nun.'

'None?' she said, surprised. 'You have nothing else suitable?'

'No, Miss McIntyre, I mean a nun; a sister of mercy.'

'Oh, yes, of course. Could I see that, please?'

'Certainly.' He heaved to one side a suit of armour that stood on a wooden box and opened the door to a cupboard. 'Were you looking for a sister who's active in her community or one who lives a cloistered life?'

'Active,' Maud said firmly. There'd be no point in the disguise if she couldn't go out in it.

'Here we are then.' Mr Mutrie pulled out a black habit. 'This should fit your requirements. It will have no objection to being folded into a bag, requires only a few accessories and one size will fit any lady.'

This last was particularly good news, as Maud was tall but Daisy was less so.

'The only other items you would require are these.' He turned back to the cupboard and drew out a dark veil, white coif and a wooden crucifix attached to a string of green rosary beads. He took them over to the counter and laid them out for Maud to see.

'The coif is worn under the veil and the rosary can hang around the neck or be secured at the waist to shorten the length of the habit to suit the wearer.'

Maud examined the items. Her fingers lightly touched the glass beads of the rosary. 'Green,' she murmured. 'What does the colour signify?'

'Each colour has its own meaning and season, but green is for ordinary time in the Church calendar.'

'I'll take this costume.'

'I've not sold a nun for a while.' Mr Mutrie began to wrap her purchases in brown paper. 'You never know what a customer is going to want when they walk through the door.'

'What have you sold recently?' She reached into her bag for her purse.

'I had a man only – let me see, it must have been a fortnight ago because that's when the wife's sister returned home – who wanted a painter and decorator's clothes.'

TWENTY-THREE

Maud paused in the middle of opening her purse. 'Painter and decorator?' Her pulse gave a little jump. 'I wonder why he came here and not to the Army and Navy Stores?'

'I thought it unsual, too, but he didn't look or sound like a tradesman and he wanted the trousers already splashed with paint.'

Her pulse quickened as she gave a small laugh, pretending amusement. 'Goodness. Did he specify the colour?'

'Brown.'

Maud felt cold spread through her body as she slowly counted out the money. The clothes sounded exactly like those worn by the man who left the train at Bridge of Gairn. 'Perhaps he was going to a fancy-dress party?'

'He certainly wouldn't pass for a painter and decorator, with those clean, soft-looking hands.' Mr Mutrie tied the parcel with string.

'There you go, Miss McIntyre.' He smiled and handed it to Maud.

'Thank you, Mr Mutrie,' she said, returning his smile. 'You've been most helpful.'

Maud left the shop with the package tucked under her arm
and her mind alive with possibilities. Was she now getting
somewhere with the Bisset case? It surely was the killer who
had bought the tradesman's outfit. It was too extraordinary a
coincidence otherwise. Not only that, but the man must know
Edinburgh well to be aware of Mr Mutrie's shop. Both the Mr
Andersons were intimately acquainted with the city, the older
Mr Anderson presumably more so.

As she mulled over what she had learned, Maud found her
footsteps taking her over North Bridge. The sun glinted off the
railway lines below. She would pop into the agency, in case
there were any letters that had not been forwarded by the
General Post Office to the Braemar Arms, as she had requested.
Then luncheon – an early one after yesterday's lack of dinner
and this morning's poor breakfast.

She made her way along Princes Street. In the gardens
below, young women strolled along, and couples arm in arm,
enjoying the warmth of the sun, the women's brightly coloured
parasols catching the light. Older men and women rested on the
benches, chatting or enjoying the display of the last of the
summer flowers. Small children skipped along the path, holding
the hands of their nannies.

It seemed almost impossible to imagine this was once a
stinking, polluted piece of water, the valley between the Old
and New Towns, used for a couple of hundred years by the resi-
dents for their rubbish and worse. Later the Nor' Loch had been
flooded to strengthen the castle's defences. Automatically she
glanced ahead, up at the castle standing on the peak of an
extinct volcano and towering over the city. Later again, the loch
was drained to make the gardens.

Maud drew level with the Scott Monument, a tall and thin
Gothic structure with a spire on top. Over two hundred feet
high, and depicted in the marble carvings were ninety-three
people, two dogs and a pig. Robbie Burns, Lord Byron, Queen

Mary, King James, Robert the Bruce, characters from Sir Walter
Scott's novels... including the pig from *Ivanhoe*.

She smiled, dodged the busy traffic as she crossed Princes
Street and turned into Hanover Street. And before long she
reached the M. McIntyre Agency in George Street.

There was no post, but the office looked a little dusty and
the aspidistra in need of water. Maud busied herself with these
and a few other jobs and soon the room looked less forlorn.

Her eyes fell on the Underwood sitting on the desk and an
idea came to her. She had a little time before luncheon and then
Aunt Sophy's funeral. She would teach herself to type. And if,
which she hoped would never happen, the agency couldn't
support itself, she could get a job as a typist.

Maud hung her hat on the peg on the back of the door, sat at
the desk and removed the cover from the typewriter. Her
fingers traced the keys. It couldn't be that difficult. And how
surprised Daisy would be! On more than one occasion she had
suggested to Maud she should learn.

Maud slid into the roller a fresh sheet of paper printed with
the name of the agency at the top and wound it on, as she had
seen Daisy do. She turned the roller until she judged the paper
was in the correct position. Settling herself more comfortably in
the chair, she held her fingers above the keyboard. This would
be fun.

The date had to go at the the top right hand of the paper.
She stared at the round keys. They were a jumble of letters.
Why on earth were they not in alphabetical order? Surely that
would make more sense?

She found the numbers at the top and with a tentative fore-
finger pressed down the one she wanted. A little hammer
moved, but no mark appeared on the paper. There must be
something wrong with the typewriter. Yet the key had moved
when she pressed down. Maud attemped the movement again,
this time watching the key arm carefully. It didn't reach the

page. She wasn't pressing hard enough. No wonder Daisy hammered the keys.

Maud pressed as hard as she could and the number appeared with a messy shadow. Not only that, it had printed on top of the agency's address. She frowned, rolled the sheet of paper a little higher and managed to complete the full date.

Peering at what she had typed, she saw the month of September was in the lower case. How did one get a capital letter? The strange thing was the letters on the keyboard were all in capitals. She sighed, pushed up her sleeves and again set to work.

Before long Maud was feeling more confident. She would now employ both forefingers. But when she did so, the two key arms met mid-air and became entangled. And when she prised the arms apart, ink covered her fingers. With the back of her hand, she brushed away a lock of hair that had come lose from her full pompadour. She sighed. Typing wasn't as easy as Daisy made it look.

Maud leaned back in her chair. She had better ask Daisy to give her a lesson or two, or take a short typist course as Daisy had done before they opened the agency.

A muffled boom penetrated the office. The one o'clock gun, fired from the castle every day, apart from Sunday, Good Friday and Christmas Day.

'Poor Greyfriars Bobby,' she murmured to herself.

The little Skye terrier had guarded his master's grave in Greyfriars Kirkyard for fourteen years until his own death. When the one o'clock gun was fired, he'd leave his post and run to the eating house he used to visit with his owner. He was fed, then he returned to Auld Jock's grave. Maud hoped someone gave him dinner on those days the gun didn't fire.

Good heavens. One o'clock. She rose and snatched her hat from the back of the door. She would need to get a move on if she were to eat luncheon and take the omnibus to be at the church for two o'clock.

The funeral went as all funerals do. Pale people clad in black, the women with veils on their hats to cover their faces, the men in black tails and black waistcoats, removing their top hats as they entered the kirk and guiding their women to a suitable pew. They all prayed and sang hymns chosen by Maud's damp-eyed father, ending with 'Abide with Me'. Maud sat with her brothers and their wives at the front of the church and wept freely when her father delivered the eulogy. What an amazing woman Aunt Sophy had been. Maud had had no idea of her boundless compassion. Sophy had been active in helping the women in the local community to set up a small industry of weaving looms, which had played an important part in modernisation of the Indian village.

On her way to Portobello, Maud had noticed the sky growing steadily more overcast, and now as they prepared to file out of the church a flash of lightning lit up the stained-glass window behind the altar.

Maud took her father's arm and, with the other mourners, they filed out into the gloomy afternoon. They walked slowly behind the glass-sided hearse, pulled by two black horses wearing black ostrich feather plumes that nodded with each sombre step.

At the cemetery Aunt Sophy's coffin was lowered into the open grave and more prayers were said. Just as the minister finished, there was a clap of thunder and Maud's father nodded. 'Her spirit has reached Heaven.'

A few rain drops fell and around them umbrellas were hastily unfurled. Maud had not brought her umbrella, so she drew under the canopy of her father's.

'It always rains when the best people are buried, Maud,' he

said, and she was pleased that the traditional thought gave him comfort.

They spoke briefly to the other mourners, who gradually moved away. As her father showed no inclination to do the same, Maud left him to his grief for a short while. Murmuring that she would be back shortly, she wandered along the path between the graves. Her eye was taken with a towering obelisk. To her surprise, given the grandness of the thing, only a few words were engraved on it. A name, the date of birth and date of death. The man had been only forty years when he'd died that May. At least Aunt Sophy, her father's elder and only sister, had lived to almost twice that age.

The rain became heavy and so Maud hastened back to her father.

'Father, we should go.' She touched his arm. 'Or you may catch a chill.'

They made their way to the road where Carstairs was waiting, the engine of the Rover already running.

'Miss McIntyre,' Carstairs touched his cap.

'Hello, Carstairs.'

'The funeral tea is at the North British Hotel,' Maud's father told her. 'Then we will go with your brothers to the office of Sophy's solicitor, where Mr Dewar will read her will. Can you join me and the rest of the family for dinner and stay the night?'

'Of course, Father.' She kissed the tip of his cold nose, red from the chilly wind off the Firth of Forth and from his sadness. 'Now get into the car quickly. The rain seems to be easing, but this wind blowing off the sea is too cold to stand here any longer.'

Carstairs helped him into the warmth of the car and while he was arranging a blanket over her father's legs, Maud dashed round to the other side and climbed in. Her brown paper parcel lay on the seat, placed there by Carstairs when she had met her father before entering the church. The chauffeur arranged a second rug over her.

They drove west, past the Palace of Holyroodhouse, home of the kings and queens of Scots since the sixteenth century. In Mary's private apartments, her Italian secretary was murdered by her husband Lord Darnley and his friends in front of her eyes. Maud shuddered as she imagined the door of the chamber bursting open and the frightened, pregnant Queen being held at gunpoint, while Rizzio was stabbed to death.

There was a form of justice, as the following year Darnley's house was destroyed by an explosion in the early hours and he was found strangled in a nearby orchard. His death was unsolved. How fascinating it would have been to investigate that case.

Now they were driving through the Palace's Royal Park. At six hundred and fifty acres, Maud knew it was almost twice as big as London's Hyde Park. What's more, she thought, it has crags and lochs, glens and ridges, basalt cliffs and patches of gorse – a wild piece of Highland landscape within Edinburgh. The park's highest peak was Arthur's Seat, which loomed behind The Sheep Heid Inn. The inn where only last month she had telephoned for the police and an ambulance after Douglas Laing's two henchmen had attempted to kill her and Daisy.

The roads grew busier and noisier, with the rumble and clip-clop of horse-drawn carriages, blaring of horns from motor cars and bells ringing on the trams.

Suddenly, Braemar seemed a long way away.

TWENTY-FOUR

The following morning Maud sent a silent prayer of thanks to Aunt Sophy as she drove the smart gold Napier Colonial Tourer through the city on her way back to Braemar. The old lady had bequeathed a sum of money to Maud, requesting she use it in the furtherance of her career. And what could be of more benefit to a detective than a motor car?

To add to her delight, Maud discovered in an Edinburgh horse and carriage repository the perfect vehicle. She'd loved the car her brother Archie had loaned her in the summer – a blue Colonial Tourer – and was disappointed when he reclaimed it on his return from working in Egypt. Now she had a motor car of her own!

The day was wonderful. Bright sunshine and a blue sky with a few fleecy clouds warmed the countryside. She had called in to her apartment and exchanged her funeral garb for a pale blue blouse with small buttons covered in the same fabric and a white lace collar and cuffs, plus a dark blue skirt. Now, with her new boater pinned securely in place, she was swept along by the south-westerly breeze.

Maud flew over the Forth Road Bridge, opened by the

King's father when she was only four years old. Gone were the days when she would have had to take a ferry to cross the water.

It seemed to take no time at all to cover the sixty miles to Dundee. After that, the next city of comparable size was Aberdeen. Once there, she would head west to Braemar. No road cut straight through the Grampian Mountains, so she would need to take a similar route to the train.

As she sped along, the scenery seemed like an endless delightful panorama. Green fields stretched away on each side of the road, hills to her left, and on her right the grey and sparkling North Sea.

After Aberdeen the road took her away from the sea and the landscape changed as the road gently climbed into the mountains. Now there were woods, and the water she glimpsed was the blue ribbon of the Dee. When she came to the village of Banchory, Maud stopped for a cup of tea and a pie at a little hotel. Then on again. Bridge of Potarch, Kincardine O'Neil, Aboyne. At Dinnet, through the trees, she caught sight of two shining lochs and was tempted to stop and explore them, but she was close to Braemar now, so she drove on. When they had solved the cases there, she told herself, she and Daisy would stop at the lochs on their way back to Edinburgh. The return railway tickets for Daisy would be left unused, but Maud cared not a jot. She smiled. Small castles dotted the landscape, pine woods and sweeping moors. And always the towering mountains of brown and pale purple, like guardians of an enchanted valley.

Maud drove by Cambus o'May and saw the gleaming white suspension bridge over the river, which she remembered from her train journey. Down the hill the motor car swooped towards Ballater. The two gallon can of petrol stored in her boot remained unused and the miles seemed like nothing.

In the midst of all this beauty, Maud realised with a shock that she had almost forgotten about the deaths she and Daisy

were investigating. Mr Bisset shot on the train and Mr McGonagall bludgeoned to death in his cottage. In the first case, she
and Daisy had five possible suspects, although only one of them,
the widow, was strong. In the second case, their two suspects
were a father and son.

She drove cautiously through the busy little village of
Ballater and felt the Napier labour as it climbed the steep hill
out the other side. Sweeping round a curve on the gloriously
empty road, she passed through a forest and out again into the
bright sunshine.

What was the connection between the two cases? Maud felt
sure there was one, but it stayed frustratingly at the edge of her
brain. No flash of insight came with the burst of sunlight.

'Come in, Maud, and quickly!' Daisy pulled her into her room
at the Braemar Arms as soon as she knocked on the door.

'What is it? What has happened?'

'Sit down and I'll tell you.' Daisy pointed to the floral
armchair before sitting on the dressing table stool to face Maud.
Her face was glowing with news.

'I was coming out of the post office – they have some bonnie
picture postcards if you wanted to buy one and they're a lot
nicer than that McGonagall's drawings – when Mr Wallace
walked past. Then came a woman who looked like she was hot
on his heels. And it wasna Mrs Wallace.'

Maud nodded for Daisy to continue.

'So I stepped back and waited inside, leaving the door a wee
bit open, and pretended to be fascinated by a display of knitting
wool. "Mrs Bisset," said Mr Wallace.'

'Mrs Bisset?' said Maud. 'What did she want?'

'I'm coming to it. He said, "Mrs Bisset" in a wary sort of
voice and went to walk on. But she put her hand on his arm to
stop him.

'"Mr Wallace," she hissed. "I want to talk to you. Where can we go to be alone?"'

'Good grief,' Maud said.

'Then,' went on Daisy, clearly enjoying herself, 'Mr Wallace said, "I don't know of anywhere," and he removed her hand.' Daisy mimicked the action and continued in a fair imitation of Mr Wallace's Highland accent. '"I'm in a hurry."

'"You're not," Mrs B said in a playful sort of way. "There's no need to be shy with me."

'"You are mistaken, Mrs Bisset. I have a hotel to run. And please stop approaching me in this way."'

Daisy paused in her account and looked at Maud. 'What do you think of that?'

'It would seem that Mrs Bisset is labouring under some delusion and that her feelings for Mr Wallace are not reciprocated.'

'Aye, me too. I mean I think the same, not that I have my eye on Mr Wallace.' Daisy smiled. 'It looks like she's after some sculdudrie.'

Was she really planning to win his heart? It wouldn't be sexual misconduct on Mrs Bisset's part as her husband was dead, but it would be by Mr Wallace, whose wife was very much alive.

'What happened next?'

'He walked away and she stood on the pavement staring after him. I noticed the postmistress was glaring across the counter at me, so I decided I'd best leave. Mrs Bisset was still standing outside, so I wished her good day. She spun round, looking awfa surprised as well she might, and pulled her coat around her, like this.' Daisy mimed the action. '"I was out for a walk, but it's such a grey day that I shall return home," she said to me. That sounds like a guilty conscience, explaining herself to an almost complete stranger.'

'Indeed.'

'Then she turned and went off towards her house. That's the end of that story.' Daisy folded her arms across her chest, to indicate that she had finished her report on Mrs Bisset's mysterious behaviour.

'We know from her comment over tea the other day that she believes she has a youthful appearance and that men admire her.'

What would Dr Sigmund Freud make of the woman, Maud wondered. Not applying his more outlandish theories, Maud thought, but those dealing with personality and the mind. It seemed the method he used was to ask his patient to lie back on a couch so that he or she were comfortable and then he would tell them to talk freely about whatever popped into their head. Whatever was in poor Mrs Bisset's head?

Maud realised Daisy was still looking at her. 'You said that was the end of that story. Is there another you wish to tell me, Daisy?'

'Aye.' Daisy paused for maximum effect. She dropped her arms. 'The news in the village this afternoon is that Lilias Bisset and Conrad Elliot have eloped!'

'Oh dear.' Maud sighed. 'Mr Elliot's disappearance will no doubt confirm the policeman's and the villagers' belief in the young man's guilt.'

'Perhaps we should visit Mrs Bisset to see if the gossip is true.'

Maud glanced at her wristwatch. 'It's tea time.' She got to her feet. 'We'll visit her now.'

Daisy rose, her face alight with the thrill of the chase. Although not exactly a chase, thought Maud, but another step in their investigation.

'I also went to the public library when you were away, to see what I could find on artists in the seventeenth century.' Daisy pinned her hat into place.

'Did you discover anything?'

'Aye. We ken that turpentine is used to clean oil paint from brushes and palettes...'

Maud nodded.

'Well, it can be added to the paint to speed up the drying time...'

Maud nodded again.

'And linseed oil can be added to oil paint to make it flow better.'

Maud smiled. 'This is exactly what we need to know, Daisy.'

'You have to get the amounts right, though, as too much linseed oil means the painting takes longer to dry.'

'So it's quite a balancing act.'

It was Daisy's turn to nod. 'And...'

'There's more?'

'Varnish is used to seal oil paintings when they are finished,' Daisy concluded with a broad smile, as she pulled on her gloves.

'Well done, Daisy!'

Her friend paused. 'Och, I'm sorry, I havena asked about your aunty's funeral yet, Maud. How was it?'

'I'll tell you on the way.'

'And was there a good spread at the purvey?'

Maud allowed herself a small smile at Daisy's wish to know about the food at the funeral tea. 'Yes, the North British did a fine table.'

The circular Palm Court had been a treat, too, with its pillars and exotic palm trees, idyllic rural scenes painted on the walls and the cupola that allowed natural light to bathe all below. The harpist in the minstrels' gallery had played a selection of works by Vivaldi – her aunt's favourite composer, Maud's father had told her.

As they hastened along the road, Maud recounted the main points of her trip south: how her father was, Aunt Sophy's bequest to her—

'You have your *own motor car*?' Daisy stopped dead in astonishment on the pavement.

Maud took hold of Daisy's arm to hurry her along. 'I have.' She smiled. 'She's a beauty; a gold Colonial Tourer.'

'That was yours parked in front of the hotel just now?'

Maud beamed. 'So you noticed it.'

'I couldna help but notice it.'

'Aunt Sophy left me money and requested I use it in a way to benefit my career.'

'And you were able to buy the motor car just like that? I mean, you didna have to wait for it to be made?'

'It was available straight away due to a cancelled order. When Mr Dewar, my aunt's solicitor, knew the situation, he let me draw on the funds immediately.' She paused, then went on, 'And, Daisy, I also have learned something of interest to our Bisset case.'

Her friend sent her a questioning glance.

'A gentleman recently bought from Mr Mutrie's a costume that fits exactly the description of the clothes worn by the Bridge of Gairn man.'

'You're telling me that someone travelled from here down to Edinburgh to buy workman's clothes? He could have bought them in the general store in the village.'

'From that we might reasonably conclude that he didn't want anyone here to see him purchasing the items. The buyer was most particular. He wanted the trousers already with brown paint stains. So the wearer would look as though he had worn them, and worked in them, for some time.'

Daisy frowned. 'A real painter and decorator wouldna do that. And nor would he buy from Mutrie's shop.'

'Our killer knows Edinburgh well, then...'

'The chances are it's one of Andersons?'

Maud nodded. 'Here's Woodend.' She and Daisy turned into the driveway of the house. 'We can tell Mrs Bisset we were just passing and thought how pleasant it would be to renew our acquaintance.'

'Aye, right, very pleasant.' Daisy rang the doorbell.

The surly maid showed them into the drawing room, where they found Mrs Bisset standing in the middle of the floor, almost in hysterics.

'A telegram from Lilias,' she cried, waving the buff-coloured piece of paper. 'She and that soldier are married! In Edinburgh! She's ruined us!'

Braemar post office obviously had no teleprinter. Maud could see the message must have been dictated over the telephone wire because it was written by hand.

Mrs Bisset staggered across the room and collapsed onto a chair, opening and shutting her mouth but making only strange little sounds.

Maud opened the drawing room door and called to the maid. 'Alice, bring your mistress a glass of water.'

Daisy snatched up a copy of American *Vogue* from a side table and was fanning Mrs Bisset with the magazine.

'Such a thing, Miss McIntyre... how could she do this to me... wasting herself on a mere subaltern.'

The maid dashed in with the water and Mrs Bisset grabbed the glass. She drank half of it so quickly that she began to hiccup.

Daisy dropped the magazine onto the table and thumped her on the back. The shock caused Mrs Bisset to gasp. Maud dismissed the maid as the hiccups subsided.

'Now then, Mrs Bisset,' Maud said firmly, 'you must pull yourself together. Sit quietly for a moment and consider that the two of them are married. It could have been a lot worse.'

She fixed Maud with a gimlet eye. 'My daughter would never do what you are suggesting. She was not brought up that way.'

'Of course.' The woman would never hear from her,

thought Maud, what Lilias had all but told her of what they got
up to in the heather. Nor did she say that a farmer's daughter
and a young soldier with prospects was not such a bad match.
She went on, 'They must be very much in love, you know, and
that is the important thing.'

Mrs Bisset snorted. 'Lilias has disgraced the family. I shall
never be able to lift my head in social circles again.'

'If you share in the work of the parish, as Mrs Wallace
suggested, and sit on committees and suchlike, you will gradually establish your own reputation as a woman of worth.'

Mrs Bisset shook her head. 'Nothing has worked out here as
we'd expected.'

That was certainly true.

'Hand me that needlework, would you?' she said to Daisy.

Daisy looked as taken aback as Maud by the woman's
sudden change of conversation and the manner in which she
addressed Daisy. Daisy stared at Mrs Bisset for a moment
before looking round the room for the needlework.

'There.' The woman gestured irritably to the low table by
her side.

Really, she could have easily reached it herself.

Mrs Bisset took the needlework from Daisy, bent her head
and began to stitch.

Daisy raised her eyebrows, and Maud indicated to her
friend they should each take a seat.

'I couldn't believe it when I heard that soldier was in the
village.' Mrs Bisset pushed the needle sharply into the fabric.
'Lilias knew neither her father nor I wanted any low-bred
soldier courting her. You know the sort of life a young man leads
in the Army.'

Actually, Maud didn't.

'He'd be better with a girl more *suited* to his class,' Mrs
Bisset went on, stitching violently.

Maud watched, certain she would soon draw blood.

'Of course, I know some perfectly respectable Army men; Colonels and – what is the rank above that? Captains.'

She clearly didn't know any Army men, for if she did, she would not have placed their ranks in the wrong order.

'But a mere subaltern...' She glanced up at Maud and grimaced, her needle poised.

Maud assumed an interested look. Encouraged, Mrs Bisset continued.

'Her father wanted a quiet place to live to begin with, saying when we had found our feet amongst the landed gentry, we would move on and buy a much bigger house in a smarter part of the country. In a year or two he intended to take Lilias to Edinburgh so that she could meet all the right people, but until then she was to get used to living here.' Mrs Bisset lowered her needlework. 'I understand that you are from Edinburgh, Miss McIntyre. You must know all the best people.'

'I'm not sure that I do.'

'No?' She lost interest in Maud as quickly as she had found it, and she shrugged. 'And now,' she went on bitterly, 'that soldier will be very lucky. Under the terms of her father's will, she will receive a substantial annuity.'

'Then she didna need to marry,' Daisy murmured.

Mrs Bisset sent her a sharp look. 'She needs to marry. How else will she have a baby?'

To Maud's relief, Daisy wisely forbore to comment on this.

Mrs Bisset sent Maud a pitying glance. 'You are not married, Miss McIntyre?'

Maud couldn't dispute it. 'I've never considered marrying.'

'I suppose I will have to remain here until the lease expires. Thank goodness it is only for three years.' Mrs Bisset sighed. 'But three years when I am in my prime. People are so envious of me, you know. I'm in my forties and look in my thirties.'

Maud stifled a gasp. Mrs Bisset was not unattractive, with her fair hair only just fading to white, and her pale blue eyes, but that she looked in her thirties was only in her imagination. Maud wasn't even sure the woman was still in her forties.

Her head bent over the stitching, Mrs Bisset continued as if Maud and Daisy were not there. 'Even if there are a few years difference in our ages, it really doesn't matter. I would make the right sort of wife to guide him and persuade him to give up running a dull little country hotel in favour of one of the better-class establishments in Edinburgh.'

Maud sent Daisy a glance. They didn't need Mrs Bisset to tell them of whom she spoke. It was clear that she wanted more than to be the chief lady of the village and that Mr Wallace was to be the stepping stone to the life she desired.

Realising she had spoken her thoughts aloud, Mrs Bisset looked up quickly. 'Thank you for calling, Miss McIntyre.' She gave a nod in Daisy's direction. 'I'm afraid I cannot offer you tea, but I am busy, as you see.'

She sent them a hostile glance and rose to summon the maid to show them out.

Mrs Bisset was certainly an unhappy woman, Maud thought, but was there more to her reaction than that?

TWENTY-FIVE

'I don't think I could have stayed another moment in her company,' said Maud, as she and Daisy made their way back down the drive. 'The woman is abominable.'

'She's an awfa silly wifie, that's for sure.'

'Good for her daughter and the soldier for doing what they wanted to do.'

'You dinna think he married her for the money, do you?'

'No, I don't. Their relationship started when they were in Inverness and her father still alive. She's an only child and so it's reasonable to assume she'll benefit financially on the death of both her parents, but that could be years away. I do believe she and Mr Elliot are in love.'

'And you dinna think he arranged to have Mr Bisset killed to get his hands on some money sooner rather than later, and that the elopement was a convenient excuse to get away from here?'

'It's possible, of course, but the letter I saw in his knapsack from Lilias in which she mentioned eloping was dated before Bisset's death.'

'What about Miss Bisset herself then? Did she arrange to kill her faither?'

'I don't think that's what happened. No, my opinion is the same. They are star-crossed lovers, but I don't believe they had any thoughts of murder locked away in some dark place of their hearts.'

'So we can take Lilias and Conrad off our list of suspects?' They reached the end of the drive and turned left towards the high street. 'That leaves the widow, the hotelier and the gardener.'

'I'm not convinced it's any of them.' Maud frowned. 'This case is proving hard.'

'But nae beyond our capabilities, Maud.'

'I sincerely hope not. What we need, Daisy, is for something to break.'

Daisy slipped her arm through Maud's and skipped a step to match Maud's stride. She grinned.

'Perhaps what'll break is your will to live. You've got the bairns' poetry reading to judge tomorrow, remember.'

The ordeal was over. As she hastened out of the school door after the recitations, Maud heard the children's voices coming from the room she had just left. They were singing in Gaelic at the top of their high-pitched voices, something that sounded like *brochan lom*, repeated quite a few times, to a jolly tune. No doubt they were as relieved as she was that the poetry competition had ended.

Maud made her way down the brae to the hotel in dire need of a cup of tea. Twenty repetitions of the poem rang in her head, although one small boy's rendition stood above the others. He'd stomped to the front of the class, folded his arms and scowled at his classmates. 'You've-hurt-your finger-Puir-wee-man-Your-pinkie-Deary-me-Noo-juist-you-haud-it-that-wey-till-I-get-my-specs-and-see.'

She'd been impressed that the little laddie had crowded the entire verse into a single breath. And that he'd gone on to dispense with the remaining three verses in the same manner. But Maud knew a recitation should not be judged on speed of delivery and so the book prize was awarded to wee sandy-haired Moilidh Macdonald.

Now, as Maud's steps took her towards that restorative cup of tea, she thought again of the session's conclusion. The class teacher had enjoined the youngsters to recite The Ten Commandments. Maud smiled bravely as the classroom worked their way through. They reached the seventh one.

'Thou shalt not admit adultery,' came a voice through the chorus of the others.

Maud blinked and shot a glance at Miss Dickson. The teacher's smile faltered a little, but picked up again.

The misrendering of the Seventh Commandment had sparked a notion in Maud's brain. What if Mrs Bisset and Mr Wallace were already having an affair and he was complicit in Mr Bisset's death? Perhaps the hotelier's apparent animosity towards Mrs Bisset, and that brief encounter outside the post office, was nothing more than a show, designed to put her and Daisy off the scent? But why would they risk it?

No, surely the idea was complete madness...

TWENTY-SIX

'I have a theory,' Maud said to Daisy, as she entered her friend's bedchamber after the poetry recitation.

Daisy grinned. 'About the puir wee finger?'

'No.'

'About the Bisset murder or the artist's murder then?'

Maud wanted to say both, but that wouldn't be true. 'Bisset.'

'It's a start,' said Daisy.

'But let's go down to the parlour first. I'm longing for a cup of tea.'

They descended the stairs and made themselves comfortable in the quiet little parlour. Most of the hotel guests were genuine tourists and spent the majority of their time out visiting places.

Their order for tea placed, Maud began. 'Is it possible that, before you overheard their conversation, either Mrs Bisset or Mr Wallace could have seen you enter the post office?'

Daisy wrinkled her nose. 'It's possible, but I didna notice them before I went in.'

'Could they have seen you about to come out of the shop?'

Daisy thought again. 'They might have. But I'd barely opened the door when they stopped outside.'

'It's the stopped outside bit that concerns me.'

Daisy drew her brows together. 'You think it might have been staged for me?'

'Yes, perhaps.'

'And if it had been, what is your theory?'

'That Mrs Bisset and Mr Wallace are actually having an affair, rather than simply Mrs Bisset planning to have one, and that the two of them acted together to kill Mr Bisset. I doubt they both murdered him, so Mr Wallace could have been the one to shoot him on the train, with Mrs Bisset's prior approval. That would make him guilty of murder and her guilty art and part, being an accessory before the murder.'

The parlour door opened and a waitress entered carrying their tea tray.

As soon as the young woman had gone, Maud said eagerly to Daisy, 'What do you think of my theory?'

'I think it's nae likely.'

'Which part do you think not likely?'

'All of it, Maud. Unless Mr Wallace is an awfa good actor, I'd say he wanted naething to do with the woman. And not only that, we have spent some time with him and neither of us has seriously thought he'd murder Bisset just because he threw the fellow out of the hotel.'

'But if you throw an affair into the mix, isn't it at least possible?'

Daisy thought for a moment. She looked at Maud and shook her head.

'Fair enough, Daisy. Have you any theories?'

'I'm beginning to think we're barking up the wrong tree.'

'That it's none of our suspects?'

Daisy nodded, as she picked up the teapot and poured two

cups. Maud sighed and took the cup Daisy handed her. 'Let's go through the list again and see what we have.' She added a little milk, took a sip of the invigorating liquid and replaced the cup and saucer on the table.

'We have – or had – five suspects in the Bisset case.' Maud looked around, satisfied herself there was no one else in the room, and continued. 'Firstly, Mrs Bisset. Motive. She disliked, probably even hated, her husband. Further, she fancies herself in love with Mr Wallace and, despite his apparent reaction, seems to believe he is in love with her. Now let's look at the means. Did she have a gun? She's a farmer's wife, so she – or Mr Bisset himself – may well have had one and, as you've pointed out, Daisy, she would very likely know how to use it. Opportunity.' Maud paused. 'But unless she travelled down to Edinburgh, went to the theatrical costumers where she bought and later dressed herself in the tradesman's clothing, committed the murder and walked across the fields back to Braemar, I can't see it.'

'Mrs Bisset doesna seem the type to walk fifteen miles across fields,' Daisy agreed. 'And she canna have walked on the road, or someone would have seen her. And what about the workman's clothes? A stranger canna have walked into the village wearing those paint-splattered breeks without someone commenting on it.'

Maud considered. 'The killer could have worn the painter and decorator trousers over their normal clothes.'

'So he would have taken off the disguise and be dressed as he usually was? That makes sense. And also makes it unlikely to be Mrs Bisset. Her skirts would be bunched up under the tradesman breeks and she'd have walked in a strange way when she got off the train at Bridge of Gairn.' Daisy grinned.

Maud smiled. 'Then we are agreed our murderer isn't Mrs Bisset?'

'Aye. At least, nae in person. And we have nae evidence for any sort of conspiracy. Next is Lilias Bisset. Motive would be her love for Conrad Elliot and her faither being dead-set against a marriage. Means.' Daisy shook her head. 'Even if she or her faither had a gun, and like her mither she'd likely be able to shoot, she didna have the opportunity. Miss B was on the same train as us and her faither was on the train coming in from Braemar. Bisset was already deid when you opened the compartment door and he fell out.'

'And by the same token, it can't be Mr Elliot. Being a soldier, he would definitely have access to a gun and be able to use it, but there's the same impossibility of opportunity.'

'Who does that leave us with?' Daisy said.

'Mr Wallace and the gardener Mr Buston. The motive for Mr Wallace could be his wish for Mrs Bisset to be free—'

Daisy snorted.

'But there's the problem of his own wife,' Maud went on.

Daisy raised an eyebrow. 'Maybe he's intending to murder her next.'

Maud passed over that comment. 'Mr Wallace may well have the means. A gun might be a useful item for a hotelier to own.'

'So he can shoot guests who don't pay their bills?'

Daisy's comments were getting ever more frivolous.

'I mean,' said Maud in a stern voice, 'to scare off intruders.'

'Like he did when Miss Lilias Bisset came back for the second stuffed bird?'

Daisy had a point. Mr Wallace hadn't mentioned owning a gun at all. But then he wouldn't have one, if he had left it on the floor of the railway compartment at Bridge of Gairn.

'As to opportunity,' Maud added, 'it must be difficult for a hotelier to leave his place of business for a period of time long enough to travel to Edinburgh to buy the disguise. Not to mention that he has no facial hair, never mind light-coloured whiskers.'

'We both ken that whiskers can be stuck on and look real enough.'

Maud knew that Daisy was referring to their clergymen disguise when they worked on the case of the stolen letters. 'True.'

'And Mr Wallace would also have needed to get away from the hotel while he carried out the murder. You'd think his wife would have noticed his absence. Unless,' said Daisy, 'you think the pair of them were in it together?'

'No.' Maud sighed. 'So it must be Mr Buston then? But all he had against Bisset was an unpaid bill for his gardening work and the humiliating way he'd been treated by the fellow. It hardly seems enough of a motive for murder.'

'People have nae doubt killed for less.'

Had they? One case came immediately to Maud's mind: that of the Dalkeith poisoner. Only some months earlier, a few miles south-east of Edinburgh, at a family party a young man had put arsenic in the coffee pot. Two men had died and most of the other sixteen guests were severely affected. That one of his victims was his father was a happy chance for the deeply in debt young man. He was prepared to kill all those at the party to achieve his aim of both profiting from his father's insurance money and obtaining his inheritance.

'Then Bisset's murderer must be *The Invisible Man*,' Daisy said in exasperation.

'A nice idea, but Mr H.G. Wells's invisible man wouldn't have needed any disguise to kill Mr Bisset. He could simply have removed his bandages and committed the crime au naturel.'

'Now there's a thought.'

'And one I'd rather not have.'

'So,' said Daisy, 'Mr Buston might have had motive,

but... just a minute. With Bisset deid, there was nae chance he'd get his money.'

'Unless he thought the widow would pay.'

'Does she seem the type?'

'Probably not.'

'What about means and opportunity?' went on Daisy. 'Wouldna it have been easier for him to dunt old Bisset on the heid with a spade?'

'Then it might be obvious it was the gardener who did it.'

Daisy shook her head. 'I canna see Mr Buston doing everything we've already agreed would be necessary to kill Bisset. The trip to Edinburgh and such like. If he could afford the train ticket, why would he be bothered about the money old Bisset owed him?'

'It might be the principle.'

'That's an expensive principle. If we dinna accept it was the invisible man, then who was it?'

'I don't know – yet.' Maud refused to be beaten. 'Shall we move on to consider Mr McGonagall's murder?'

Daisy huffed. 'Why not?'

Maud wouldn't let herself be sidetracked by Daisy's obvious dismay at their lack of progress. 'We are agreed that the most likely suspects in this case are the Andersons, senior and junior?'

'Aye.'

'Using the same approach as we have just employed in the Bisset case' – Maud paused for Daisy to finish groaning – 'Mr Anderson the elder stays in Edinburgh and so would have easy access to Mr Mutrie's theatrical outfitters. He comes up to Braemar once a month and his movements might not be of as much interest as those of a stranger to the village. Do you agree so far?'

Daisy nodded.

Maud went on. 'He would be concerned that his son's repu-

tation in the art world, and by extension his own, would be
ruined if it got out that David Anderson—'

'Was paying for paintings knowing they were forged.'

'Worse,' Maud said, 'in that that he was probably commis-
sioning Mr McGonagall to produce the fakes. This means that
the older Mr Anderson had motive, means and opportunity. I
suspect that either he spoke to the artist in an attempt to end the
arrangement, or that David Anderson tried to pull out of whatever agreement he had with McGonagall. And that Mr McGonagall retaliated by trying to blackmail—'

'Pay up or he would go to the police?'

Maud nodded and took a gulp of her tea.

'But if the artist did report him to the police, then McGonagall himself would be charged with forgery,' Daisy pointed out.

'It seems more likely that it was David Anderson who
visited the artist, and that the artist threatened to tell David's
father and demanded money for his silence.'

'Then the killer is David Anderson?'

'Mr McGonagall made it clear to us that he wanted to live
in Paris. The money he received for the fakes would have made
a useful contribution to his travel fund, but not give him enough
to live the life he wanted when he got there.'

'Not if he carried on putting away the drink, it couldna.'

Maud put down her cup and saucer. 'Once he'd realised
how much more he could make from blackmail...'

Daisy had brightened considerably at the prospect of
solving at least this case. 'David Anderson goes down to visit his
faither from time to time, and the gallery here doesna have
regular opening hours, so his presence wouldna be missed in the
village. I canna think the two men are in it together, though.'

'I agree. Mr Anderson senior seems a decent sort, although
that's just the impression I've formed.'

'Impression is as good as anything, since we have naething
else but our brains. Pale whiskers and paint-splashed breeks are

nae much to go on, I ken, but it fits the description given by the stationmaster at Bridge of Gairn.' Daisy smiled. 'It's Mr Anderson the younger all right.'

Maud picked up her cup and finished her tea. 'It feels as if we are getting somewhere at last.'

TWENTY-SEVEN

On Saturday night, Maud and Daisy walked up the path to the village hall, a pretty little building painted in green and white. Two questions were on their minds: could they prove it was David Anderson who had murdered Mr McGonagall, and who had killed Mr Bisset? They had only three days left of the fortnight Maud had allowed to solve the Braemar case. Cases, as it turned out.

She opened the door. A rush of hot air hit her face and a cacophony of sounds greeted her ears as they entered the brightly lit hall. A trio consisting of fiddle, accordion and bodhrán was playing a lively tune on the stage, and in the centre of the room people spun round in the Gay Gordons.

People, tables and mugs of beer seemed to be everywhere. Maud was glad she had saved for the occasion her lilac silk gown with sleeves to the elbow, over a cream blouse with a high lacy collar. She had exchanged her sturdy boots for the ivory kid-leather shoes with straps across them. Daisy had also kept her favourite costume for the ceilidh, a rich brown silk dress with cream facings and cuffs.

'I canna wait to dance,' Daisy said excitedly, her eyes shining, as she gazed round the hall. 'Who can I get to ask me?'

Maud smiled at Daisy's enthusiasm as they made their way to an empty table and took seats. A few of the better-off men were wearing kilts, but other than that everyone was wearing their Sunday best. Suits with waistcoats for the men, their faces already red in the heat, and simple cotton dresses with bright sashes at the waist for the women. There wasn't a hat in sight.

Maud removed her straw hat with its pink ribbon and placed it on the table. Daisy did likewise. Maud felt a little self-conscious at the two of them sitting there alone. She also noticed that theirs was the only table not covered with mugs of beer.

'Where do we find the wine, do you think?' she shouted at Daisy above the hubbub.

At that moment, the music came to an end and Maud held her breath, waiting for all eyes to turn to her. But the good-natured clamour of voices was almost as loud as the band had been.

'Looks like nae wine,' Daisy shouted back. 'The beer is over there.' She nodded to a row of kegs on a trestle table standing against one wall. 'Shall I get us some?'

'Would you?' Maud wasn't sure she would like the taste, but she needed something on the table to avoid looking like a sourpuss.

Daisy pushed back her chair and gamely elbowed her way through the folk milling about on the edge of the dance floor, waiting for the band to strike up again.

A man with his sleeves rolled up to the elbows and his shirt open at the neck stood near one of the barrels. He turned and helped Daisy with the tap on the keg, filling two mugs for her. He said something to her and she gestured to where Maud was seated. He looked over and gave a smile of recognition.

It was the young man who'd given her a lift to the start of

her Callater walk. Maud returned his smile. What was his
name? Something to do with a poet, or perhaps poetry. He was
making his way over to her, carrying the mugs for Daisy.

Rabbie, that was it! Like the poet, Rabbie Burns. Only he
was Rabbie Geddes.

'Hello again, Miss McIntyre.' He gave her a broad grin.
'Nice to see you and your friend Miss Cameron at our ceilidh.'

'You couldna keep us away.' Daisy winked at him and
laughed.

Goodness, the girl hadn't even drunk any alcohol yet.

'Do please join us for a moment if you have time, Mr
Geddes,' Maud said.

'Thank you.' He held Daisy's chair for her as she resumed
her seat and then took one for himself.

'Are you here with a friend?' Daisy gave him a look of innocent enquiry.

'Just my wee sister, Shona. She's over there.'

Daisy gave a satisfied nod. Maud followed his gaze and saw
a little girl she recognised from the school poetry recital. Shona
was chatting with a group of other girls at another table and
drinking what Maud assumed was lemonade.

The band was preparing for another dance. 'Ladies, take
your partners for the Eightsome Reel. Yes, that's right,' called
the fiddler, 'it's a ladies' dance.'

Before Mr Geddes could say a word, Daisy jumped to her
feet and held out her hand. 'My dance, I believe?' She grinned.

He smiled, took her hand and placed it on his arm, and they
joined the other couples on the floor. Maud watched as circles of
eight were formed effortlessly. The band struck up a strathspey
reel and with loud whoops the dancers were off. Hands were
joined and circles danced, first one way and then the other; they
formed cartwheels with their hands, set to their partners, went
hand in hand in a great chain, linked arms and twirled, and took it

in turns to enter the middle of the circle. As far as Maud could tell, the purpose of the reel as it was danced here was for each man to swing his partner so wildly that she had difficulty keeping her feet.

Through the mass of dancers, Maud saw Daisy's red head bobbing up and down. Hers wasn't the only red head in the hall, but it was the most active. She was laughing and twirling, determined to stay upright as she hung on to Rabbie Geddes's muscular arms. A great roar went up whenever some unfortunate female spun across the floor. But it was all good natured and there was no shortage of men vying to give the sliding woman a hand up.

By the time the reel had come to an end, Daisy's face was as red as her hair. Mr Geddes returned her to the table and she dropped into the chair.

'Would you do me the honour of the next dance?' he asked Maud.

She hesitated. The same dances in Edinburgh were performed a lot more stately than here. Imagine if she lost her footing and flew across the floor!

'We can wait for a Military Two Step, if you would prefer,' he added, sensing her unease.

'That would be very pleasant, Mr Geddes. Thank you.'

He left, promising to return later for the two-step.

Daisy fanned herself with her hand. 'They dance much better up here than in the city.'

'It's certainly different,' Maud admitted. She took a sip from her mug of beer. This was different too. It had a rather strange, peaty taste. The musicians had begun to play a foot-tapping little number that was new to her.

'I don't know this one,' she said to Daisy. 'What is it?'

She continued to fan herself. 'Nae idea.'

'Ladies and gentleman,' called the man playing the squeeze-box, 'we are going to do a couple of new dances tonight. The music is known as ragtime and it's very popular in the United States. I'll talk you through each one.'

Almost immediately the floor filled with people eager to try a new dance.

'This is the Bunny Hug,' the musician called out.

Following the man's instructions, the dancers began to behave in a most extraordinary manner. Maud watched in astonishment. The couples faced forward, cheek pressed to cheek, their arms around each other's neck, doing a sort of hopping dance with their bottoms sticking out.

'It's not exactly elegant,' she remarked to Daisy.

But Maud couldn't stop her foot tapping. She took another tentative sip of beer.

The dance finished and another lively tune began. She was beginning to enjoy the evening.

The next moment, she was aware of a tall, kilted gentleman standing by their table.

'Good evening, Miss McIntyre.'

His deep voice was very familiar. Slowly, Maud's gaze travelled up from his black brogues with their buckle, the silver skean dhu tucked into the top of one long sock, a pair of strong legs, the blue and green tartan of his kilt, the sporran, doublet with silver buttons, white shirt, black bow-tie... and a warm smile on his handsome face.

'Lord Urquhart,' she said, accepting the inevitable.

'I thought it must be you sitting here when I saw Miss Cameron dancing with a young gentleman.' He turned and bowed to Daisy, who giggled. 'How delightful to find you both here and how charming you both look.'

'Did you bring the King?' asked Daisy, her face glowing as she cast her gaze about the room.

'Alas, no. His Majesty was unable to attend.'

'Or any of the royal family?' Daisy continued, looking hopeful.

He shook his head. 'I've no doubt they would be here if it had been possible.'

Daisy sighed.

Maud was still a little stunned by Lord Urquhart's Highland evening wear. 'I wonder you are not also wearing a Highland bonnet, Lord Urquhart,' she found herself saying.

The smile fell from his face. 'Highland bonnets are not for indoors.'

'No,' she muttered.

'I was about to ask if either of you ladies would like to dance, but perhaps I am not suitably dressed for you, Miss McIntyre.'

He turned to Daisy and held out his hand. 'Miss Cameron?'

Maud sat there feeling like a complete fool, her face as red as Daisy's had been a short while ago. What had made her say such a ridiculous thing? For goodness' sake, she knew that Highland bonnets were never worn indoors. She took a couple of deep breaths; she must compose herself before he and Daisy returned to the table.

Mr and Mrs Wallace danced past and gave her a cheery wave.

Barely had the music ended when Mr Wallace approached and asked her for the next dance. With gratitude – for she was dreading the embarrassment of having to converse with Lord Urquhart – Maud accepted the hotelier's hand and was relieved to find the dance was a sober waltz.

'I wanted to thank you again for finding my stolen birds,' he said, as they danced. 'Miss Bisset arranged for the return of the merlin yesterday.'

If only she could solve the other crimes so easily, Maud thought.

'The village is awash with talk of the elopement. I can't say I'm sorry to see the back of that girl,' Mr Wallace continued. 'The family have been nothing but trouble since they took

Woodend. With the girl as well as Bisset gone, I don't expect the
wife will stay on until the lease expires.'

It didn't seem as though the hotelier had any fond feelings
for Mrs Bisset.

'Sorry, Miss McIntyre, I realise that sounds harsh, but the
woman has been plaguing me almost since they moved here.'

'Oh, in what way?' Maud asked, her tone innocent, as he
guided her expertly around the floor.

'She has got a notion into her head that I am fond of her – in
a romantic sort of way, you understand.'

'How mortifying for you.' A thought came to Maud. 'And
for your wife. Does Mrs Wallace know of this?'

He gave a chuckle. 'Oh yes. Naturally, I told her – I
couldn't have anyone else noticing Mrs Bisset's behaviour and
informing my wife – and she thought it most amusing. Not
making fun of Mrs Bisset, you understand, but tickled that I
might still be thought handsome enough to be a good catch.'

Maud was relieved that Mrs Wallace was aware. For a
moment, she had wondered if Lilias Bisset could have tried to
extort money from the hotelier for her elopement. Not that it
would have given him a stronger motive for murdering Mr
Bisset.

When Mr Wallace escorted Maud back to her table, it was
empty. Daisy was nowhere to be seen. Then Maud noticed,
through the mass of men, women and children, Daisy chatting
to the dominie Mr Shepherd at another table.

She glanced around to see who else she recognised. Mr
Buston the gardener was there, talking to a group of men of his
own age, beer mugs in hand. David Anderson, in a blue and red
tartan, was in a set of six dancing with Rose. Maud resolved to
speak to the girl as soon as the Dashing White Sergeant ended.

Lord Urquhart was also on the floor, partnered with the
young woman Maud had last seen sitting astride a runaway pig
and now looking very pretty in a lemon dress with a pale sash.

But it was Lord Urquhart Maud could not keep her eyes from. To her surprise, he danced with both enthusiasm and grace. And the swing of his kilt as he performed the reel of three was quite... delightful.

The dance ended, and with a start Maud realised that Rose was no longer to be seen. The musicians began to play a Military Two Step and, as good as his word, Rabbie Geddes reappeared to claim her for the dance. Chiding herself for taking her eyes off Rose and missing an opportunity to speak to her, Maud accompanied Mr Geddes onto the floor.

'Did you enjoy your walk to Loch Callater, Miss McIntyre?' he asked, as they danced in couples round the edge of the floor.

Maud smiled. 'I did, thank you. It was kind of you to give me a lift.'

'Och, it was no trouble at all. Sorry,' he added, as they failed to turn in time and almost bumped into the next couple. 'I'm happy to help anyone. It was only, what, three days earlier, on the day that awful Bisset was found dead, that I gave a hurl to Mr Anderson,' Rabbie Geddes went on conversationally.

'Mr Anderson?' Maud tried to subdue the fluttering in her stomach to speak casually. 'Which one?'

'The younger one.' He twirled her under his upraised arm.

And was David Anderson wearing painter and decorator's clothing? she wanted to ask, but that would have sounded strange. Then she could not speak, for she and the other women were twirled by their partners.

As soon as they were back in pairs and dancing around the room in a large circle, she asked in an idle sort of way, 'Mr Anderson had been out to enjoy a walk?'

Rabbie Geddes laughed. 'I don't think I'd use the word enjoy. I picked him up at the Brig o' Dee. It's only three miles outside the village, but he looked worn out, and he must have forgotten he'd have to walk back.'

David Anderson would certainly look exhausted if he'd had

to walk across country from Bridge of Gairn to the Dee bridge, given he spent his working days sitting in a gallery.

'Perhaps he wasn't suitably dressed for a walk?' Maud asked lightly.

'Aye, that suit he wore couldn't have been too comfortable for rambling in the country.'

He wasn't wearing the paint-splashed trousers. He could have removed them if his usual clothing was underneath, as she had suggested to Daisy, and hidden the other trousers under a hedge on his way back. Perhaps, too, an old thick shirt, if that had blood on it. Would she and Daisy have to search in all the hedgerows over those twelve miles? Oh, if only sheep could talk.

The dance came to an end, and on returning to their table, she found Daisy gone again. How frustrating, when Maud was desperate to tell her friend what she had learned. Her assistant was spending too much time this evening enjoying herself...

'Miss McIntyre?'

It was Lord Urquhart again.

'Would you care to dance?'

Maud hesitated. The trio of musicians were tuning up and had just announced this would be the last dance of the evening before a break for refreshments with a piano accompaniment by the laird and then singing by those who wished to perform.

She noticed that almost everyone had scrambled onto the floor for this final dance, including those children who hadn't yet been whisked home by a parent.

'Take your partner in the position for a waltz,' shouted the caller above the ever-present din in the hall.

A waltz cannot hurt, Maud thought. She accepted and let Lord Urquhart lead her onto the dance floor.

Immediately the dance began, they were instructed to walk backwards and forwards, do some strange little hop kicks and stick out their backsides.

It was too late, she was on the floor, so in for a penny, in for a pound, and off they went.

'This is our second number this evening from across the pond,' called the accordion player, 'and it's called the Turkey Trot.'

'Why doesn't that surprise me,' Maud laughed, as they all strutted up and down.

'I hear there's also the Grizzly Bear,' Lord Urquhart smiled, 'the Duck Waddle—'

'Stop.' Maud laughed. 'It sounds more like a farmyard than a dance floor.'

'You're not far off. As you can see, it's a case of imitating the particular animals.'

Maud wasn't sure she'd ever seen a turkey doing what they were doing. On the other hand, it was fun. Before long, she was glowing nicely and knew she had a large smile on her face.

'Your recent notice in the *Edinburgh Evening News* caught my eye,' he added.

The smile fell from Maud's face as she thought of her new advertisement. *McIntyre for Hire. No Case Too Big or Too Small.* Those words had been suggested by Lord Urquhart when she'd been investigating a case in Edinburgh.

As if he knew what she was thinking, he went on, 'How are your current investigations coming along?'

'Very well, thank you, Lord Urquhart.'

'I'm glad to hear it, Miss McIntyre. I know there's no better private detective in the whole of Scotland.' He shot her a smile. 'When you took on my case, you made it clear you wouldn't let anyone get in your way.'

Had she actually said that? She certainly wouldn't let Lord Urquhart get in her way. She knew how much he liked to... interfere... in the work of her agency.

'That is correct, Lord Urquhart.'

'Please call me Hamish. After doing this silly dance, I think we're past formal address, don't you?'

The music ended on a crescendo and she was spared the necessity of a reply.

When he returned Maud to her table, it was once again empty of Daisy.

'Allow me to bring you a plate of whatever refreshments are on offer,' he said.

She thanked him, and as he went off to collect two plates of food from a newly erected trestle table, she looked around for Daisy.

To enthusiastic applause from the gathering, a distinguished-looking elderly gentleman in Highland evening dress had moved to the piano on the stage. The laird played a beautiful lilting tune which Maud did not know. Some of the women in the hall put their forks aside and sang in Gaelic. It was a sweet sound and touched Maud. She brushed aside a tear. How ridiculous she was behaving over a song. Perhaps it was the evening itself that was having this effect on her: the genuine pleasure she could see on people's faces, whether they were singing, eating, chatting to friends or simply listening to the laird play.

She pulled herself together. She wanted to tell Daisy what she had learned and she hoped her friend had news for her too. Where *was* Daisy?

With a sigh, Maud touched the oval filigree brooch on her high lace collar to ensure it was still in position. She envied the other women in their simple but pretty dresses. She would wear one of those next time; it would be easier to dance in...

Maud stopped this line of thought. There wouldn't be a next time, at least not here in this Highland village with Lord Urquhart.

A thud on the chair beside her indicated Daisy had returned.

'There you are,' Daisy said impatiently, as if it were Maud who'd been away from the table all evening instead of her. 'I have something interesting to tell you.'

'And I you, Daisy.'

Her friend leaned towards Maud's ear. 'I've spoken to Rose—'

'Ah, Miss Cameron, you are also here.'

Maud and Daisy broke apart. She looked at the two plates Lord Urquhart had set on the table. Each held something brown which looked like it had been dropped from a great height. Her stomach turned.

'Stovies!' Daisy said with glee. 'My mither used to make them.'

'I will fetch another plate for myself,' Lord Urquhart said.

'There is no need,' Maud said faintly. 'I find I am not hungry.'

Daisy stared at her. 'You havenae tried it yet.'

'What exactly is it?'

'Tatties, onions and meat stewed together.'

Maud gingerly picked up an oatcake set on the side of the plate and nibbled it. Lord Urquhart laughed and went off to procure a third dish of stovies. Daisy glanced round the hall, where most people were now seated at the tables or standing in groups at the edges of the room and eating from piled-up plates.

'I've been dodging that night porter all evening.' Daisy turned back to Maud and pulled a face. 'Anyway, now his lordship's gone, I can tell you what I've discovered.' She put a large forkful of the mixture into her mouth, savoured it and swallowed. 'Mmm, the dish of the gods.'

That was taking it a bit too far, Maud thought. 'Tell me quickly what Rose said before he returns.'

'Mr Anderson the elder had gone back to Edinburgh, as arranged, on the Wednesday, the day we spoke to him, so he definitely wasna up here on Sunday night when the artist was killed.'

'Or if he was, he didn't go to the family house.' Maud tentatively forked up a tiny amount of stovies.

'Aye, but he would have had to sleep somewhere, and I canna see him dossing down in a steading.'

Neither could Maud. She tried to picture Mr Anderson sleeping in a barn with farm equipment or animals about him and decided that theory was not feasible.

No, the trail was surely leading them to David Anderson.

TWENTY-EIGHT

Maud woke from a deep sleep, sighed and stretched. She lay in the generous bed and smiled to herself. She had enjoyed the whole experience last night. Even the stovies.

Lifting her wristwatch from the nightstand, she looked at the time. Eight o'clock; later than she would have liked. She rose to wash and dress. If she hurried, there was just time for breakfast before church. She was reaching into the wardrobe for her dark blue suit and matching coat when Daisy burst in.

'Maud!' She was breathless from running. 'David Anderson is on his way to the railway station.'

Maud's pulse jumped. 'He must be allowed to catch a train, I suppose.'

'No, he *mustna*. He has a suitcase with him and he seemed awfa agitated.'

Still she sought a reasonable explanation. 'He might simply be going to Edinburgh.'

'Or he might be fleeing.' Daisy's voice was urgent.

She frowned. 'How do you know where he is?'

'Because I've just seen him!'

'What were you doing out so early?'

'I had a wee bit of a sair heid after last night, so I went out for some fresh air. Never mind all these questions,' Daisy said, exasperated. 'You have to make a citizen's arrest!'

'How can I do such a thing? I would need to witness him committing a crime.' Maud's eye fell on the nun's habit, hanging on the rail in the wardrobe. It was tempting, very tempting... 'For that matter, why couldn't you have arrested him?'

'Maud, we both know that a word from a fine lady will always carry more weight with the police than from someone like me. For goodness' sake, hurry. We're wasting time here, while he's getting away.'

David Anderson's running away probably *was* a reasonable explanation. Maud's eye was still on the disguise she had bought in Edinburgh.

Daisy followed her gaze and her thoughts. 'Put that on and follow him.'

Maud hesitated. 'You don't think I'll be damned for wearing it, do you, and especially on a Sunday?'

'God is merciful.' Daisy raised her eyes heavenwards.

'Then, my friend, the game is afoot!'

Maud snatched up the black habit and drew it on over her undergarments. Daisy dug out the other items Maud had bought from Mr Mutrie.

'Here.' She held out the coif and Maud attempted to secure it over her low pompadour. Daisy tutted. 'That's nae use. Sit down. Quick.'

Maud hastened over to the stool at the dressing table and watched Daisy's expert hands hurriedly unpin her hair and coil it up again in a tight bun before pinning the white cotton cap on Maud's head. Then she settled the short cape over Maud's shoulders and secured the black veil on top, so that it hung down the back of her head.

'There's nae time to tie the rosary at your waist. It'll have to hang around your neck.'

A quick glance in the mirror told Maud she looked sufficiently like a nun so as not to attract suspicion.

'Is there a back way out of the hotel?' she asked.

'Follow me.'

She was close on Daisy's heels as her friend pushed open a
door marked Hotel Use Only. They ran down the narrow staircase and out into a yard.

'This way,' said the ever-resourceful Daisy. 'But dinna run
now. That'll draw attention to you. I've never seen a nun run.'

'And yet they must have to sometimes,' murmured Maud,
hastening after Daisy. 'When they have to catch a train, for
instance.'

Within minutes the railway station was in sight, a plume of
steam rising from the track behind. The train was already there,
waiting at the platform.

'Hurry!' Daisy handed Maud her purse, as a sudden burst
of steam indicated the fireman on the footplate was shovelling
on more coal. 'There must be a pocket somewhere in that
costume.'

They reached the door to the station. Daisy opened it and
gave her a shove. 'Good luck.'

She stumbled on the hem of her habit and almost landed
face first on the floor of the ticket hall.

She heard Daisy call, 'Sorry!' as she caught her feet in the
nick of time, straightened and came face to face with the ticket
man. He peered at her through his hatch.

'Yes, miss? I mean, sister.'

Maud could see the train on the platform, while the hiss
of steam was growing louder as the engine prepared to
move off.

'Ballater, please.' She fumbled with the purse and found the
coins she needed. 'Thank you.' She slid the money across the
oak counter and took the ticket. 'Bless you,' she added, feeling it
was required.

'Thank you, sister,' the ticket man called after her, as she hurried onto the platform.

There was no sign of David Anderson. He must be already on the train. Or had Daisy been mistaken and he wasn't intending to board at all, but was merely one of those men who liked to watch locomotives? But that couldn't be right, as he'd been carrying a suitcase.

There was no time to waste. Maud had to get on now before it drew out of the station. And she needed to be in the same compartment as David Anderson. She hastened along the plat-form, her wide black skirts flapping about her legs. In one compartment sat an elderly minister and he looked up hope-fully as she passed by his window. Having no desire at this moment for a discussion on theology, she hurried on.

The guard's whistle blew and he gestured to her to get onto the train, just as she caught sight of her quarry. She wrenched open the door, jumped in and threw herself onto the seat oppo-site him.

David Anderson muttered an oath, leaned forward to swing the door shut and the train began to move away. Finding at last a pocket in the volumious folds of her habit, Maud slid in the purse and folded her hands in her lap in what she hoped was a pious position.

He had turned away and was staring out of the window with his brows drawn together, as they left Braemar behind.

'It's a bracing day,' Maud began, in a voice she hoped sounded different from her own.

He looked at her in an unfriendly way. Had he seen through her disguise? She adopted a saintly expression and continued to gaze at him, while desperately thinking what her story would be if he asked why she had been in the village. There was no convent, but there was a Roman Catholic church. That was it; she'd been visiting a sick fellow member of the church. With a start she realised she had no luggage. Not a long visit then, just for the day. But this was a morning train, so it would have been a flying visit.

She needn't have worried. David Anderson had no interest in her. He said only, 'No doubt snow is on its way,' and turned again to stare out of the window. His legs were crossed and the top foot bounced in an agitated manner.

'Surely not yet.' She had to keep him engaged in conversation, to find out where he was going.

He shrugged without taking his gaze from the landscape they were passing. 'Snow is inevitable up here.'

Maud looked up at his suitcase on the rack. 'I see you have some luggage.' Too late she realised she shouldn't have drawn attention to that fact, given she had none. 'Perhaps you are going somewhere nice and warm?' She smiled encouragingly.

He turned his head to stare at her. 'You are very nosy for a nun.'

Maud flushed. 'Forgive me. We do not talk much in the convent, you know. It's not encouraged.'

'I can see why,' he muttered.

'So it's refreshing,' Maud ploughed on, 'to have a wee chat with others sometimes.'

'If you think you're going to have "a wee chat" with me, you're mistaken.'

Before she knew it, the words were out of her mouth. 'You sound as though you are in pain, my son. Your soul is not at rest.' Goodness, did she really say that? 'May I be of any assistance?'

He started in his seat and, for one dreadful moment, Maud was afraid he was about to strike her. She held her breath and kept in character.

He sank back in his seat. 'I'm sorry, sister, you are correct. I am in pain, as you put it.'

She softened her voice. 'Can you tell me what ails you?' She was getting rather good at this. Perhaps she had missed her vocation, she wondered.

He shook his head. 'It would shock a woman of the cloth.'

'You are wrong, sir. There is nothing you could tell me of which I am not already aware.' That was certainly true.

He hesitated. The train rumbled on in silence, and Maud began to fear the moment had passed and he would not reveal what he had done. She could not risk this happening.

'I believe the next stop is Bridge of Gairn?' she said.

It worked. David Anderson turned slowly towards her, his face white. 'I wish to God I'd never heard of Bridge of Gairn.' He slumped, his voice bitter.

'Surely a simple country railway station cannot have harmed you in any way?'

'Ha! You cannot imagine how it has changed my life.'

'I cannot.' When he said nothing else, she tried again. 'Is it, perhaps, related to the pain you feel?'

He stared at her. 'How did you know?'

She had to choose her words carefully. 'It was a guess, sir. One that was not hard to make.'

Now was the moment; she must get him to admit to his crimes. 'I'm sure you would feel better, my son, if you confess whatever is on your mind.'

A look of hope crossed his face. 'Anything I tell you would be in confidence? I thought that applied only to priests and the confessional box.'

'In the Catholic Church, it is the duty of the person who hears a confession not to disclose it to another.' Maud was pretty confident that was the case.

'So my secret would be safe?' He leaned forward in his seat.

Maud inclined her head, at the same time crossing the fingers of her hand lying under the other in her lap.

David Anderson gave a deep sigh. 'Very well,' he said. 'I must unburden myself. I confess that I have killed two men.'

He was watching her face closely. Maud blinked, but kept her outward composure. But her heart thumped. So the killer *was* David Anderson! She had his confession... but what now? No one else was there to hear it. She needed more information from him.

'That is indeed a heavy burden to bear,' Maud said gravely. 'Can you tell me how it happened?'

He shrugged. 'The first man was on his way to Edinburgh, to tell my father something I wished kept a secret.'

So Bisset had discovered the art forgeries. Oh, the irony of Bisset on his way down to Edinburgh to reveal all to Mr Anderson senior, while the gentleman himself was on his way up to the village.

'I tried to reason with him, but he wouldn't have it, so I had to kill him.'

There was no 'had to' about it, she thought, keeping a neutral look on her face. 'And the second man?'

'I wanted to end an agreement I had with him and he refused. If I hadn't killed him too, that would have been the end of my career.' David Anderson shot her a defiant look.

'I see,' Maud murmured. What should she say now? She needed him to spell out what had brought about the murderous state of affairs. 'Are you able to tell me this secret you mention?'

'Why not?' He shrugged again. 'I've already told you the worst of it. I commissioned the second man to paint forgeries of certain works of art.'

At last! Maud's pulse gathered speed. 'It is easy to stray off the straight and narrow path, my son. But what catastrophy brought you to this?'

'No catastrophy.' He gave a short, harsh laugh. 'I wanted to impress my father. He thought I wasn't up to the job of finding valuable paintings – and he was right.' That harsh laugh again. 'My father has the ability to pick the best paintings from those people who wish to sell, and to make money and a reputation for his gallery in Edinburgh. I, on the other hand, have been given a small gallery to run in Braemar and I can't even manage that successfully. Or I couldn't, until I found Mr Mc–' He faltered. Clearly naming the artist was a step too far for him.

'When I found the second man to paint those fakes for me,' David Anderson continued, '*then* my father was impressed by what I was achieving at the gallery.'

Maud almost felt sorry for Anderson the younger. To have your father scorn you must be a bitter pill to swallow. But it could never excuse murder.

'The first man wasn't interested in money. He was just bored and looking for something to amuse him. The second man, the artist, said if I tried to stop our business arrangement, then *he* would reveal all to my father unless I paid him a large sum of money.' He buried his head in his hands.

'You were indeed caught between the devil and the deep blue sea.'

He raised his head and shot Maud a surprised look.

'As it says in the Scriptures,' she added.

David Anderson nodded. 'So you see, I had no choice really but to kill him too.'

Maud shook her head slowly, hoping he would take her gesture as agreement that a blackmailer deserved to meet such an end.

She glanced up at his suitcase on the luggage rack. 'And now you are a fugitive on the run?'

'I suppose I am. A couple of damned private detectives have worked out the situation and are closing in on me. I don't intend to wait until I'm arrested.'

'So what do you intend to do?' Maud asked.

'I know what I intend to do to at least one of them, Miss McIntyre.'

Maud got to her feet as David Anderson leaped to his.

'Did you think I was such a fool as not to recognise you?' he sneered. 'Oh, I didn't immediately, I admit, but then.'

They stood facing each other on the swaying train, the wheels rolling over the track suddenly too loud in Maud's ears.

She felt a stab of fear as the train went into a tunnel. She was as good as blindfolded. Four walls hemmed her in, and within that compartment David Anderson wanted to find her. He had only to brush against her and she would be caught. She thought she felt his breath on her cheek and she began to tremble...

Maud put out a hand and felt for the seat behind her. An instant later she was crouching beneath it, with both hands stretched out. She had not long to wait. He began to edge his way round the compartment, feeling for her.

'Oh, sister,' he called softly, in a voice reminiscent of a child playing hide-and-seek. It chilled her blood. She forced herself to concentrate on what she was waiting for. She didn't have to wait long. The cuffs of his trousers brushed her hand.

In a flash she had him by the ankles. Jerking his feet from under him, she brought him crashing down.

Maud scrambled out from under the seat and sat on him. He writhed and twisted, and tried to kick his way free, but his legs were caught under the seat and he could not draw them back. All her weight was on him in the dark compartment and she pummelled the back of his head mercilessly with her fists. He was strong, but so was she thanks to the Indian club training.

Seconds later, daylight flooded back into the carriage and she saw her enemy's face as he turned towards her. His face convulsed, his eyes blazing, as he arched his back and she felt herself slipping. She went to regain her position, but as she did so, he sprang up and she fell back onto the floor.

'So you intend to murder *me* now?' Maud's heart thudded, but she managed a sneer. 'And after me, who will be next? My assistant? Perhaps the policeman she has already told by now?

Or maybe you'll turn on your own father because it will be the only way you can stop him from learning the truth?'

'Damn you, you leave me no choice!'

He wrenched open the compartment door and stepped out into nothing but the rushing air.

TWENTY-NINE

Maud scrambled up and ran to the open door banging rhythmically against the outside of the train. She looked to the rear, expecting to see David Anderson's broken body on the track, but he was on the running board, clinging to the curved brass handle next to the door, making his way along the outside of the coach.

She put out a foot, touched the running board and let herself down onto it. The skirts of her habit flapped in the wind as the train rushed along. Her heart thumped so loudly that Maud could barely hear the clanking of the wheels on the rails. She clung on to the brass handle he had used seconds before, as he grabbed the next one.

The whistle sounded and steam hissed from the engine as they approached a level crossing. The train began to slow. Not far ahead she could see the station. As they approached, Maud watched in horror. David Anderson jumped onto the platform from the still-moving train.

The portly stationmaster stepped out of his office, shouting at the fool who'd just risked his life to alight from the train in that manner.

'Stop that man!' Maud shouted. 'He's a murderer!'

David Anderson scrabbled to his feet, pushed past the astonished stationmaster and ran off down the empty road. The stationmaster gathered his wits and lumbered after him. With a squeal of brakes, the train drew into the station.

Maud jumped off the running board, as behind her the train juddered to a halt and there came the sound of running footsteps. Someone else had gamely joined in the chase.

She sprinted past the stationmaster and onto the road, after David Anderson. Little by little she was gaining on him, his breathing more laboured the further they pounded along the road. Maud gave a flying leap and brought him down.

He slammed hard onto the ground. She felt the breath forced out of her lungs as she landed on top of him. She gasped, blood pounding in her ears. They both lay still for a moment, then David Anderson groaned and suddenly they were struggling again, scrabbling and flailing in a tight knot. They rolled over in the middle of the road, the voluminous folds of her habit tangling about their legs. She tried to poke a finger in his eye. He put his hands around her neck and attempted to squeeze the breath out of her. She kicked him. He fought back.

'Stop. Oh, do stop!'

Maud heard the tremulous tones at the same time Anderson did. They both looked up into the horrified face of a minister.

They fought on. She struggled, grasping at Anderson's jacket. He twisted and was on top of her again, trying to pin her arms to her side. Her coif had come unpinned and her hair was in her eyes, obscuring her vision. There came a blessedly familiar voice.

'Get off her!' shouted Daisy, her face as fierce as her voice.

Maud felt her friend pulling at Anderson's jacket in an effort to drag him away. He kicked out at Daisy.

Suddenly, Maud felt him fall back and go limp. She pushed him off and scrambled to her feet.

'Oh dear, oh dear,' said the minister, wringing his hands as the stationmaster puffed to a halt beside them.

Maud sat on the dusty ground, dragging in gulps of the sweet fresh air.

'You must get up, sister,' said the stationmaster, reaching out to help her to her feet. 'It's not a good idea to sit in the middle of the road.'

The minister stared at David Anderson, still lying flat on his back in the road, breathing deeply, and turned to Maud, admiration in his voice. 'You have subdued the devil who possessed that man.'

Maud's coif was dislodged and filthy, and her cape torn. The wooden crucifix hung down her back. Her cheekbones felt bruised. David Anderson's face had a few marks of its own. He attempted to climb to his feet, then swore loudly and moaned before sitting back down on the ground.

'I think my arm is broken.'

'Haivers, man!' Daisy said. 'It's naething more than a fracture.'

Maud was fairly sure that was the same thing.

'You're a most unusual nun.' The stationmaster pushed his cap to the back of his head as he looked at her.

Maud straightened her coif and dusted down her habit.

'That's because I'm not. I'm really a private detective,' she said proudly. She hadn't missed her vocation.

'A private detective.' The stationmaster looked at her in wonder. 'I've never seen one dressed as a nun before...'

'The police have their methods, stationmaster; we have ours. Miss McIntyre and her assistant Miss Cameron at your service.' Maud smiled at Daisy.

Then she turned to stare at the man sitting in the road, nursing his arm.

'The police must be informed,' Maud said.

'What? Because I had a fight with a woman disguised as a nun?' David Anderson gave a scornful laugh.

'Because you are a double murderer.'

'So you say.' He shrugged and caught his breath as the movement hurt his arm. 'But where is your evidence? I'll be bringing a charge of assault against you both.'

Daisy glared at him. 'Och, I'm feart.'

Maud now noticed there was another man present, standing a little way back. 'Mr Geddes!' she exclaimed. 'How very pleasant to see you again, but why are you here?'

He touched his cap. 'I met Miss Cameron outside the hotel. She told me what had happened and I offered her a hurl.'

'I was awfa worried about you, Maud,' Daisy said, 'and I felt I should be here.'

'And thank the Lord you are, Daisy. You arrived just in time.' Maud turned to Mr Geddes. 'You have transport?'

He nodded.

'Can I trouble you to take me, Miss Cameron and this *gentleman*,' Maud gestured to David Anderson, his head bent, 'to the police office in Braemar?'

Mr Geddes looked apologetic. 'I'm sorry, miss, but there's room for only two.'

Behind her, Daisy made a noise that sounded like a stifled laugh. Maud could only imagine that Mr Geddes had brought her here in his horse and cart.

'You go with Mr Geddes, Maud,' Daisy was saying. 'I'll bide here with the prisoner, while the stationmaster goes back to the station and telephones for the police officer. I'll come back with Constable Oliphant and the prisoner. I expect the policeman will get a car from somewhere.'

'I *would* like to wash and change,' Maud glanced down at herself, 'but I can't leave you here alone.'

'Dinna worry,' Daisy said with a smile. 'I've got the minister to protect me.'

The Adam's apple in the elderly man's throat went up and down as he swallowed.

'And you,' Daisy folded her arms and addressed Anderson, 'can shoogle along on your bumbaleerie to sit at the side of the road. Try any funny business and I'll break your other arm.'

Oh, it was a break now, was it? Maud thought to herself.

'If you're sure, Daisy, then thank you and I'll see you back at the hotel.'

Maud followed Rabbie Geddes a short distance along the road before he came to a halt. She looked about and drew her brows together. 'Where is your horse and cart?'

He pointed to a bicycle leaning against the drystone wall. 'That's my transport, miss. The horse and cairt belong to my employer, and I'm not on his business today.'

'How are we both to travel on that?' She nodded at the bicycle.

He grinned. 'I'll show you. It's easy. I'm used to giving my sister a hurl, and you can't be much heavier than her.' He frowned as he looked Maud up and down. 'Although perhaps a wee bit taller.'

A wee bit? Shona was some nine years old and at least a foot shorter, Maud thought. No matter. The fictional but resourceful detective Miss Gladden would not be daunted and neither would she.

She took a deep breath. 'Very well.'

Rabbie Geddes snatched up the bicycle and turned it round in the road, threw a leg over the saddle and stood with his feet firmly on the ground either side of the contraption. He patted the metal bar in front of him which ran the length of the machine to the handlebars. 'Hop on, miss.'

Hop on? That was the last method of mounting she had in mind. It was a relief to Maud that she wore the voluminous skirts of the habit. Although the divided skirts recommended by the Rational Dress Movement would have been preferable.

'You sit on it side-saddle, like on a horse,' he added helpfully.

Riding side-saddle was a symbol of male domination. Maud eyed the metal bar. On second thoughts, perhaps that was the best approach in the circumstances.

'Or,' he went on, 'you could sit on the handlebars.'

'That sounds better,' she said, only slightly convinced.

He held the bicycle steady between his legs. 'Turn with your back to me.'

'Goodness.' Maud gasped as he lifted her so that her bottom was on the handlebars.

'Keep your feet – and your dress – away from the wheels,' he cautioned, and in an instant he pushed off.

She gathered up the folds of her habit and gripped the handlebars for dear life as he pedalled and the machine bumped along the road. Once her heart had stopped thudding, she found with the breeze on her face the ride was exhilarating. She must learn how to bicycle.

A motor car went past with Constable Oliphant in the passenger seat.

'There's the police officer,' Maud called to Rabbie Geddes over her shoulder. 'He should be there soon.'

'Keep still, miss,' came Rabbie's concerned voice. 'I can't see over the top of your head so I have to look round you. And you don't want to upset the bicycle and have us both in a ditch.'

'Indeed not,' she managed to say.

She kept very still and thought about David Anderson. It looked as though he was not going to admit his crimes to anyone but her. Maud hoped the police officer could gather enough evidence to charge him. Scots law required corroboration: at least two independent sources of evidence in support of each crucial fact before an accused could be convicted. How frustrating it would be if the jury was not convinced of Anderson's guilt and returned a verdict of not proven. It had the same legal effect as not guilty, and Sir Walter Scott had famously called it 'that bastard verdict'.

Maud was considering this when a two-seater overtook them with a burst of its horn. The bicycle wobbled under her, she caught her breath and the occupants of the motor car gave a merry wave as they disappeared into the distance.

'We're almost there!' Rabbie Geddes called to her.

'Thank goodness,' she murmured between gritted teeth.

A short time later, Rabbie cycled into the village. He drew up outside the police office. Maud jumped down from the handlebars, glad to be back on solid ground.

'Thank you very much, Mr Geddes. I will never forget that journey,' she said with feeling, resisting the urge to rub her backside.

'My pleasure.' He laughed and pedalled away.

The door to the police office was locked. As Maud sat on the doorstep and waited for the return of Constable Oliphant and Daisy with the prisoner, she was already putting the final pieces of the jigsaw puzzle together in her head.

THIRTY

Bathed and changed into a pale blue blouse with white lace collar and cuffs and her dark blue skirt, and with a delicious dinner of rabbit pie inside her, Maud knocked on Daisy's bedroom door. Daisy appeared, neatly attired in her pale green chiffon blouse and dark green skirt. Maud linked her arm through Daisy's and together they walked down the staircase. In the hall a small group stared up at them. Good, she thought, Mrs Wallace had arranged for the relevant people to attend, as Maud had requested.

Rose Gilmour, who had started them on the road to Brae-mar, could not be included in the gathering as she needed to remain anonymous. But Maud and Daisy would contrive to meet her before their journey back to Edinburgh and tell her all that had happened.

'Good evening,' Maud said to the assembly, as she reached the bottom of the stairs, 'and thank you for coming. Could everyone please come into the parlour. Mrs Wallace has kindly agreed to ensure we will not be disturbed.' She nodded at Mrs Wallace, who hovered with the rest of the little group.

Daisy ushered everyone into the parlour, where a bright fire was burning, the curtains drawn and the lamps lit. All was cosy. It felt a little unreal to Maud that she was about to recount the facts that had led to two bloody murders.

The murmurings died down as everyone took their seats and waited expectantly. Maud checked they were all there. Mrs Bisset in a large purple hat with matching feathers and looking resentful, Mr Wallace glancing at his pocket watch, Mr Buston ill-at-ease in his Sunday suit. Mrs Wallace, in her rich blue silk day dress, sat by the door and produced her knitting. She must have finished the little pink bonnet, Maud thought in passing, as she was now working with a ball of soft lemon wool.

Suddenly, the door opened.

Maud glanced round. 'I asked for no—' She broke off as in walked Lilias Bisset and Conrad Elliot. No, that should be Mr and Mrs Elliot. And...

'Good God, it is my husband's murderer!' cried Mrs Bisset, rising from the armchair and pointing to Conrad Elliot. 'Mrs Wallace, send for the police!'

'I doubt that would make any difference,' Maud said soothingly. 'Constable Oliphant has this afternoon made an arrest in connection with the murders of Mr Bisset and Mr McGonagall.'

'McGonagall?' Mrs Bisset wrinkled her nose. 'Who is he?'

'The artist who was murdered.'

'Oh, him,' she said disparagingly.

Maud returned her gaze to the tall, dark-haired man dressed in a cream suit, white shirt and cream waistcoat, who had entered with the Elliots and now stood behind the young couple. She frowned. Lord Urquhart. What was he doing here? He smiled blandly back at her.

'Lord Urquhart, your presence is a surprise.'

'But not an unwelcome one, I trust?'

'What is your purpose here?' Maud stared at him coolly, waiting for an answer.

He gave a theatrical sigh. 'The agreeable young lady pig-owner I danced with at the ceilidh last night informed me of the elopement of these two turtledoves and that it was the talk of the village. She had earlier made Miss Bisset's acquaintance and knew where Mr and Mrs Elliot were staying in Edinburgh. With a little inducement, she was persuaded to tell me their address.'

Maud raised an eyebrow.

'If you are wondering what the inducement was,' went on Lord Urquhart, his gaze on Maud, 'it was merely that I pointed out how much better it would be for the young couple's future if they could reconcile with Mrs Bisset. I simply telephoned their hotel and persuaded Mr and Mrs Elliot to return for that purpose.'

He smiled at Maud, a little smugly, she thought.

She noticed the girl sent a hopeful glance towards her mother, who refused to meet her daughter's eye.

Lilias added in a sullen voice, 'And I wanted to be sure that Conrad's name was cleared. Lord Urquhart picked us up from Ballater railway station in his motor car.'

'A very sensible decision.' Maud gave a brief nod to Lord Urquhart. 'I'm glad you are here, Mr and Mrs Elliot. The timing may be coincidental for this evening's gathering, but it is perfect. Congratulations to you both, by the way.'

'Thank you, Miss McIntyre, on behalf of my wife and myself,' said Conrad Elliot, and Lilias gave him a shy smile.

Yes, they may do very well together, Maud thought. Perhaps there was hope for the girl, away from her family.

She cleared her throat. 'I believe you all know, apart from Mr and Mrs Elliot, and Lord Urquhart, why I have asked you here. It concerns, of course, the deaths of Mr Bisset and Mr McGonagall.'

'I don't see why we had to rush here this evening,' grumbled Mrs Bisset.

'As Burns said, "If a thing were done, then best it were done quickly," or words to that effect,' said Daisy.

'I think you'll find the quotation in Shakespeare's *Macbeth*,' Maud said, 'but the sentiment is correct.'

'But I don't understand,' continued Mrs Bisset. 'What has this artist got to do with my husband's death?'

'If you keep your mouth shut,' Daisy said, 'you'll find out.'

Mrs Bisset glared at her, but held her tongue.

'Mr Bisset was found dead in a railway carriage that arrived at Ballater station on the Tuesday before last.' Maud glanced at Mrs Bisset. Had she said that too bluntly? Mrs Bisset looked at her impatiently, so Maud continued. 'At first it seemed that he had taken his own life—'

'It seemed that to the police, but nae to us,' put in Daisy.

Maud nodded. 'We learned that a man had hurried off the train when it drew in at Bridge of Gairn. It was Miss Cameron's and my belief that this man, in the disguise of a painter and decorator, had murdered Mr Bisset on the train somewhere between Braemar and Bridge of Gairn.'

'A tradesman! Ridiculous notion,' Mrs Bisset scoffed.

Maud ignored the interruption. 'Our investigations led us to suspect one, or perhaps two, of five people. These were Mr Buston because Mr Bisset had refused to make payment for gardening work done at Woodend and had humiliated the gentleman in the process.'

'I expect I would have been paid in the end...' John Buston turned his cap over in his hands.

'Perhaps you would have been. But you were never a serious suspect. Mr Wallace,' Maud turned to him, 'you were also on our list.'

Mrs Wallace's needles paused.

'I cannot imagine why,' said her husband.

'How about because you'd thrown old man Bisset out of the lounge bar and warned him never to come back, or else?' said Daisy.

'That's not quite what I said. I told him if he didn't behave himself next time, then at the very least he'd be banned.'

'At the very least?' Daisy raised an eyebrow.

'I meant I'd get him charged with breach of the peace. It's not unusual for a publican or hotelier to make such a threat.'

'Maybe not in Glasgow, but here?'

Mr Wallace shrugged. 'Bisset was a thoroughly unpleasant character.' He turned to Mrs Bisset. 'I'm sorry, but it's true.'

'I know that better than anyone. I had to live with him.'

'Mrs Bisset, you were also a suspect,' Maud said.

'I thought I might be. I made no attempt to hide that I'm glad he's dead. I married too young to a puffed-up, tedious little man and we had nothing in common. But I didn't kill him.'

'I overheard you and Mr Wallace outside the post office, when you said you wanted to talk to him privately,' Daisy said.

'She fancied herself in love with me,' added Mr Wallace. 'The feeling was not mutual.'

Mrs Bisset coloured. 'I may have a few years on you—'

'A *few* years!' He laughed.

'My dear,' murmured Mrs Wallace, as she bent her head to her knitting. 'Be kind to the poor woman.'

Mrs Bisset sent the older woman a furious glare. 'Don't patronise me. My social standing is vastly superior to yours.'

Mrs Wallace raised her eyebrows and continued with her knitting.

Mrs Bisset turned back to Mr Wallace. 'You have made a mistake in refusing me. I intend to be the chief lady of this dull little village. Think what I could have done for your career!'

For your own career, thought Maud. Perhaps the woman really did believe herself in love with Mr Wallace, or perhaps she saw him as a stepping stone to the position she desired. Either way, the woman was to be pitied.

'That's three of us,' Mrs Bisset said sharply. 'Who were the other two you suspected?'

Maud's sympathy for her evaporated. 'Your daughter Lilias and Mr Elliot.'

'That man is a bad influence on Lilias,' said Mrs Bisset.

'Perhaps it's the other way round, that she's a bad influence on him,' Mr Wallace muttered.

Mrs Bisset spun round to face him. 'What exactly do you mean by that?'

He shrugged. 'Like mother, like daughter.'

'Mr Wallace,' murmured Mrs Wallace in a rebuking tone, her eyes never leaving the stitches she made with each twist of the yarn.

Conrad Elliot got to his feet. 'You are talking about my wife.'

'Please,' Maud said, 'let us all remain calm. Neither Mr nor Mrs Elliot were responsible for the murders of Mr Anderson and Mr McGonagall.'

Conrad Elliot reluctantly resumed his seat. Lilias reached out and took his hand.

'If it wasn't one of your five suspects, then who was it?' Mr Buston looked confused.

'It wasna one of the five suspects in *Bisset's* death,' Daisy said.

'Exactly so.' Maud gazed round the room at them all, feeling the air of expectancy. 'It was our suspect in the case of Mr McGonagall's murder.'

'How can there be any connection between the two?' Mrs Bisset demanded. 'I've never even heard of the man, let alone met him.'

'Ah, but your husband had,' said Maud quickly.

Mrs Bisset frowned.

Daisy picked up the thread. 'Aye, he had found out a secret of the artist's and was threatening to reveal it.'

'Blackmail? Why on earth would he do that? We have enough money.' Mrs Bisset's face had turned red.

'It wasna blackmail. It wasna about money at all,' Daisy added. 'Your husband was bored and when he fell across a forgery duo, he thought he'd amuse himself at their expense. It's common knowledge in the village that your husband took plea-sure in belittling the menfolk who live here.'

'I don't like your tone,' said Mrs Bisset, recovering herself.

'And I dinna like yours,' Daisy muttered.

'But what is this about forgery?' It was Mr Wallace's turn to look confused.

'McGonagall was being paid to paint fakes, which were sold through the art gallery in the village,' Maud explained.

'With naething to do with himself all day, Mr Bisset must have been awfa pleased when he learned that,' added Daisy.

Mrs Bisset's frown deepened. 'And how did he discover such a thing?'

'That's something we can't yet be sure of,' said Maud, 'but Miss Cameron and I believe your husband must have seen the artist emerge from his cottage late one evening carrying a parcel and followed him. Mr McGonagall had to pass Woodend each time he went to the village. Very likely Mr Bisset then saw a new painting in the window of the gallery and his suspicions were aroused.'

'You are saying that *Bisset* murdered McGonagall?' Mr Wallace frowned. 'That's not possible because Bisset was already dead by that time.'

'He was, right enough,' said Daisy. 'We're saying that David Anderson killed Bisset.'

Mr Wallace looked from one to the other. 'Mr Anderson of the gallery? I don't understand.'

Daisy sighed. 'Try and keep up.'

'It *is* a little confusing, Daisy.' Maud again addressed the assembly. 'Mr Bisset was threatening David Anderson with informing his father of the forgeries. We know that the younger Mr Anderson was desperate to impress his father with his business acumen. Should Mr Anderson senior have learned of his son's skulduggery, it would have been the end of the young man's career in the art world. Indeed, if it got out, then the father's reputation would be as ruined as his son's and possibly they would both go to prison.'

'So the younger Mr Anderson killed Mr Bisset to keep his secret safe?' asked Mr Buston.

'As safe as it could be,' Daisy pointed out. 'The artist, of course, still knew.'

Maud nodded. 'David Anderson began to be afraid, knowing the net was closing in on him. He went to Mr McGonagall's cottage that night to tell him their arrangement was at an end.'

'But McGonagall didna accept that. He wanted money to flit to Paris, where all the famous artists stay apparently. McGonagall tried to blackmail him, threatening to clype on him to his faither.'

Mrs Bisset sniffed. 'How can you possibly know all that?'

'David Anderson confessed to me this morning,' Maud said, 'and then he attempted to run away. He is now in police custody and should be charged soon.'

Maud hastily considered the evidence: Mr Mutrie's sale of the paint-splashed trousers to the man he would surely be able to identify as David Anderson, the stationmaster's glimpse of him at Bridge of Gairn, the clothes which should be found hidden in a hedgerow probably not far from the station, the lift Rabbie Geddes gave to David Anderson... The murder of Bisset might be easier to establish than that of McGonagall, but one death made sense only with the other...

'I thought this was supposed to be a nice quiet little village,' Lord Urquhart murmured to her, and she became aware that the little gathering was breaking up.

'Shall we go outside for a moment?' he said. 'I feel the need for some fresh air.'

Maud nodded; she felt the same. They made their way out of the hotel. Light fell from the windows, and by unspoken consent they moved away from the building and stood in the clear starlight. It looked as though David Anderson was right, and that snow was on its way. It certainly felt as though there would be at least a frost tonight. She breathed in the crisp cold air. It was a relief after all that had happened.

'Why did you come back?' she asked Lord Urquhart.

'As Mrs Elliot said, because I wanted to encourage a reconciliation between mother, daughter and son-in-law.'

Maud looked at him. 'Anything else?'

'Perhaps also to see you again.'

'Perhaps?' Goodness, was she almost flirting with him?

'Definitely.'

Yes, she was definitely flirting with him. And it was rather pleasant.

'Miss McIntyre, you are a very intelligent woman.'

'And so I cannot imagine why I am standing here with you.'

'Would you like me to show you why?'

She gave a soft laugh. 'Now is hardly the time or place.' It was indeed a cold night. She rubbed her arms through the sleeves of her blouse.

He noticed her shiver. 'Allow me.' He removed his jacket and slipped it round her shoulders.

The hotel door opened and out came Daisy.

'There you are, Maud,' she called. 'Come in for a moment. Mrs Wallace wants to thank you.'

Maud slid the jacket off and passed it back. 'We will no doubt meet again, Lord Urquhart.'

He smiled. 'You can be sure of it.'

She walked back to where Daisy stood at the entrance to the hotel and murmured, 'Your timing is impeccable, as always, Watson.'

Daisy grinned. 'You know my methods, Holmes.'

A LETTER FROM LYDIA

Thank you so much for reading *Murder in the Scottish Hills*. As with The Scottish Ladies' Detective Agency, I write to entertain – myself and, I hope, others.

If you enjoyed this second book in the series and would like to keep up to date with my latest releases, please sign up at the following link. Your email address will never be shared and you can unsubscribe at any time.

www.bookouture.com/lydia-travers

One of the great rewards of writing about Maud and Daisy is hearing from and replying to readers. I appreciate the kindness of those who take the time to let me know they have enjoyed the pair's adventures.

If you liked *Murder in the Scottish Hills*, and I really hope you did, I would be very grateful if you could leave a short review to help other readers discover my books.

Thank you for reading.

Love

Lydia x

KEEP IN TOUCH WITH LYDIA

www.bookouture.com/lydia-travers

facebook.com/LindaTylerAuthorScotland

twitter.com/LindaTyler100

instagram.com/lindatylerauthorScotland

ACKNOWLEDGEMENTS

Huge thanks go to a number of friends. Firstly to my writing buddy Julie Perkins for the crucial combination of our brain-storming sessions and her deeply insightful readings – I couldn't have written Maud's adventures without her; and to Joan Cameron for her enthusiastic support of Maud's exploits from the beginning and her many wonderful plot suggestions – I'm only sorry that I couldn't use them all.

I am also grateful to the following friends for their invaluable help and suggestions: artist Trina Stark for guiding me through the materials and techniques of the art world, Lynda Leslie for the Braemar walks, Vicki Singleton for avian information, former Procurator Fiscal Depute Laura Sharp, Sheila Gray who read the early draft of the novel, Jon Tyler for his advice on railways and Beth Keshishian Tyler who wanted me to give Maud a case to solve in Braemar.

I am indebted to Alastair Dinsmor MBE, Curator of the Glasgow Police Museum, and to Museum guides Robert Barrowman and Edward Haggarty.

Thanks also go to the team at Bookouture.

Other influences on my writing have been the work of comic genius P.G. Wodehouse and of course the various detective stories beloved by Maud.

Some liberties have been taken with the jurisdiction of the Scottish criminal justice system in 1911. Sadly, Queen Victoria did have her way and the Deeside Line terminated at Ballater; a motor bus service took passengers on to Braemar. Any mistakes are my own.

Made in the USA
Las Vegas, NV
23 August 2024

94323109R10166